TEN FEET TALL

Center Point
Large Print

Also by Wayne D. Overholser and available from Center Point Large Print:

The Durango Stage
Proud Journey
Pass Creek Valley
Summer Warpath
Fighting Man
Ten Mile Valley
High Desert
The Waiting Gun
Guns in Sage Valley

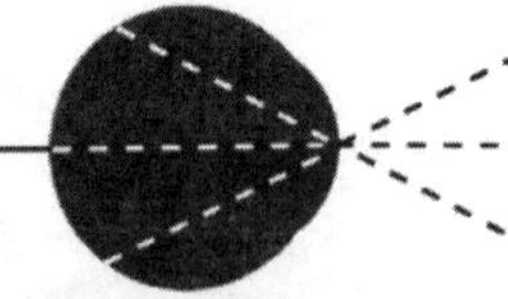

This Large Print Book carries the Seal of Approval of N.A.V.H.

TEN FEET TALL

COLLECTED STORIES

Wayne D. Overholser

EDITED BY
STEPHEN OVERHOLSER,
WITH AN INTRODUCTION BY
DANIEL J. OVERHOLSER

CENTER POINT LARGE PRINT
THORNDIKE, MAINE

This Circle V Western is published by
Center Point Large Print in the year 2019 in
co-operation with Golden West Literary Agency.

Copyright © 2019 by the Estate of Wayne D. Overholser.

All rights reserved.

First Edition
January 2019

Printed in the United States of America
on permanent paper.
Set in 16-point Times New Roman type.

ISBN: 978-1-64358-065-4

Library of Congress Cataloging-in-Publication Data

The Library of Congress has cataloged record
under LCCN 2018045181

Additional Copyright Information

"The Woman from Cougar Creek" first appeared in *Big Book Western Magazine* (51). Copyright © 1951 by Popular Publications, Inc. Copyright © renewed 1979 by Wayne D. Overholser.

"The Price of Pride" first appeared in *Thrilling Western* (6/47). Copyright © 1947 by Standard Magazines, Inc. Copyright © renewed 1975 by Wayne D. Overholser.

"The Devil and Old Man Gillis" first appeared in *Best Western* (9/51). Copyright © 1951 by Western Fiction Publishing Co., Inc. Copyright © renewed 1979 by Wayne D. Overholser.

"Shooting for a Fall" first appeared in *10 Story Western Magazine* (6/50). Copyright © 1950 by Popular Publications, Inc. Copyright © renewed 1978 by Wayne D. Overholser.

"It's Hell To Be a Hero" first appeared in *New Western Magazine* (4/49). Copyright © 1949 by Popular Publications, Inc. Copyright © renewed 1977 by Wayne D. Overholser.

"The Tongue-Tied Cowboy" first appeared in *Golden West Romance* (Fall/50). Copyright © 1950 by Standard Magazines, Inc. Copyright © renewed 1978 by Wayne D. Overholser.

"From Hell to Leadville" first appeared in *Fifteen Western Tales* (2/48). Copyright © 1948 by Popular Publications, Inc. Copyright © renewed 1976 by Wayne D. Overholser.

"The Deputy with a Past" first appeared in *Popular Western* (8/50). Copyright © 1950 by Beacon Magazines, Inc. Copyright © renewed 1978 by Wayne D. Overholser.

"Judge Peterson's Colt Law" first appeared in *Exciting Western* (5/48). Copyright © 1948 by Better Publications, Inc. Copyright © renewed 1976 by Wayne D. Overholser.

"The Breaking of Sam McKay" first appeared in *Fifteen Western Tales* (3/48). Copyright © 1948 by Popular Publications, Inc. Copyright © renewed 1976 by Wayne D. Overholser.

"Fugitive From The Boothill Brigade" first appeared in *Ace-High Magazine* (5/48). Copyright © 1948 by Popular Publications, Inc. Copyright © renewed 1976 by Wayne D. Overholser.

"The Man Ten Feet Tall" first appeared in *Fifteen Western Tales* (1/49). Copyright © 1949 by Popular Publications, Inc. Copyright © renewed 1977 by Wayne D. Overholser.

Table of Contents

Introduction

In the 1940s and early 1950s, magazines of all descriptions published adventure fiction—mystery, science fiction, romance, Western. Most were pulps, so named for the quality of paper. With prices ranging from fifteen to twenty-five cents the magazines were available to everyone.

In the pulps the quality of the stories varied widely, but the hallmark was action. Exciting events held readers' attention, and kept them coming back for more.

My father, Wayne D. Overholser, wrote Westerns. At first he wrote part-time while teaching social studies in the junior high school in Tillamook, Oregon and the high school in Bend, Oregon. As his sales increased, he sensed that he could make a good living as a full-time writer. He had taught for nineteen years and was ready for a change.

He was successful, and as it turned out, the magazines of this era launched him into the growing market for full-length novels. By the mid-1950s, after his move to Boulder, Colorado, the magazines faded and he was publishing Westerns in hardcover and paperback editions. By the time his career ended some thirty years later, he had written over one hundred novels. He won numerous awards, was active in the Western Writers of America—a professional organization he helped found in 1953—saw two novels made into feature-length films, and thoroughly enjoyed his career.

But before that, on an old Royal typewriter, he wrote three hundred and fifty short stories and novelettes for the pulps. Nearly all of them appeared once and only once. That was the nature of the business. Pulp magazines came out every week, month, or quarterly, and of course they were constantly replaced by new issues—a great, churning river of fiction.

The stories in this collection have not been available to readers since they were first published. They reflect not only traditional Western situations and characters, but the author's research. As a trained historian, Wayne D. Overholser liked to incorporate a measure of reality into his fiction. In addition to being entertained, readers of these stories will learn of stagecoach and freight lines in mountains and plains, mining in the Rockies, cattle and sheep ranching, farming, land disputes, and town life in the American West of the period ranging from the 1860s to the late 1890s.

A stock character in literature the world over is the Old Man. He is variously portrayed as rich or poor, kindly or mean, wise or foolish. In several of these stories by Wayne D. Overholser, the

Old Man plays a pivotal role. This is in keeping with the author's research. He was well aware that the first white men to settle in the West were by nature sturdy, strong-willed characters who survived against great odds to establish ranches, farms, mining empires, and towns. In a lawless land, they set their own rules—and enforced them. As time went on, though, these men were challenged by younger men. Adventure fiction is energized by conflict, and the role of the Old Man fit perfectly while being historically valid.

Westerns are also noted for picturesque writing. Wayne D. Overholser knew how to set a scene vividly. His large and small landscapes will draw new readers into new adventures. Read on. Enjoy.

Stephen Overholser, Editor

My brother Steve put together this collection of Dad's short stories several years ago. He wrote this introduction explaining how Dad would research and write these stories. Those stories always had a lot of action and quite a bit of historical detail. Our father was one of those lucky individuals who loved his work. Writing was very fulfilling for him throughout his life.

Steve Overholser was an accomplished author in his own right. And like our father, he loved his writing career. When he was a teenager he decided he wanted to write books just like Dad. This was truly a lofty and difficult goal. After college Steve joined the Army and went to Vietnam. When he returned from the war, he began his writing career. As with most beginning artists he about starved to death. He worked nights as a school janitor and plied his craft during the day. It was at this job that he met the love of his life, the school librarian. A marriage between an author and a librarian is about as perfect a match as could be found.

Steve's work was similar to our father's in that he always strived for historical accuracy. And he always researched his stories in great detail. But his writing style was distinctly his own. In 1974, he won the Western Writers of America Spur award for his first book *A Hanging in Sweetwater*. This is a very prestigious award. After this award he sold every book he wrote. Steve published eighteen novels. Sadly, his career was cut short due to Parkinson's disease. Steve passed away in April of 2017 due to complications from this terrible disease.

I take great pride in seeing my father and brother's legacy live on through their books. Their work in Western literature is admired by their peers and those who have read their books.

Daniel J. Overholser

The Woman from Cougar Creek

It was a dusty Phip Callahan who rode a sweat-stained horse into Cherry Wagner's place on Cougar Creek at dusk. He'd left Gunnison early that morning and had piled up more miles than a man should have to ride in a day, but time was of the essence.

He dismounted, his gaze sweeping the familiar scene: the dark bulk of the roadhouse with lamp-lighted windows staring at him like unblinking yellow eyes, the low log barn, the scattered sheds, the network of corrals.

Phip watered his horse at the trough, stooping to drink from the pipe, and as he straightened, old Frank Hayes, Cherry's handyman, came from the barn, a lantern swinging from his hand.

"Staying overnight, mister?"

"You bet I am, Frank."

Hayes held the lantern high, its light falling across Phip's wide, freckled face. "Oh, hell, I guess my eyes are getting bad. Didn't recognize you, Phip."

"It's me, right enough," Phip said. "How's business?"

"Good. Too good." He paused, then added with some bitterness: "I'm doing two men's work, but

Cherry can't get nobody else to help out around here."

"You know what gold does to a man, Frank. Nobody wants to work for wages when he hears about the strikes they're making down the creek."

"Yeah, that's right. Sometimes I wonder why I stay. Not that I'm thinking of quitting, mind you. I'll stick as long as Cherry needs me."

There was a moment of silence except for the rattle of dishes from the road-house kitchen and the distant growl of the creek as it tumbled down from the high country to the east.

"Guess Brownie's got his fill," Phip said. "Got a vacant stall?"

"Sure. Half a dozen tonight."

Phip followed the old man into the barn. Hayes hung his lantern near the door and motioned to the third stall. "In here. I'll get some oats."

Phip stripped his brown gelding, dropped the saddle onto a peg, and rubbed the horse down. Hayes had returned to stand in the runway, a tired, stooped old man, the murky light of the lantern falling across him.

Phip gave his horse a pat, thinking of Cherry Wagner as he did most of his waking hours. He didn't understand her and he wondered if it was given to any man to really understand the woman he loved. He wondered, too, if Cherry would ever be serious about a man, and if she did, whether he would be the man.

But that was not the immediate problem that had brought him. He had come this time strictly on business, and the prospect was not a pleasant one.

"I reckon you figure to sign Cherry up," Hayes said somberly.

Phip stepped from the stall into the cone of light falling from the lantern. He was a medium tall man, red-headed, with pale blue eyes puckered by the sharp Colorado sun. He was a practical man, disciplined by years of hard work. Now, not yet thirty, he had what he wanted at last, a partnership with Matt Lane in the Colorado Stage & Freight Company, a small business rich with promise. There was striking irony in the fact that Cherry Wagner held the future of the CS&FC in the hollow of her slim-fingered hand.

"I aim to try," Phip said. "Think she's ready to sign?"

"Damned if I know," Hayes said. "Sometimes I just can't make her out. Talks a lot about women's rights."

"Maybe Gale's in the way."

"I reckon he is, at that. Anyhow, he's here, talking smooth and sweet the way he does, and all dressed up like he was going to a funeral."

Something tightened inside Phip Callahan. He knew Randy Gale, knew him too well. He muttered: "It may be his funeral."

"Yeah, if you don't fix it for him, I will," Hayes

said. "I've stood by Cherry because her pappy was my best friend. He was on his deathbed last spring when I promised him to stay on. But I dunno." He rubbed his leathery face. "I just dunno. Well, you better go in and eat."

Phip understood how it was. Hayes and Cherry's father had come to Colorado twenty-odd years ago with the rest of the fifty-niners; they had watched the disappointed go-backs return to their homes, cursing the stories they'd heard of Colorado's gold, but Frank Hayes and Bill Wagner had stayed. Wagner had married and made his strike in Gregory Gulch, but Hayes had nothing but bad luck, and wound up working for Wagner. Only two years ago he had bought the toll road down Cougar Creek and built this layout. Then he'd died, and everything had gone to Cherry.

There was nothing Phip could say to ease the bitterness in the old man's heart. Cherry had made mistakes that could have been avoided if she'd listened to Hayes, but she wasn't one to listen.

Phip said: "Might as well see if they can rustle some grub, I reckon." Then he turned toward the door. That was when the gun sounded from the other end of the runway.

Phip felt the breath of the bullet, and wheeled, drawing his gun as he turned. Hayes had been hit, but there was no time to look at him. Phip glimpsed the shadowy figure of the gunman. He fell flat into the litter of the stable floor as another shot came, the sound of it beating against the walls, thunder-loud in this confinement. Then Phip brought his gun into play, adding to the racket.

Phip laid two shots at the man, fast. The second was a waste of lead, for the bushwhacker had been slammed against the back wall of the stable by the first bullet. He bounced off and sprawled face down. Phip waited a moment, but there was no movement from the man.

Hammer back, Phip lunged toward him, keeping low and taking a zig-zag course. Then he saw the gun three feet from the motionless body and slowed his pace, dropping his own .44 into leather. Kneeling, he turned the man over and flamed a match beside his face. It was Jupe Klein.

For a moment Phip knelt there. He knew Klein almost as well as he knew Randy Gale, a trigger-happy killer, hardly more than a boy, who had hung around the saloons of Canyon City and Pueblo. It had been his brag that he'd have as many notches on his gun as Billy the Kid did by the time he was twenty-one.

Phip was sure, or as sure as a man could be of something he couldn't prove, that Klein had belonged to Gale, but even if he had the proof, he doubted that Cherry would believe him.

Hearing a groan, he remembered suddenly that Hayes had been hit. Phip rose and ran back along the runway to him.

"Take it easy," Hayes said. He had pulled himself into a sitting position and was leaning against the wall. "He just tagged me."

Phip grabbed the lantern and said: "Let me have a look."

It was a flesh wound in the old man's left shoulder, a ragged hole bleeding badly. By the time Phip had wadded a bandanna and pressed it against the wound, Cherry had come running out of the house with Randy Gale and half a dozen others.

"What happened?" she called out.

She came into the barn, recognized Phip, and in the same instant saw that Hayes had been hit. "Frank, is it bad?"

"Naw. Randy, you ought to have your boys practice before they try a set-up."

They crowded through the door, Gale's handsome face suddenly ugly. "What are you laying it onto me for, Frank? I didn't have anything to do with it."

"He's out of his head, Randy." Cherry motioned to the men. "Help him inside. Missus Decker will patch him up. She's as good as any doctor."

Gale stayed behind, and when the rest had gone, he asked Phip: "Who did it?"

"Klein."

"I don't believe it."

Phip motioned to the other end of the runway. "Go have a look."

Gale took the lantern and strode toward the dead man. Phip remained near the door, watching, and when Gale returned, he asked: "Believe it yet?"

"I believe what I see. Who'd he shoot at?"

"I wonder," Phip said.

Gale stood motionless, black eyes on him. *Smooth,* Phip thought. *Even now he seems unruffled.*

"Callahan," he said, "if I have to kill you, I'll do it."

"This is a good time to try."

Gale shook his head. His mouth curled into a smile, but his agate-black eyes were cold. "No, this ain't the time."

"Maybe later. A shot in the back."

"Maybe."

"Funny thing, Randy. I've had to fight someone ever since I was big enough to walk, but I never met up with anybody before who had no honor about the way he fought."

"Honor?" The smile remained on Gale's lips. "What's your notion of honor?"

"I wouldn't try to explain it to you."

"I know what it is, Callahan. A damned nuisance. I get what I want, and the way I get it ain't important."

"And you want Cherry?"

Gale shrugged. "My stage company needs this spot, Callahan. I aim to get it. If Cherry goes with the deal, why, that's all right."

Phip sucked in a ragged breath. Wheeling, he strode out of the pool of lantern light, and went on to the house.

Phip had often wondered whether it had been foresight or plain fool luck which had prompted Bill Wagner to buy the Cougar Pass toll road and build this layout two years ago. The road had been little more than a goat trail over the Continental Divide, and there had been only a cabin and a log shed where the big roadhouse and barn stood now.

But Wagner had often bragged that all he had to do to strike ore was to stick a pick into the ground, so perhaps he had smelled gold on down the creek. At any rate, the strike had been made, people had poured in, and within a matter of days Bill Wagner could have sold out for ten times what he had paid. That's exactly what he would have done if he had lived. Now Cherry flatly refused to sell for any price.

When Phip came into the dining room, Mrs. Decker, Cherry's cook, poked her head out of the kitchen.

"Howdy, Phip. What'll you have . . . steak?"

"Sounds good." He hung his hat on a nail. "Thought you'd be with Frank."

Mrs. Decker shook her head. "I took a look at

him. He didn't need my doctoring. Cherry can do it. Tough as a boot heel, that old varmint. Looked to me like his hide was so tough the bullet bounced off him."

Phip sat down and rolled a smoke. Mrs. Decker shoved wood into the firebox and there was a clatter of stove lids being dropped into place. A moment later he heard the sizzle of grease.

Mrs. Decker poked her head out again. "Biscuits are plumb cold, Phip. Couldn't you get in here any sooner?"

"Stayed too long in the barn talking to Frank."

She drew back into the kitchen and presently came out with a thick steak fried the way Phip liked it, and biscuits, butter, and a dish of grape jelly. She poured steaming coffee into the cup, set a thick slab of apple pie in front of him, and dropped heavily into a chair across the table.

Mrs. Decker was fat, forty, and good-natured. She had gone through three husbands since she was fifteen. She was the best cook Phip knew, and she had been with the Wagners ever since he'd known them. Like Frank Hayes, she'd stayed on with Cherry because Bill Wagner had asked her to. Now she leaned across the table, big hands folded.

"Phip, I'm worried."

"I'm going to eat," he said. "Go ahead and tell me about it."

"Nothing much to tell. It's just Randy Gale and

Cherry. I'm scared he's going to smooth-talk her into marrying him, and I'm pulling for you."

Phip grinned. "Thanks, but it's not just a matter of marrying her."

"I know. Well, I like Matt Lane, too. You boys need this spot for your business. Cherry knows how it is." She shook her head. "Seems like Cherry just wants to try her wings."

"I reckon."

"Oh, Frank said it was Jupe Klein who tried to get you."

"That's right."

"Then Bucky Quinn must be around."

Phip nodded. "I didn't ask Gale. Didn't figure he'd tell me, but there's a good chance Bucky is close by."

Mrs. Decker rose. "It's a terrible country, Phip. Every day I promise myself I'm going back to Iowa where folks don't go around shooting each other." She tramped into the kitchen.

Phip finished his meal. Later, as he lingered over his second cup of coffee, Cherry came in. She stood in the doorway a moment, the lamplight full upon her. Phip pinned his gaze on her, telling himself she was the most beautiful woman in the world. She stood there, smiling, as if sensing his admiration.

Cherry was a tall woman with dark brown hair and a warmly molded body that never failed to bring men's eyes to her. She had worn Levi's and a man's shirt when Phip had seen her in the barn, but since then she had changed to a freshly starched pink dress with a snug bodice and a skirt that made a tight fit around her hips.

"I didn't thank you," Cherry said, coming across the room to his table. "You saved Frank's life."

"Maybe I saved my own life. Maybe it wasn't Frank that Klein was shooting at."

She frowned. "Why would he shoot at you?"

He asked: "Question is, why would Klein shoot Frank?"

"You know the answer to that," she replied. "I couldn't run this place without him. I'd have to sign up with somebody."

"Meaning me? Or Randy Gale?"

"I'm not meaning anything just yet. Come upstairs. Frank said you're here to talk business. I'm ready."

He rose and came around the table.

Smiling, she laid a hand lightly on his arm. "I'm a businesswoman, Phip. I have the right to make the best deal I can. You're like most men. You think a woman should stay in the kitchen or sew or have babies. But the day is coming when a woman can do anything a man can."

"Anything?"

"Just about. In Wyoming, women even have the right to vote."

"A mistake," he said.

They went up the stairs together, her hand still on his arm. He had never kissed her. He had never even told her he loved her, although she must have sensed his feeling for her.

Until he had thrown in with Matt Lane he had always worked for someone else and she had been Bill Wagner's daughter, not rich perhaps, but well-fixed by frontier standards. There had been that wall between them, a matter of pride with Phip Callahan and perhaps a foolish thing, but very real.

He glanced at her, unsettled by her nearness and the soft pressure of her hand on his arm, and he wondered now, with her father gone and Frank Hayes on his back, if she felt the need of a man's help. She had been so sure of herself. Her remark about being a businesswoman was typical of that self-assurance.

They walked down the hall to the front corner room Bill Wagner had fixed as a parlor for his daughter when he'd built the house. The furniture was walnut; the maroon rug and white lace curtains were expensive and had been carefully chosen in Denver. In the corner stood a piano that had been freighted over the pass from Canyon City.

She motioned toward a chair. "Sit down, Phip." Then, stepping back into the hall, she tapped a closed door. "All right, Randy."

Mechanically Phip reached for paper and

tobacco, not liking this. Randy Gale came in, every black hair in place, his brown broadcloth suit immaculate. Phip knew he needed a shave; his clothes, ordinary range duds, were dusty after the long ride from Gunnison. Alongside Randy Gale, he knew he looked like a saddle bum.

"Sit down, Randy." Cherry moved to a desk, pulled open a drawer, and lifted a sheet of paper from it. "I have Randy's contract offer here. Have you drawn one up, Phip?"

"No."

"Guess I win the pot," Gale said.

"Not until Cherry signs with you," Phip said. "Gale, I've been wondering about Klein's body. Did you take care of it?"

Gale's smile faded. "Why should I?"

"It's been taken care of," Cherry said. "One of the freighters will take it to Gunnison."

She sat at the desk in the center of the room. "Now, we all know I have the facilities a stage company needs for a home station. The toll you'd have to pay would break you unless you make a favorable deal with me." She tapped the paper. "Randy came prepared with a contract. He owns the Pueblo and Western, as you know, Phip. In other words, he has no partner to satisfy."

Phip fired his cigarette. What she said was true. Phip had a partner and at times Matt Lane could be stubborn. It was his money that had launched the CS&FC. Phip's contribution had been his knowledge of the freight business and his willingness to do the riding and the fighting to keep the business alive.

"There is also the matter of a mail contract," Cherry went on. "I assume whoever proves to the government that they can stay in business will get that contract."

Gale said: "You're smart as well as beautiful."

"Thank you, Randy." Cherry tapped the paper again. "What's your offer, Phip . . . if you and Matt have decided on one."

Gale plucked a cigar from his coat pocket. "Whatever his offer is, I'll top it."

"I might point out," Cherry said, "that next year the new camps down the creek will have ten times as many people as they have now. The freight company that signs with me will have a monopoly on a million dollar business."

She sat back. "I don't aim to be a hog. I just want my share."

Phip slouched in his chair, cigarette smoke curling up in front of his face. He was licked before he opened his mouth. He had everything lined up for the stage and freight line except this one spot, purposely holding it to the last because he had hoped Matt would sweeten the pot. But he had heard nothing from his partner.

Before he had left Canyon City, Lane had said: "You've known Cherry Wagner for years, so you ought to be able to wrangle a good deal with her. Offer her anything up to five thousand. No more."

Now Phip got up and strode to the window. He tossed his cigarette stub through it and wheeled back. "Cherry, did it ever occur to you that there are some things in this deal that are worth more than the money involved?"

She laughed softly. "Randy has argued along those same lines. He's been here two days making lovely talk and promising to marry me." She shook her head. "I haven't been interested, Phip. The money looks good. I told you I aim to have my share."

There was no use to tell her that the company that signed with her might not make the million dollars she talked about so glibly, that there were risks which could not be foreseen, and there would be a big payroll to meet and equipment to buy, and a possibility that other roads would be opened which might have an easier grade than hers. No, those things would mean nothing to her. She had to demonstrate that she was a businesswoman.

"Go ahead, Callahan," Gale said. "Make your offer."

"Just a minute." Phip came to stand across the table from Cherry. "I wasn't thinking about making pretty talk."

Her eyes were on him, very dark and very lovely, and he was as stirred as no other woman's eyes had ever stirred him. For just a moment the hardness dropped from her; the armor of her self-assurance seemed inadequate.

She said very softly: “No, I didn’t think you were. It’s just the money with you, too, isn’t it? You and Matt Lane.”

“No,” he said more vehemently than he intended. “There’s something else. You know me, Cherry, and you know Matt Lane by reputation. Missus Decker knows him very well. We’ll keep any bargain we make. No lies. No cheating. No back-shooting like happened tonight. Isn’t that something to consider?”

Gale rose, cigar tilted upward. “All right, Callahan. I wanted to save her this, but I can’t. You’ve called. Make your play.”

Phip made a half turn, facing Gale. There wasn’t even a hint of a smile now on Gale’s face. His dark eyes were as menacing as a thunderstorm blowing up over the Continental Divide.

In Pueblo and Canyon City they said Randy Gale was deadly fast with the gun he carried in a shoulder holster, but he seldom used it. Buying men like Jupe Klein and Bucky Quinn was cheaper and less dangerous than risking his own life. But now Klein was dead and Quinn was not around, so it was strictly up to Gale. His bleak face left no doubt of his intent.

“No!” Cherry said sharply. “You’re like two

dogs with hackles up and teeth bared. I didn't call you in here to act like dogs. Sit down, Randy."

Just for a moment he stood glaring at Phip, cigar still held at that cocky angle. Then he swung to Cherry, bowing stiffly. "We are two dogs, Cherry. You might as well recognize it, but I was man enough to at least try to settle our differences away from you."

"You have a veneer of culture," she said tartly, "or perhaps you only pretend to have one."

He flushed. "That wasn't kind. I have great respect for a woman. I should think that would be more than a veneer." He spread his soft white hands. "At least I didn't come to a woman in clothes I've lived in for months, smelling of sweat and horse. . . ."

Phip took two long strides toward him, but Cherry moved between them, very angry. "I guess this wasn't a good idea. You're still acting like a dog, Randy, and dogs have no veneer at all."

"What I said was true, wasn't it?" he demanded.

"I've grown up in mining camps, Randy. I know men, I think. At least I know what Dad used to tell me is true. The difference between them is something inside that you can't see. You have to feel it. It's not the clothes they wear or the way their hair is combed."

Phip took her hand and turned her toward him. He said: "I'm sorry. I can't give you sweet talk like Gale, and I don't have any of that veneer you're talking about." He swallowed, searching for words that would not come. "I can't even say what I want to in front of him."

She smiled. "We'll take a walk along the creek, Phip. Maybe then you can think of what you want to say."

She picked up Gale's contract and put it back in the desk drawer. "I'll tell you what I will do tomorrow, Randy. Wait till I get a wrap, Phip."

After she had gone, Phip asked: "Where's Bucky Quinn?"

"Around," Gale said, adding: "He was Jupe's friend, you know."

"I know."

In front of the house was a small bar that opened into the dining room. While Phip had been eating supper, he'd heard the steady run of talk from the barroom, the clink of glasses, the rattle of chips at the one green-topped poker table. Now the room was deserted. Even the lamps had been blown out.

It struck Phip as being queer, for it was still early. Then he dismissed it from his mind, for most of the men he'd seen were freighters bound downstream to the new camps, and they would have to be on their way again before sunup.

Phip went on through the barroom to the front porch and rolled a cigarette, thinking of what he'd say to Cherry. He had not expected it to go quite this way, for he knew now that she understood Randy Gale, and that surprised him. He'd taken it more or less for granted that Gale's smooth talk, fine clothes, and grand manner had blinded Cherry to the man's real intent, but it wasn't so. Bill Wagner had been a shrewd, honest man, and regardless of her stubborn pride and self-assurance, Phip realized those qualities had come down to his daughter.

She joined him a minute later, a shawl over her shoulders, a scarf around her head. It had been a warm, Indian summer day, but at this altitude the heat fled the moment the sun dropped from sight. Now the air held a sharp chill, a portent of winter that lay but a few days ahead.

"These freighters are making the last trip of the season," Phip said. "You got all the supplies you'll need?"

"We're ready for a tough winter," she answered. "You won't operate until spring?"

"No. Not stagecoaches, anyway. If we have to bring mail, a man will do it on Norwegian snowshoes."

They were silent for a moment. There was no sound but that of horses kicking in their stalls, the roar of the creek in the Canyon upstream, and the whisper of aspen leaves in the night breeze.

She said: "Let's go down to the creek."

He put his hand on his gun butt, remembering

Gale's admission that Bucky Quinn was around. The man would make his try sooner or later, but probably not when Cherry was around.

"All right," he said, and gave her a hand down the step.

They walked across the yard and on through the aspens to the creek, angling upstream.

"I'm waiting, Phip," she said.

"All right." He took a long breath, trying to still the panic in him, for the knowledge was a pressing weight against his mind that if he did not make her see this thing as he saw it, both of them were ruined, and Matt Lane as well.

"I can't offer you the money Gale did, Cherry. You see, this isn't a million-dollar business as you think. It's a gamble. These camps may peter out. Colorado has been full of strikes that look big one year and are nothing the next."

"I know that," she said.

"Matt isn't a young man. Maybe I did wrong, but I sold him the idea of pioneering stage lines. If we lose, he's wiped out. That's pretty tough for a man of Matt's age when he's put his life savings into something."

"You can't convince me on the basis of sentimentality, Phip."

"I'm not trying to. I wanted to explain why we can't offer you what looks like a good deal alongside Gale's." He paused, trying to think how to say it without forcing her into a position where she felt she must defend Gale. "Well, it's like I said. You know me and you know Matt's reputation. We'll keep an agreement regardless. What I'm trying to say is you'd be better off making less money and knowing you'll get it, than signing with Gale."

"I see," she said coolly. "You're thinking of me."

"I'm thinking of all of us."

She was leaning against an aspen trunk, her face a pale oval in the darkness. He could not see her expression, but felt he'd convinced her of nothing.

"There is a place for sentiment," she said finally, "and a place for business. I'm not in a position to think about Matt Lane and his savings. You know as well as I do that there'll be a narrow gauge rail line into this country before long. I've got to make my pile before then."

"It won't come until these mines show more permanence than they do now," he said. "Cherry, we'll send men to work for you . . . men you can trust to keep your road up and your corrals and barns in repair. All you'll have to do is collect tolls. You'll make plenty from your meals, bar, and rooms. Frank will be able to take it a little easier, too."

"So he's been crying to you, too," she said. "Listen, Phip, I'm running this business. Not

Frank. Not Missus Decker, either. If they don't like it, they can quit."

"They won't," he said. "You know that."

"Why? They don't love me that much."

"Maybe they do. Maybe it's loyalty to your dad. Either way, you can make a mistake that will wipe out everything you own. Loyalty is something you can't buy."

"Oh, hell!" she said in disgust. "You're trying to sell me a bill of goods on the basis of loyalty and promises made on Dad's deathbed. I know all about those promises, Phip. I appreciate what Frank and Missus Decker have done for me, but that's got nothing to do with this. What I want from you is a figure that you'll offer for a year's use of the road and facilities here."

He could dodge it no longer. "Five thousand."

"Half of what Randy offered," she said derisively. "Maybe I'll just hold out and make my deal with a bigger company than either one of you."

"The big boys don't gamble, Cherry. Set too high a figure, and they'll build their own road."

"Then I'll sign with Randy."

He could think of nothing more to say. He could have recited chapter and verse to prove Gale was crooked, but she wouldn't believe him. Nor would she believe Gale hired Jupe Klein and posted him in the barn, knowing Phip Callahan must come soon, for time was short. The mail contract would be awarded before long. Randy Gale had expected to get it by default.

"Maybe men are more alike than I thought," Cherry said. "You don't believe a woman can manage a business. That's what it boils down to. You think the world runs on brawn and guns and violence. You think a woman has no place in it. Well, I'll show you you're wrong."

He thought then of the one thing he hadn't said. Not that it would make any difference. She had misjudged him, and would go her own stubborn way until it was too late to take the right path. Still, he had to say it.

"I love you," he said. "I had a notion we could be partners on the toll road and the stage line. There will be some fighting to be done, and I can do that. I can't run a roadhouse, but you can. I thought out marriage could be a partnership, but I guess you don't see it that way."

"So you love me," she said. "That's the way Randy works."

He was angry then, wildly and bitterly angry. He thought of the lonely nights he'd spent riding the high country or camped beside a fire with the spruce wilderness crowding him, of the hours he'd sat on the high box with the ribbons in his hands, tooling a Concord over narrow mountain roads with a high cliff on one side and empty space on the other. Through those hours he had pictured her face, her dark hair and eyes, her graceful body, and he had dreamed of someday possessing her love. It was that dream that had driven him to Matt Lane, that dream which had given him the words to persuade Matt this business of pioneering stage lines could be profitable.

The anger built a fire in him that he could not hold back. He had repressed it too long. A man can have his dreams and live by them for so long. Then if they are wiped out, there is nothing left, nothing for him to hold to or live for.

He moved forward and put his arms around her. In that moment he was a crazy man, crazy with the want of her, hating himself for being a fool so long, hating her because she did not understand and had no faith in him.

"You're the low one, Cherry. You're stubborn and selfish and you don't have sense enough to recognize a man's honest love when he offers it to you."

She struggled to break away from him. "Stop it, Phip. Let me go."

But he didn't let her go. Not then. He kissed her, holding her close. Suddenly she quit fighting him, her arms tightened around his neck and she was kissing him with the same passion that was in him. He felt the warm pressure of her breasts; he tasted the sweetness of her lips. It seemed to him that she could not get enough of him, but that was crazy. She must hate him. This was not the way he had planned to kiss her; it had not been the way he planned to tell her he loved her.

It was the gun pressed against his spine that jarred him back to reality, the sound of Bucky Quinn's soft voice: "I reckon she don't like that, Callahan. Let her go."

Phip dropped his arms. He had no illusions about Quinn. He had been a fool for coming out here, knowing the gunman was around. He said: "Go back into the house, Cherry."

For a moment she stood there, staring into the darkness at Quinn's tall form. "Who is it, Phip?"

"Bucky Quinn."

"It's all right, Quinn," she said. "Leave us alone."

He laughed. "No, it ain't all right, ma'am. You go in. Don't go to yelling, or I'll blow his backbone in two."

Phip said: "Do what he says."

She ran then. Presently Phip heard her steps on the porch and heard the door slam shut.

Quinn pulled Phip's gun as he said: "We'll wait a while, Callahan. We'll wait long enough for you to think about Jupe."

There are times in a man's life when he feels the imminence of death and each moment becomes a year. In this brief span that he waits for the end to come, he relives the high spots of his life, the mistakes and disappointments, the victories and satisfactions that come from worthy accomplishments.

It was so with Phip Callahan. But one big disappointment overshadowed everything. Cherry hadn't believed him.

Phip heard a cry from the house—Cherry's voice, high and frantic. There was no thinking on Phip's part then. He whirled, a swift, involuntary action prompted by the note of urgency in Cherry's voice.

Quinn swore softly, his attention diverted for that one moment. As Phip turned, the gun in Quinn's hand roared. White heat lanced along Phip's back. But the bullet had not blown his backbone apart as Quinn had threatened. It had merely slanted along a rib.

Phip's left hand slapped Quinn's gun arm down, his right fist hammered the man's nose, and Quinn staggered back, a grunt of pain escaping him. Phip closed with him then, left hand gripping the gunman's right wrist. Quinn fell, Phip on him, and they rolled over, fists slashing each other. There was no light here at the edge of the aspens. They fought by feel, Quinn not even cursing, for he had no breath to waste in futile words.

They were like two animals of the wilderness, fighting without rules. Only one would survive. It was fist, knee, and boot. There was the taste of blood on Phip's lips; he was jarred, bruised, and cut, but he didn't give up his hold on Quinn's wrist and the gunman wouldn't loosen his grip on the Colt.

They rolled over again, Phip's right hip feeling the bruising pressure of the gun that Quinn had dropped. He tried to smother Quinn with his weight, tried to hold him there while his right hand groped for the gun. Quinn jabbed a thumb at his eye, and missed, the point driving against his nose and sending a wave of pain through him. Then he had the gun and leaped away, releasing his hold on Quinn's right wrist.

Phip dropped so that he wouldn't be silhouetted against the pale sky. This was the finish; he knew it and he wanted it to be that way, for Cherry's scream seemed to be echoing and re-echoing across the Canyon.

Quinn got his gun into play first. It was the wild and frantic shooting of a desperate man intent only on firing first. He was successful in that, and because of his success he died, for Phip, less than twenty feet from him, targeted the gun flash. Bucky Quinn must have died in that first burst, for his own gun was silenced.

Phip jumped into the aspens and crawled behind Quinn, but there was no stirring in the grass, just the hard labor of a dying man fighting for his last breath. It came, and after that there wasn't even the sound of air sawing out of his lungs.

Phip crawled to him and struck a match. By that tiny flame that blazed into darkness, Phip saw Quinn's bruised face, the bubbles of blood on his lips, the slack look of death.

There was no sound now from the house. Phip ran toward it, pushing shells into the cylinder as he ran. He hit the porch and plunged on into the barroom.

Mrs. Decker called: "Wait, Phip!"

He lunged through the door into the dining room and stopped. The darkness was so thick that he could see only the vague outline of the cook's big body. "Where's Gale?"

"I don't know," she replied. "I'm scared. I heard Cherry yell and I got up. My room's back of the kitchen. I started up the stairs and Gale yelled for me to stay down here."

Phip moved across the dining room and looked up the stairs. The door at the top was closed, but a thin rectangle of light showed around it. A man would be blown to pieces the instant he came up the stairs and threw the door open.

"Gale's a damned fool," Mrs. Decker said bitterly. "He sure kicked this into the open."

"Maybe not such a fool. He was sure Quinn would take care of me. All he wants is Cherry's name on that contract. Then a fire in this house would destroy evidence."

For a moment Phip stood staring at the line of light around the door. There was no sound.

That was hard to understand, for freighters were asleep in those rooms, and the wounded Frank Hayes was in one of them. Some of them, Hayes anyway, should be giving Gale trouble.

"This is the only way to get up there?"

"The only way," the cook answered, "unless you take a ladder and climb . . ."

"Where's any ladder?"

"There's one leaning against the back of the house. Frank made it, so if our roof ever caught fire . . ."

Phip gripped her arm. "Listen," he whispered, "have you got a gun?"

"Just a scatter-gun, but it's loaded with buck-shot. . . ."

Phip tightened his grip. "The freighters up there must be Gale's men, or they'd have sided with Cherry by now. How many are up there?"

"Six. They ain't all Gale's bunch."

"Some might have got the drop on the others," Phip said. "Give me five minutes. Then get that scatter-gun and tell Gale you're coming up the stairs."

"All right," she said. "Get moving."

Phip ran back through the barroom and onto the porch. He circled the house and felt along the back until he stumbled against the ladder. Five minutes had been too short a time. He pulled the ladder down, swayed under its weight for a moment, then started back around the house to the front. The minutes were falling away. Anything could happen once Gale was sure Callahan was alive.

Phip got the ladder up against the front wall of the house. He went up, gun in hand, his eyes on the lighted window. He was opposite it when Mrs. Decker bellowed: "I'm coming up, Gale! I've got my scatter-gun and I'm going to blow you into Kingdom Come in three pieces."

Gale shouted: "Cherry gets it, if you do!"

Phip kicked glass out of the window and slid into Cherry's parlor. He ran into the hall. Gale was standing at the stairs, a gun in one hand, Cherry clutched in front of him with the other. A freighter stood just beyond him, his .45 palmed.

Stairs creaked under the weight of Mrs. Decker. "Open the door, Gale!" she hollered. "You ain't getting out of this because you've got Cherry!"

Cherry cried: "Randy, I'll take your deal! Let Missus Decker go!"

Phip moved closer. "Turn around, Gale."

Randy Gale wheeled. Cherry threw herself sideways as he turned. Both guns roared, thunder-loud in the narrow hall. Phip walked into the ballooning smoke, the smell of it a stench in his nostrils. Gale, a bullet hole in his head, went down on his face, falling against Cherry and knocking her off her feet.

Phip had made that one clear shot at Gale and he had made it good, but there was the freighter, and Phip hadn't been fast enough to take the two of them. The freighter fired, his bullet walloping Phip in the chest. He threw a shot, a wild one, for he was fighting to stay upright.

The door to the staircase slammed open. Mrs. Decker let go with the shotgun. Another freighter had run out of a room farther down the hall. Phip, with one shoulder against the wall, aimed, and dropped the man in his tracks. Then the tide washed in around him. Phip's legs refused to hold his weight. His last memory before the blackness took him was Cherry's voice.

"Phip, you can't die. You can't."

There was no knowledge of day or night in Phip Callahan for a long time, no knowledge of anything except pain and gray figures that moved around his bed in a world of vague unreality. Then the gray figures became distinct and the vagueness was gone. He was looking up into Cherry's dark eyes.

She pressed the tips of her fingers against his lips. "No talk, partner. You've been a long ways into the valley."

He slept again, and when he woke, his first memory was that of Cherry saying *partner*. He wondered why she had used that word. From his bed he could look out upon a sun-drenched earth. There was snow on the ground sparkling in the light.

He lay there a long time thinking about how he had failed, thinking of Matt Lane and the stage company and the mail contract they had missed. Then Cherry came in, saw that he was awake, and came to his bed.

"The doctor said that as soon as you were able to listen, I was to tell you that everything is all right . . . although he doesn't know why, except you're too tough to die."

"Everything couldn't be all right," he said.

"Yes, it is." She drew up a chair and sat down. "I came upstairs that night to get a gun, Phip. I was going back down to help you, but Randy came into my room and asked again if I was going to sign with him. I said no, and he drew a gun on me and said I had to. He showed me another contract, one that was worded in a way that if, through sickness or death, I was unable to manage the roadhouse and toll road, he was to take over. I refused to sign it, and he got rough with me. I guess . . . I guess I screamed."

She wiped a hand across her face. "Two of the freighters were his men. They corralled the other four in Frank's room. That's the way it was when you came up the ladder and Missus Decker showed up with the shotgun."

She smiled. "Well, it's over, Phip. One of the freighters left that night to get a doctor from Gunnison, and I hired another to take my signed contract over the pass to Matt Lane in Canyon

City. It wasn't much of a contract, but it was the best I could draw up. Since then we've heard your company has the mail contract from the government."

He could only lie there and stare at her. She leaned forward and took his hand.

"There's one thing I want you to understand, Phip. I knew what Randy Gale was, all right, but I wanted to keep it on a business basis and I thought I could use Randy to force a better deal out of you and Matt Lane. Then after you kissed me, I . . . well, I changed my mind. I did recognize a man's honest love when I saw it."

Then Phip Callahan found the right words to tell her how much he loved her, the words he had thought about as he'd sat beside a hundred campfires or clung to the high seat as he'd tooled a Concord around the hairpin turns of a narrow mountain road.

She leaned down and kissed him, murmuring: "A partnership, Phip, a real one that will last a lifetime."

The Price of Pride

Big Doug Lindsay was on the sidewalk when the stage pulled into Prineville. John Prater, in the coach, eyes searching the crowd before the stage stopped, picked Lindsay out as the man he was seeking, and felt the prickle of uneasiness travel along his spine. Nature had not been altogether kind to Prater, having dealt more brain than brawn, more nerve than good looks, and in that instant Doug Lindsay looked as tough as a grizzly bear and almost as big.

Lindsay came pushing through the crowd when the passengers stepped down, eyes briefly on the woman, the whiskey drummer, and finally on Prater.

"You're John Prater?" he said, and held out a huge hand, disappointment shadowing his green eyes.

"I'm Prater." He stood before Lindsay feeling like a mouse beside a Newfoundland dog, his small hand gripping the big one briefly.

"You don't look like I guessed you would," Lindsay said. He picked up Prater's two suitcases, jerked his head toward the buckboard across the street, and plowed through the crowd. "We'll get rolling. Long ways to go up to Ochoco."

Lindsay didn't say anything more until they

were out of town heading east into the Blue Mountains. He drove fast, cursing the horses occasionally or flicking them with the whip. Prater, glancing at him sideways, felt that domineering arrogance that great size sometimes gives to men, and he wondered if he had done right in making this choice.

"I hope you ain't got no uppity notions," Lindsay said suddenly. "I won't send my boy down here to school because he'd get 'em, and I made my money raising sheep, and Bud's going to raise sheep, too."

Prater said nothing. He rubbed a thumb over a chin that was not as big as it should have been, pulled his hat a little lower over his eyes, and leaned his thin shoulders against the seat. He would be as much out of place here on the Ochoco as Doug Lindsay would have been in town, and he wondered what had got into him to make him resign a teaching job in Portland high school to tutor Doug Lindsay's boy, Bud.

"Well, have you?" Lindsay demanded.

"Have I what?"

"Got any uppity notions?" he repeated roughly.

"I'm not sure what you're driving at."

Lindsay glowered. He pulled a plug of tobacco from his pocket, gnawed off a chew, and replaced the plug.

"You like mutton?"

"Why, yes." Prater didn't. He even hated the smell of it cooking.

"You'll be eating some. I had a female woman last year teaching Bud, and she didn't like mutton." Lindsay spat over the wheel. "Blast a finicky woman. Kicked all winter about not having fresh vegetables. Didn't like potatoes and beans and biscuits." He shook his head. "Good thing all people don't live in town."

"I guess so," Prater agreed.

"You'll have three students," Lindsay went on. "My Bud, and Ginny Webb . . . my cook's girl . . . and Roy Adams. Roy's only ten, but a mighty smart kid. He belongs to one of the herders. Now if Bud shoots off his mug in the wrong direction, you blacksnake him. I ain't standing for no funny stuff."

"You wrote that Bud was doing high school work," suggested Prater.

"Yep. I'm aiming to see he gets a good education. I don't know what good Latin and geometry and history is on a sheep ranch, but he's sure as shooting going to get it."

"Education includes socialization as well as book learning," Prater said tentatively.

"Shucks . . . give it to him," Lindsay said heartily.

"Socialization isn't something you give a boy, Mister Lindsay. It's something he has to learn, indirectly I'd say, and not as a result of direct teaching. The best way to get it is by association with other people."

"We ain't hermits," Lindsay grunted. "We come to town regular, ever' Fourth of July. Everybody." He eyed Prater a moment and asked softly: "You aiming to say I should move him into the town school?"

"I wouldn't say anything about what was best until I know Bud."

"You'd better not say anything about going to town!" Lindsay bellowed. "You'd just better not. Uppity ideas is one thing I'm going to keep out of his head if I have to blacksnake him every day. Savvy?"

"Yes," Prater said.

Lindsay lapsed into silence, apparently having said all that he wanted to right then, and did not speak until it was nearly dark. He motioned then toward a ranch that lay across the creek.

"That's the Bryan outfit. They'd make some money if old Sam had sense enough to raise sheep."

Prater held his silence, thinking that he might fare better at the Bryan table than he would at Lindsay's. He gazed at the shadowy buildings, saw a lantern moving across the yard beside a man's tall figure, saw the bright shine of lamplight in the front windows of the ranch house. He heard a child cry: "I've got King's X! You can't catch me now!"

"Danged fool, that Sam Bryan," Lindsay muttered. "Just plain, stubborn fool. He's talking about sending his boy, Vance, off to college this fall. He'll ruin every kid in the county if he does. They'll all want to go."

A horseman loomed ahead in the dusk. Lindsay cursed and, drawing his gun, laid the barrel across his lap.

Prater stiffened. "What's that for?"

Lindsay didn't answer until they had passed the rider. Then, relaxing, he slid the gun back into leather. "I figured maybe it was Sam Bryan. Never know what that *hombre*'s going to do when I meet up with him. I told him the other day I'd shoot him if he sent Vance to college."

"That the only trouble between you?"

"Well now, he's been kicking about my sheep crossing the creek, and I told him to go to thunder. When he owns that land, I'll keep my sheep on this side. As long as he don't, I reckon it's free range." He laughed softly. "Kind of rough country up here, Prater. You know how to shoot?"

"I've done some deer hunting," Prater answered carefully.

"You may be shooting at something else before the winter's over. Last time I saw old Sam he told me he was fixing to get his boys together and burn us out. I told him to come ahead. Reckon we could hold out a long time in my house, and if we got him, I'd buy a good outfit cheap from his widow."

It was nearly midnight when they reached the Lindsay place and drew up beside the barn.

"I'll put the horses away," Lindsay said. "Then I'll show you your room."

Prater waited in the gloom of the barn while Lindsay unharnessed the horses, the smoke-darkened lantern swinging from a nail overhead. Lindsay blew it out, and picked up Prater's suitcases.

"Come along," he said.

It was a log house, the front room big and sparsely furnished. Prater's room at the east end of the wing was even more sparsely furnished. There was a bed, the springs sagging, one straw tick with a few ragged quilts spread over it. A bureau stood against the wall, a basin and water pitcher on it, and a rickety chair in the corner.

Doug Lindsay had lighted a lamp, set the suitcases on the floor, and moved back to the door. He stood there a moment, taking off his hat, and ran a hand through hair that was mixed with brown and gray.

"Bud's given me a pile of trouble here lately," he said suddenly. "But maybe you can learn him. I got him the fastest horse in the county, bought him the best danged rifle I could find, and still he ain't satisfied." Lindsay shook his head and said doubtfully: "Maybe you can learn him."

Prater did not unpack his suitcase that night. He undressed and, killing the lamp, crawled into bed between the blankets, dust rising from the tick and bringing a series of sneezes from him before it settled. His mind reached back over the long stage trip from Shaniko, beyond that to the job he had quit for no better reason than wanting something different that did not hold him in a city's shackles.

He wondered how much better off he had made himself. He had something that was different, but he was still bound by shackles, those which were the ignorance and narrowness of a stubborn man. . . .

Out of deference to his weariness, the cook let Prater sleep until eight. He had breakfast alone, shaved before a mirror hung between the two kitchen windows, and went across the grassless yard to the building that once had been a granary, and was now a schoolhouse. There were four double desks, a scarred blackboard on the front wall, and a battered desk in front for the teacher. The air was musty and smelled of chalk.

The two children in the room were Ginny Webb, a fifteen-year-old girl with pigtails down her back, the consciousness of approaching maturity in her, and a red-headed boy who promptly announced that he was Roy Adams, that he was in the fifth grade, and that he hated fractions.

"Where's Bud?" Prater asked.

Roy snickered. "He don't like school."

"He's in the barn," Ginny said. "He's got a dog he's nursing."

"Why would he nurse a dog?" Prater asked.

"He's bent on being a doctor," the girl answered, "and he says he's got to practice. Seems like he's always taking care of something that's sick or hurt."

Prater glanced at his watch. "It's almost nine. Do you want to go after him, Ginny?"

"No." Ginny looked at the floor. "You ring that bell on the desk. His dad will bring him."

Prater picked up the bell and, moving to the door, gave it a vigorous ring. He stepped back to the desk and sat down.

"I'm in the eighth grade," Ginny said without being asked. "Next year I'm going to high school in Prineville."

The girl had said it a little defiantly, watching Prater as if she expected him to explode.

"That's fine, Ginny," he said, and smiled.

"Mister Lindsay says town schools give you uppity ideas," she said.

What next? thought John Prater. *What next?*

Prater was saved the difficulty of making Ginny Webb a tactful answer, for Bud Lindsay came in then, his father behind him. Bud was big, taller than his father and almost as heavy, and except that his eyes were brown instead of green and his chin not quite so wide and blunt, he was a carbon copy of the older man.

"This is Bud, Mister Prater," Lindsay said. "He's seventeen, and I reckon this is the last year we'll have to have a teacher for him. He's been doing high school work for two years, so I figure you can give him all he'll need come spring."

"He can't give me nothing I need," Bud said sourly.

Rebellion was on the boy's wide face, the kind of rebellion that promised momentarily to break into some unpredictable act of violence. John Prater, reading the tension that was in Bud Lindsay, knew that in his ten years of teaching he had never been up against a tougher job than this.

"You'll learn and behave," the older Lindsay said, "or he'll blacksnake you. There's one in the barn, Mister Prater. If you need it, go get it."

"He don't wear big enough britches to whip me," Bud said.

"I don't think a blacksnake is a necessary concomitant for learning," Prater said easily. "We'll get along."

"All right," Lindsay said, and wheeled out of the room.

"Sit down, Bud," Prater said.

"You going to make me?" he demanded.

"No. But you may stand all day, if you want to."

Bud scratched his head, looked at young Roy Adams who was grinning expectantly, then at Ginny who was frowning and shaking her head at him, and finally at Prater. Without a word he sank into one of the double desks.

"I don't believe in much work the first day of school," Prater said. "I'll give you an arithmetic assignment, Roy, so you'll have something to do this afternoon. In fractions. We'd better find out what your trouble is. You know a good doctor has to diagnose a case before he can cure the patient."

His eyes touched Bud briefly, and saw the flicker of attention brighten the boy's face. Then he nodded at Ginny.

"I'll give you some work, too. One of our main jobs is to get you ready to pass the state examinations this spring." He paused, his eyes coming to Bud again. "You're different since you're doing high school work. We can work out a course of study that will interest you, and we'll do it together. What do you want to be?"

"Nothing."

"That isn't so, Mister Prater!" Ginny said fiercely. "Don't you believe him, Mister Prater."

"We all want to be something," Prater said. "Funny thing. When I was your age, Bud, I wanted to be an explorer, but instead I wound up a teacher."

He reached for a fifth grade arithmetic. “Well, about those fractions, Roy.”

Prater held them fifteen minutes, and let them go. He glanced through the eighth grade books, and left the schoolhouse, sauntering across the yard. He looked at the pine-clad mountains rising on both sides of the creek, and then went into the barn.

Bud was crouched beside a box in the corner, and when he heard Prater, he looked up, scowled, and looked into the box.

“Hello, Bud,” Prater said.

A black and white hound pup was in the box, one leg in splints, and when he saw Prater, he cowered back into the corner, his eyes raised to Bud’s face in the pathetic, unquestioning way a dog does when he places faith in a human who loves him.

“A broken leg?” asked the teacher.

“Yeah. I fixed it. I think he’ll be all right.”

Prater knelt beside the box, his hand feeling along the splints.

“A good job, Bud. Maybe you never thought about it, but a lot of people couldn’t do that. A doctor has to have certain peculiar talents. I don’t mean all doctors have those talents, but the good ones do.”

“What kind of talents?” Bud asked.

“Well, patience, for one thing, and faith, and mostly, I think, a desire to prevent suffering.”

"You think I could be a doctor?" Bud asked.

"I'd have to know you better before I'd try giving you an answer. In fact, I'm not sure you really want to be a doctor."

"I want to be one, all right. Wanted to ever since my mother died. She wouldn't have died if we could have got a doctor in time. But Dad says I've got uppity ideas. He says I'm going to herd sheep after this year."

"I'll tell you what we can do," Prater said. "I know a doctor who will send us some medical books. I'll write him a letter today. Meanwhile, we can work on science and Latin."

Hope brought a brightness to the boy's face. But then it faded. "Dad will kill you if you get me some medical books."

"I don't think so," Prater said. "I'll write that letter now. Where can we mail it?"

"There's a post office at the Bryan place. I'll saddle a horse for you, and we'll ride down there." Bud rubbed his chin. "Dad won't like it."

John Prater knew Lindsay wouldn't like it, and he didn't care to think what the big man would do when he heard, but there was such a thing as professional integrity, and adherence to it was a driving force in Prater.

It was noon by the time the letter was slipped through the post office slot in the Bryan living room. Bud stepped back into the saddle, and patted the stock of his Winchester.

"Let's take the trail on this side of the creek," he suggested. "We might jump a buck."

Prater nodded. "Lead out."

They didn't go far—around the house and past the corrals and into a hay field. Then a rifle cracked from the kitchen, the bullet zinging like an angry hornet between them.

"Come back here, you cussed Lindsay pup!" a man yelled. "You've got a right to mail your letters here, but you sure ain't got no right sashaying across my range."

"Old Sam Bryan," Bud muttered, reining his horse around. "Didn't reckon he'd be home this time of day."

They rode back to the house. Old man Bryan, bare-headed, was standing in the yard, the hot September sun falling on him, a cocked Winchester held at the ready. He was an older man than Doug Lindsay, a little on the scrawny side with deep lines in his weather-beaten face. A boy was standing behind him in a poplar's shade, a lad a little older than Bud, Prater guessed, and a good deal smaller. He was smiling as if quietly amused, and Prater, glancing at Bud, saw that he, too, was smiling. It struck Prater that these boys were untouched by the hatred which was prodding their fathers into a killing feud.

"What was you up to, Lindsay?"

"Nothing. We just figured we'd ride home on this side of the creek."

Bryan's eyes came to Prater. "Who's this peanut?"

"The new teacher," Bud said.

Bryan's lips curled, and he spat into the hoof-churned earth of the yard.

"Your dad thinks he's smart, hiring a special schoolmarm. He couldn't send you to a regular high school, could he? A Lindsay'd be too good for that."

"You're insulting, and I'd say plain ignorant," Prater said sharply. "I am neither a peanut nor a schoolmarm, and it strikes me as being out of place for a man like you to be calling other folks names."

Bud snickered. The boy under the poplar laughed silently. Bryan's stubby face turned a darker red. He raised his rifle, then slowly lowered it.

"You'd better drift," he said, "and don't never forget you got no rights past the post office."

Bud made no answer. He nodded at Prater, and they rode past the house and across the creek.

"Old Sam ain't used to being talked to like that," Bud said, and laughed. "He and Dad call each other names all the time, but nobody else around here does." He sobered then as if thinking of his own problems. "Ginny usually gets the mail. We'll have to tell her about those books, or

Dad will get his hands on them, and I'll never see them."

They rode in silence for a time, a growing grimness on the boy's face.

"Someday I'm going to lick Dad!" he suddenly burst out. "I'm not going to keep on being walloped with a blacksnake. He always says a man has to depend on his fists or a gun, and that's all that counts."

"I don't think licking him is the answer, Bud," Prater said.

"You'll find out when you know him better!" the boy cried.

An hour later they reined into the Lindsay yard.

"I have a biology book in my room," Prater said. "I'll get it. After you put the horses away, come into the schoolhouse."

Bud nodded, his face softening. "I'll be over as soon as I take a look at the pup."

John Prater had got off to a good start with Bud, a better start than he had expected when he had seen the boy that first time.

One morning before Bud came into the schoolhouse Ginny said: "I've read about men who did miracles. You know, like vaccination for smallpox. I don't suppose you'll ever be written about in a reader, but you've done a miracle with Bud. You should have seen the trouble the teacher had with him last year."

But nobody knew better than John Prater that he was no miracle man.

In that first week Prater saw what Bud had meant when he said Doug Lindsay believed in his fists and his gun. The big man paid little attention to Prater or the children. He was seldom home, but when he was, his presence was like a chill frost. In a way Prater felt sorry for him. He had never seen a clearer case where a man's sorrow was brought on himself by his own faults.

Not that Doug Lindsay would have admitted any feeling that was close to sorrow. To those around him he appeared entirely self-sufficient, battering down his opposition by force or the fear of force. But John Prater saw through him, and he was not surprised when Lindsay called him into his office one evening.

"Sit down." Lindsay waved to a chair, and when he leaned forward and brought his face into the lamplight, Prater saw the bruises on it.

"I had a fight with Bud tonight," Lindsay said heavily. "We're moving the sheep, and we're short-handed. I was going to send him along for a week, and he said he wouldn't go. He wouldn't miss school." He leaned back, slumping a little, as if some of the strength and certainty had gone out of him. "What have you done to the kid, Prater?"

"It seems I've made him like school."

Lindsay's fingertip touched a cut on the side of his face.

"No kid of mine's going to tell me he won't do what I tell him," he said in a blaze of anger. "I started to blacksnake him, and he took it away from me. I licked him with my fists. I had to do that, didn't I, Prater?"

"No."

"Then what kind of home have you got if you don't have obedience?"

"What kind of home have you got now?"

Lindsay didn't answer. He got up and walked to the window and stood there, staring into the dusk. Then he wheeled.

"Prater, you're a smart man. If I'd had you here five years ago teaching Bud, we wouldn't be where we are now. But instead I had women teachers, and not one understood the kid. I don't know how you've done what you've done, but I wish to blazes I could do the same thing."

"I understand the boy and what he wants to do," Prater said. "If you could bring yourself to do that, you'd have no more trouble."

"Huh, he wants to be a doctor!" Lindsay came back to the desk and pounded on it. "I won't stand for him being no cussed sawbones. He's my only heir. I built this place out of nothing, and when I die, I'm going to leave it to somebody who knows how to run it."

"You're a fool, Lindsay," Prater said, "but I don't know what it would take to make you see it."

"Don't you talk that way to me!" Lindsay came around the desk, fists balled. "You're not even the beginning of a man."

"You just said you wish you could do with Bud what I've done," Prater said.

Lindsay paused a step from where Prater sat. He stared down at the teacher, breathing heavily, his hands slowly opening. Presently he turned and, lumbering back to his chair, sat down.

"Yeah, that's right. I'm a fool. I know it, but I didn't think anybody else knew it. Folks don't talk like that to me. You've got more nerve than I gave you credit for, Prater."

It was the first admission of any weakness Prater had heard from Doug Lindsay, and he widened the opening he had made.

"I'd never seen you before the stage got into Prineville, but I knew who you were. Just from the way you wrote, I thought you'd be the kind of man you are."

"I don't savvy."

"You think that money and strength will make people admire you, but it won't get you anything but fear and hatred." He asked: "Is there anybody in the world who loves you, Lindsay?"

"No," he said hoarsely. "Nobody."

"You see how it is. You've let your own

strength and toughness keep the very thing away from you that you've most wanted."

For a long time they sat in silence, the ticking of the clock on the shelf above Prater an ominous and rhythmical break in the silence. For the first time in Doug Lindsay's life, somebody had talked to him honestly, and Prater, watching him could not tell how the big man would react.

"You're talking straight," Lindsay finally said grudgingly. "I loved my wife, but I guess I never showed it in a way she could understand."

Prater held his silence, seeing the naked look of regret on Lindsay's face, the clock's tick-tick-tick a steady clatter in the room. It was not likely, Prater thought, that Lindsay had ever unburdened himself like this before.

"Bud's all I've got of her," Lindsay went on. "I've done what was best for him. If he's going to run this place someday, he's got to know how." He pinned his eyes on Prater then, and he said defiantly: "Sure, I've been tough on him, and it hurt me like all get-out to do some of the things I have, but he's got to be tough, too. That's what I aim to make him. I won't have a weakling for a son, Prater."

"In some ways Bud is less of a weakling than you are, Lindsay," Prater said.

"What do you mean?" he demanded.

"If I've got the boy judged right, you're having your last chance with him right now."

"Last chance?" he asked uneasily.

"A lot of kids Bud's age want to be something one day and something else the next. It's different with him. I never saw a boy who had his heart set on something like he has, and I don't think he'll change. You're the one who's got to change."

"If you mean about him being a doctor," Lindsay bellowed in a quick surge of anger, "you're crazy as a loon! And if I find out you're helping him in this doctor business, I'll make you sorry you ever saw this place!"

"The thing you're forgetting," Prater said, "is that Bud inherited a chunk of your stubbornness."

Prater rose and left the room, Lindsay's puzzled eyes on him until he closed the door.

Thinking about it a long time that night, Prater guessed Lindsay was torn between a genuine love for Bud, and the hard, tough standards he had set. He doubted Lindsay could break down the wall he had built between him and his son.

The medical books came the next day. Ginny brought them from Bryan's and took them directly to Prater's room before she put her horse away. She must have told Bud because he was knocking on Prater's door within five minutes from the time she had left.

Prater had opened the package and spread the

books across the bed. Bud grinned, immediately sat down on the bed, and began thumbing through them.

"There's a lot in those books I don't understand," Prater said. "You won't, either, but they'll help you know what it's all about. One of these days you'll have to make a decision. . . ."

"I've made that decision," Bud said. "I was fixing to pull out this fall, but now that you're here, I'll stay till spring."

"You dad's a hard man to understand. In his way, he thinks a lot of you."

"In his way." Bud laughed shortly. "He just wants to kick me around."

He put his hand to a scab on his cheek where his father's fist had cut him. "I don't have to take it. Some of the men with families figure they have to put up with his cussedness, but not me. Come spring, I'm pulling out."

So, through no seeking on his part, John Prater found a strange responsibility resting on his shoulders. He felt no sympathy for Doug Lindsay, but he did for Bud, and he saw no way to break the deadlock.

Short-handed or not, Bud did not help move the sheep. He stayed in school, and spent his evenings in Prater's room poring over the medical books. It was better, Prater decided, not to take the books to the schoolhouse. The one thing that would blow the top off was for Doug Lindsay to see those books.

That was the way things stood the evening Lindsay and Roy Adams's father got back to the home ranch. The sheep had been moved down the creek, and Lindsay had brought Adams back to take a wagonload of supplies to the sheep camp the next day.

Lindsay was in his office and Prater was sitting on the front porch, smoking, when Bud came through the door and hunkered for a moment beside Prater.

It was a warm night with a thin moon in the sky and a smoke haze in the air from a forest fire that was burning somewhere east of them.

Bud asked: "Did you hear a whistle a while ago? Some kind of bird maybe?"

Prater took his pipe out of his mouth. "Guess I did, now that I think of it. Over there across the creek."

"Thanks," Bud said, adding: "Don't say anything to Dad."

Bud disappeared into the darkness. Prater sat for half an hour wondering about it before Bud came noiselessly out of the night. He hunkered down beside Prater again.

"That was Vance Bryan out there," he said in a low tone. "I thought I heard him when I was in your room reading, but I wasn't sure about it."

A pulse quickened in Prater. He'd sensed from

the first that Vance and Bud were friends, but Bud had never said so, and he had never asked.

"I suppose your meeting up with Vance wouldn't hit either his or your father very well."

Bud's laugh was short and without mirth. "They'd bust a button. One reason Dad hires a special teacher for me is because it makes old Sam mad. Then Sam announced Vance will go to college . . . because that'll make Dad mad. Their feud goes back for years. Started over a piece of land down the creek."

Prater sat with his back to a post, knees pulled up in front of him, drawing steadily at his pipe. He figured it took a powerful reason to bring Vance Bryan up here in the middle of the night. He watched Bud in the lamplight that washed out through the open door, and saw him glance toward the lighted window of the office.

Bud was fighting his mental battle, and Prater, knowing sooner or later he would seek an adult's advice, held his silence.

"A fellow setting out here in lamplight makes a target for a bushwhacker over there in the willows," Bud said suddenly.

Prater tapped his pipe against the top step. "You reckon somebody's out there?"

"If there isn't now, there will be by morning. That's what Vance came to tell me. Seems like Dad took the sheep down the Bryan side of the creek just to be ornery. They didn't do much damage, but got into Bryan's garden and messed up a ditch or two . . . enough to set the old man off. He's coming up here sometime tonight." He glanced toward the office window again. "I don't know whether to tell Dad or not. He probably wouldn't believe Vance, anyhow . . . or if he did, he'd go to war."

Prater looked at him. "How are we fixed for a siege?"

"All right. We have food and ammunition. Dad figured this would happen sometime."

Prater held his silence, then said: "Suppose you and I sit up all night?"

Bud nodded slowly. "If Bryan comes, a few bullets in his direction might change his mind. That's what Vance said. He figures his old man won't do anything more than fire a few bullets through our windows."

Prater said: "But if your dad knew, he'd get his men from the sheep camp, and there'd be a fight to the finish. Is that it?"

"That's it," Bud replied. "There'd be no stopping him. He's been wanting Sam to start shooting, so he'd have an excuse to wind it up."

"What about Ginny and her mother and Roy?"

"Guess we'd better tell them so they can sleep in the cellar tonight."

Prater rose. "Bring a rifle and some cartridges to my room. With a window open, I don't think they'll get in without us hearing them, and if they just want to shoot the place up, no great harm done."

Ten minutes later Bud brought a .30-30 and two boxes of bullets to Prater.

"I'll bar the door as soon as Dad's in bed," he said quietly. He stood in the doorway a moment. "Dad's going to raise a rumpus when he finds out."

"I'll give him all the reasons we didn't tell him," Prater said. "If it means a trip back to Portland for me, that's all right."

"I'll be going with you," Bud said.

He went down the hall toward his own room, and, watching him, Prater felt a surge of satisfaction. Then for a moment panic washed through him. This cure was stiff medicine. It might bring death to any of them.

The moment passed. Prater shoved bullets into the Winchester, and sat down beside his open window.

It was nearly midnight when Prater heard Lindsay go to bed, and the house became still. Presently Bud came into the doorway.

"I don't think I'm going to be able to stay awake," he said.

"Lie down on the bed in here," Prater said. "I'll wake you if I hear anything."

"I won't sleep long," Bud promised.

But Bud slept through the night while Prater

stayed at the window, ears keening the air for unnatural sounds. It was not until dawn had begun to spread a gray light over the meadow between the house and the creek, though, that Prater heard the thud of horses' hoofs, the faint mutter of talk.

Prater shook Bud. "They're out there," he whispered.

Bud came awake at once, grabbing his Winchester and sliding the barrel through the window.

"Wait a minute," Prater said, holding the boy's arm. "No sense of wasting your ammunition. The minute you fire, you'll bring a dozen bullets through this window."

The tension went out of Bud. "Have you ever done any fighting?"

"No. That's just common sense not to draw their fire."

"Yeah," Bud said. "I'll wait."

The light became better as the minutes dragged by.

"I suppose they'll try getting around on both sides of the house," Prater said.

"Yeah, I hadn't thought of that." Bud remained motionless, staring at the creek. "Wonder if Vance came with them."

"He's a pretty good friend of yours, isn't he?"

"He's the only friend I've got . . . except you."

It came then, a volley from half a dozen rifles

driving lead into the center of the house. Prater and Bud answered, and dropped flat on the floor as bullets whined through the open window or slapped into logs outside.

"Let's get back to the front room," Prater said.

Doug Lindsay was there when Prater and Bud came into the living room. The sheepman was in his underwear, hair awry, his curses fervent and varied.

"So old Sam finally done it!" Lindsay bellowed. "I didn't think he had the nerve. Adams"—he motioned to the herder who had come from a back room—"watch the other side of the house. There's about six men out here in front, but Sam's got more. Chances are, they'll try to get in through the back."

Lindsay shoved a rifle through a bullet-shattered window, and laid his fire along the creek. He pulled his Winchester back as lead screamed past him to rip into the back wall. He reloaded, and suddenly paused, eyes pinned on Prater.

"Who was answering their fire?"

"Both of us," Prater said. "From my room."

"How come Bud was in there?" Lindsay demanded. "And how come you was firing back so quick?"

"I stayed up all night," Prater said. "Bud gave me a rifle, so I was ready for them."

Lindsay drove three more bullets at the Bryans,

and ducked back. He scratched his head as though a multitude of unanswered questions had gathered there.

"Prater, why in tarnation was you staying up all night, and why did Bud bring you a rifle?"

"Vance came."

"Hey, what do you know about that?" Lindsay brought his rifle up again. "Just like shooting ducks on a lake."

Old Sam Bryan's shrill cry sailed out across the meadow. "Get back, Vance! Get back!"

"Don't shoot, Dad!" Bud shouted.

At first Prater, crouching at the window, couldn't see what was happening, but he did now. Vance Bryan, for some reason, had broken away from where he had been hunkered behind the horse trough and was racing toward the house. Doug Lindsay, satanic malice stamped upon his face, had brought his rifle to his shoulder. He squeezed the trigger just as Bud shouted.

Vance's left leg gave with the shot. He went down as if a giant sickle had cut it away from him and he fell full out, his hat rolling off his head, dust boiling up around him. Bud let out a choked cry, and, running to the door, he raised the bar.

Lindsay was lining his sights on Vance for another shot. Just as he thumbed back the hammer, Prater said: "If you shoot that boy again, Lindsay, I'll kill you."

Lindsay's eyes came momentarily to Prater,

blinked when he saw the rifle in Prater's hands.

"What the devil is this?"

"Hold your fire!" old Sam Bryan's shrill voice cut across the meadow again.

Lindsay's eyes turned to the yard. "Bud's bringing Vance in here," he whispered in disbelief. "He's bringing the boy I shot."

His rifle still covering Lindsay, Prater said: "I told you the other night you were having your last chance with Bud. Either you make up to that boy for what you've done to him, or you'll never see him again." He added: "Vance warned Bud what his father was going to do."

"Why wasn't I told?"

"Would you have believed Vance?" Prater demanded. "He said old Sam wasn't going to do any more than shoot out a few windows. But if you'd known, you'd have sent for every man you had and wiped out the Bryans . . . and hanged for it, likely."

There was silence outside. Bud had one of Vance's arms over his shoulder, and he was helping him across the trodden yard, a blood red trail behind them.

Prater, still uncertain what Lindsay would do, edged to the door. "Bryan! Come in here! Send your men home. Vance is hit!"

They came through the door, Vance and Bud, the first time in his life Vance had been in the Lindsay house. From the way the boy was bleeding, Prater knew an artery had been cut.

"Lay him on the couch," Bud Lindsay said.

Prater, watching from the door, saw the Bryan men ride away along the creek, saw old Sam Bryan come across the meadow, his Winchester cradled in his arm. When he dismounted and entered the house, Prater stepped back and kept his rifle ready in case the old flame of hatred was fanned into another shooting.

"I was trying to get in to warn you, Mister Lindsay," Vance said. "When I came up last night, Dad was just aiming to shoot out your windows. Then he got some more men, and he was figuring on killing you and Bud."

Bud swung away from the couch. "I got a tourniquet on his leg. It'll hold the bleeding until we get him to Prineville. We need to hurry. I'll stay with him and loosen the tourniquet once in a while to keep the circulation going."

Neither Lindsay nor Bryan spoke. They stood motionless, staring at one another.

"It would be a good thing if you two would go outside and shoot yourselves," Prater said to Sam Bryan and Doug Lindsay. "Your kids are friends, and I'm thinking that would be the best thing you could do for them."

Then Doug Lindsay did a strange thing. He stepped around Bryan and went to the door that led into the back of the house.

"Adams," he called, "hitch up the team to the

buckboard! We've got to get young Bryan to town . . . fast."

Lindsay wheeled and came back. "Sam, I've been thinking that since you're sending Vance to college, it would be a smart idea to send Bud along so's he could go to school. Seems like he's got a lot of uppity ideas that I can't get out of his noggin."

Bryan held out his hand hesitantly, and Lindsay took it.

"I'm ready to bury the hatchet," Bryan said. "But I figured you was too stubborn and mean ever to do it. We should have done this long ago."

Later, with Ginny standing beside him in the doorway, Prater watched the buckboard wheel away down the creek, with Adams driving, Bud in the back beside Vance, Doug Lindsay and Sam Bryan riding horseback on either side.

"I still say you're a miracle man, Mister Prater."

"No, Ginny," Prater said. "Not a miracle man. All I did was help Lindsay swallow a pill. When he knew that Vance was trying to help him, and saw Bud risk his life to bring Vance to safety, there wasn't much he could do but swallow it."

He paused, then added: "And that medicine will make a different father out of Doug Lindsay, to boot."

The Devil and Old Man Gillis

The Tenmile folks allowed that the universe was a triangle, the three corners being the good Lord, the devil, and old man Gillis, but young Sheriff Jim Waldron had a different notion. He figured the universe was a straight line with the Lord on one end of the rope, Gillis on the other, and the devil in the middle. For downright cussedness, Jim contended, the old man threw a shadow plumb across purgatory.

Fred Gillis, the old man's boy, was in town with the Circle G crew loading a bunch of steers. He stopped at the sheriff's office, and said sort of offhandedly that his dad wanted to see Jim. About that time Jim let out a blast of sulphur and brimstone that would have done the old man proud, but Fred just grinned and walked off. Fred was all right except for the fact that Gillis was his pa, and you couldn't blame Fred for that.

Jim went across the street to the post office, telling himself he'd just forget Gillis's request, which, in plain Tenmile English, was an order. He unlocked his post office box, took out his mail, and got a second jolt. There was a letter from Martha Bilbo. No, Martha Gillis it was, or should be.

Jim walked back to his office, staring at

Martha's fine Spencerian handwriting. Coming from the river bottom as she had, Martha never had a chance for much education, but she could write a mighty pretty hand. Just like in the copybook Jim had when he was in school. Then he noticed the postmark—Tenmile! And the letter had been mailed the night before.

It took a little doing for Jim to hang onto his sanity. When Martha had left the county four years before, she'd sworn she would never come back. The way Jim got it, she'd told off old man Gillis in a manner to which he was not accustomed. But she was back, or she'd had someone mail that letter for her.

Jim went through the rest of his mail. Reward dodgers. A couple of bills. A letter from a ten-cow rancher on the other side of the range asking him to look into some rustling. That was all, except Martha's letter.

He stared at it a full minute before he worked up enough courage to open it. There had been a time when he'd been in love with Martha himself, but that had been five years ago when they were both kids. Before he'd known what was happening, she up and married Fred Gillis.

Now, staring at the name on the envelope, Jim thought about the bundle of letters he had in his trunk, written with the passion of a sixteen-year-old girl who thinks she's in love. Well, she hadn't been. Not with Jim Waldron, anyway, or she wouldn't have run off to Durango and married Fred Gillis. He thought of the letters he himself had written, the ring he had bought and never given her, the kisses under the cottonwood trees beside the Dolores River.

This wasn't good. She had no right to come back into his life.

Jim ripped open the envelope, took out the single sheet of paper, and flattened it on the desk.

> Dear Jim,
> I have no right to ask you for a favor after what has happened, but I have never forgotten that you liked me once. Besides, you are the sheriff. I must see you. I am at the old Penrose cabin. Don't tell anybody.
> Martha

You liked me once.

He crumpled up the paper and threw it across the room. He had loved her. He still did, even after she'd married Fred Gillis, given him a son, and then run off. Now she had the gall to say it.

You liked me once.

He rose, picking up the wad of paper, and stuffed it into his pocket. Well, he'd see her. That ten-cow rancher on the other side of the range could wait. Everything used to wait for Martha. It still would. And old man Gillis could wait, too.

Jim was buckling on his gun belt when

someone came in. Turning, he saw it was Betty Miller, pretty and cool in her ruffled pink dress and smiling in that comfortable way she had. She had been waiting a year for him to ask her, but she might as well forget it. Martha was a fire in his veins, a fire that five years had not put out.

"Howdy, Betty."

"Good morning, Jim." Her blue eyes ran down his long-boned frame, the smile lingering. "Going somewhere?"

"Taking a ride," he said.

It came to him then that he had not been fair with Betty. He'd taken her to dances and eaten the fudge she'd made for him Sunday afternoons in winter and drunk the lemonade she'd made in summer. It was natural enough for her to think he was courting her.

The devil with it. He'd just been lonely, and she'd helped him pass the time. It was her bad luck if she had counted on him. He never said a word about loving her. Never kissed her. Well, he would cut it off right now, and she would forget him. There were plenty of single men around Tenmile; she had her pick of the lot.

"Will you be back tonight?" she asked.

"I'm not sure."

"I was going to ask you for supper." The smile ran across her full lips again. "My fryers are big enough to eat. And I'll bake a chocolate cake."

That was like a woman, he thought sourly. *Trap*

a man by the stomach. He'd had supper at her place more than once and every time he came close to foundering on her chicken and chocolate cake, but that was past.

"I may be gone a couple days."

"Well, I'll go ahead and fix supper. If you do get back, it will be ready."

"Don't count on me," he said, and walked past her out of his office.

He saddled his roan and took the upriver road. The Penrose cabin was in some rough country on High Mesa. He wondered what Martha was doing there and why she had not come into town to stay. Why hadn't she come to see him if she'd been in Tenmile to mail the letter? Did she think he didn't have anything to do but ride all over the county when she sent for him?

He grinned sourly. She knew he'd come. Maybe he had a chance with her now that Fred was out of her mind. Anyhow, he came any time she wiggled a finger. That was the kind of hairpin he was.

Three miles above town he passed the lane that turned off to Circle G. Old man Gillis would be lying in bed just the way he had been for the last six months. Paralyzed from the hips down. Crazy, the old man had been. Thought he was still spry enough to bust the wild ones, but he'd found a big black gelding that had busted him. Jim had not seen him since the accident and he didn't want to. The old man hadn't changed, and he never would.

Jim was fifty yards past the turn-off when he thought of something. There might be a connection between Martha's letter and the old man's order to see him. Gillis hated her even more than he hated other folks, and Martha had plenty of cause to hate him. When he heard Fred and Martha were married, he'd turned the air blue all the way from the ranch to Tenmile.

Jim reined around and took the lane to the Circle G. Might be a good idea to see the old man before he went to the Penrose cabin. If Gillis knew Martha was in the region, he'd want her arrested on some trumped-up charge or another. That would be like him, but this was the morning Jim would tell him where he could head. He'd always wanted to. Just let the old reprobate come up with one of his ornery schemes and see how far he'd get.

The Circle G buildings were scattered in a bunch of pines about half a mile from the river, low log buildings that were comfortable enough for men, but never a place for women, and the old man hadn't changed a thing for Martha. He'd been rough on her from the start. To make it worse, she was pregnant the first month, and the bigger and sicker she got, the meaner the old man was. It all wound up in a fine blaze two months after the baby came, and Martha pulled out. Fred stayed. Old habits were too strong, Jim guessed. The old man had beaten Fred down for twenty years, and when Martha left, he didn't have the guts to go with her.

Jim racked his roan in front of the house and went up on the porch. Old Charley Manders, the cook, answered Jim's knock.

He said: "Come in, Sheriff. Gill's waiting for you."

Jim crossed the big living room, taking a quick look around. It had been a long time since he'd been here, but there was no change. A couple of bear rugs on the plank floor, the old leather couch and the pine table, some chairs, guns on the wall, saddles and bridles tossed into the corners. It was a good bet, Jim thought, that Martha hadn't been able to change a thing in the year she'd been here.

The old man's bedroom was at one end of the living room, and when he heard Jim's spurs, he bawled: "Where the devil you been, Waldron? Took you a year to get out here."

Jim went on into the bedroom. The old man was flat on his back, a blanket spread over him, legs as useless as two sticks. His face, Jim saw, was thinner than it had been before the accident, but the long sweeping mustache was the same, the sharp green eyes, the petulant scowl that creased his high forehead and reached down to twist his lips under the mustache. The old man was as mean as ever, which was exactly the way Jim expected him to be.

"Get down off your high horse," Jim said. "I had a notion not to stop by at all."

"Oh, you did, did you?" Gillis bawled. "Well, let me tell you something, kid. You're up for election next year." He waggled a bony finger at Jim. "I may be laid up, but I can still pin the sheriff's star on the man I pick. I got you elected, and I can get you licked."

Jim was sore, right down to his boot heels. He was twenty-five and he didn't like being called *kid*. Besides, he didn't figure the old man had anything to do with his election. Then he thought of Martha and forgot about himself. If old man Gillis were anything but what he was, he'd have been happy just seeing Martha around.

"What do you want?" Jim asked.

The old man put his hands down against the mattress and shifted his shoulders. "You're going to do a job. I don't want no back talk about it. I heard you was sweet on that no-good filly before Fred married her. . . ."

"What do you mean . . . no-good?" Jim said, anger stirring in him again.

Gillis snorted. "All right. All right. Reckon you're still sweet on her. I wish to blazes she'd married you instead of Fred. She would have, too, if you had a pa who owned a spread the size of Circle G. Knew a good thing when she saw it, but it didn't do her no good. She didn't get a blamed nickel when she left." Gillis laughed. "Well, she pulled out and it was good riddance. Now Fred gets a letter from her the other day. She's working in Denver. Claims she can make a home for the boy."

"She's his mother," Jim said.

"Mother! Now, if that ain't the dangedest word to pin on her. Even if she is, she don't get Freddy. Not by a jugful, she don't. That's where you come in. She may want to go to court, which same won't get her nowhere, but she'll kick up a stink. Cheaper just to stop her before she gets started."

No, Martha would not get anywhere in a court in Tenmile. Not with old man Gillis owning the judge the way he did. He'd own the jury, too—through his money or one way or the other. You couldn't find twelve men within fifty miles of Tenmile who'd vote against the old man.

"What do you want the boy for?" Jim asked.

"Want him? Why, you blamed ignorant, chuckle-headed idiot, he's my grandson, ain't he? I aim to raise him like a Gillis, not like none of the river-bottom trash that woman came from. If she shows up, you get rid of her. Make love to her if you want to. Pay her. Threaten her. Throw her into jail. Just get her out of here." Gillis scratched thin hair. "Do the job, and there's a thousand dollars in it for you."

This was the time to tell Gillis where to go, and he would have if the boy hadn't run in. The child had grown a lot since Jim had seen him, a fine-looking kid with Martha's dark eyes and black hair and sharp little nose.

"Look, Grampa." The boy held up a grass-hopper. "I catched him."

Then Jim saw a miracle. The old man's face softened, the scowl fled, and his voice was tender when he said: "Well now, if that ain't the dad-gummedest hopper I ever seen. I'll bet you had a tussle with him."

"Sure did," the boy said proudly. "I cut sign on him and trailed him clean across the pasture."

The old man dug under his pillow and brought out a battered sack of horehound. "Here, you take a piece of candy and go out and catch another hopper. I'll have Charley fix you up a fishing pole."

The boy stuck a grubby hand into the sack and popped a piece of horehound into his mouth. "You bet, Grampa." He ran out of the room.

Gillis lay listening until the sound of the boy's steps had died. Then he cleared his throat and looked at Jim, scowling again. "Well, you heard what I said."

"I heard all right," he said. He added: "Cute little tyke."

"Sharp as a tack," Gillis said. "Chip off the old block. Rides a horse like he was born on one. She ain't getting her hands on that boy. Now, you hit for town and keep your eyes peeled. If that woman shows up . . ."

"Gillis," Jim said, "I don't give a hang what you can do to me when election comes up. That's Martha's boy. She'd got a right to him, if she wants him."

"Why, you blasted . . . ," Gillis began.

Jim walked out, leaving the old man sputtering. When he swung into the saddle, he saw the boy pursuing another grasshopper across the horse pasture.

It was nearly noon when Jim reached the top of High Mesa and rode through the aspens. The first frost had turned the leaves orange. They fluttered above him in the chill wind, ceaselessly turning in the delicate way they had. Some had already fallen and lay tinder-dry in the trail so that his horse's hoofs made rustling sounds on them, the noise running out through the brittle stillness.

Martha must have heard him for she was waiting in front of the cabin.

Jim reached the clearing and reined up, the noon sun falling sharp and bright upon Martha. Her red lips held a wistful smile. For a moment neither spoke. He had seen her only once after she had the baby. Four years ago. She'd been seventeen then. Twenty-one now, four years younger than Jim and Fred Gillis.

The years had not taken anything from her. They had added something, he thought, perhaps maturity and deeper beauty.

"Jim," she said.

He swung out of the saddle and she ran to him. There was no holding back. There never had been any holding back with her. Her arms came around his neck. She kissed him and clung to him; he felt the soft roundness of her breasts, and for this moment the bitterness that five years had brought to him was swept away. There were just the two of them in a world surrounded by aspens. Nothing else mattered.

She drew away, a hand coming up to caress his cheek. "I knew you'd come, Jim. I knew."

He looked at her, the certainty that had been in him for the one short moment suddenly gone. He didn't know why. One kiss could not bridge five years. She had run off with Fred Gillis when she was engaged to Jim Waldron.

Old man Gillis's words came back into his mind: *I wish to blazes she'd have married you instead of Fred. She would have, too, if you'd had a pa who owned a spread the size of Circle G.*

Jim remembered other things, too: expensive things she'd wanted, and telling her he'd buy all of them. Fool! His folks had been as poor as the

Bilbos down in the river bottom. But nothing had seemed impossible when he had been twenty, and in love.

Martha hooked an arm through his and led him into the cabin. "I knew you wouldn't fail me, Jim. I've thought of you so much all these years."

He sat down in a rawhide-bottom chair, ill at ease now. He had discovered something he should have known all the time. A man could not go back. She had married Fred, she had given him a son. All this time Jim had been thinking about her, dreaming about her, nurturing something he thought was his love for her. Well, he had it straight now. It had been nothing but his battered pride. He'd held her in his arms and kissed her, but it hadn't been the same. Suddenly he felt like a free man.

She was bustling around the stove, filling the firebox with chunks of aspen, shoving the coffee pot to the front, slicing bacon, and now and then throwing him a smile. He remembered that smile. Sometimes it had been for him, and sometimes when they were dancing it had been for another man. He remembered how many times he had been forced to surrender her to another's arms. Then he'd gone outside and sulked. Maybe had a few drinks and usually wound up fighting the fellow she'd danced with.

"I'll have dinner right away," Martha said.

"Tell me all the gossip. What's been going on? How are your folks?"

"My folks died last winter," he said. "Influenza. A week apart."

"Oh, I'm sorry. I hadn't heard."

Silence then, except for sizzling bacon. She popped a pan of biscuits into the oven and set the table. He began noticing things that struck him as being queer. As far as he knew the cabin had not been lived in for years, but the stove was clean, there were dishes and pans for several people, and shelves were stocked with cans and sacks of food. The pile of wood behind the stove had been freshly cut.

Jim rose. "I'll tend my horse," he said, and went out.

There was a spring behind the cabin. He saw, with growing concern, that several horses had been watered here. Recently, too. He left his horse in the log shed. Just one other animal there now, but there had been two more. A half-filled sack of oats stood in the corner. He returned to the cabin, puzzling over what he had found, and not liking the conclusion he was forced to make.

"Almost ready," Martha said cheerfully. "I expect you're hungry."

He stood in the doorway. "When did you get here?"

"Yesterday. I rode into town last night and mailed that letter. I was afraid to look for you."

She straightened and faced him. "Jim, I'm just plain scared of old man Gillis. That's why I wrote the letter. I . . . I didn't want him to see me in case he was in town."

"He wouldn't have been in town," Jim said, and told her about the accident.

"He deserved it," she said. "I know that's not the right attitude, but I don't care. You know how he treated me." She turned to the stove, suddenly close to tears. "Maybe I didn't deserve anything better after what I did to you. I've made an awful mess out of my life, Jim. I . . . I hope I haven't made one out of yours."

He didn't say anything. There was nothing he could say. She'd messed up his life plenty, but there was no use telling her.

"You aren't married?" she asked.

"No."

"You will. You'll find the right girl and you deserve the best. I wasn't. I mean . . . it wouldn't have worked with us, but that doesn't excuse me for what I did."

She took the biscuits out of the oven and poured coffee.

Jim asked: "Who's with you?"

She whirled, the coffee pot in her hand. "Nobody. Why?"

"Plenty of sign."

"Oh, someone was here just before I came. I don't know who." She set the coffee pot on the stove, eyeing him. "I've been in Denver, you know. Working and saving all the money I could."

"That your horse in the shed?"

"Yes. I bought him in Durango." She forked bacon onto a tin plate and set it on the table. "I bought some grub. I knew about this cabin, and when I got here, I saw someone had been living here, but no one was around, so I moved in. It's all right, isn't it?"

"I reckon."

She motioned him to the table. "I hope whoever was here doesn't come back."

They ate in silence, Jim watching her and trying not to let her know he was. If she was aware of his covert glances, she gave no sign. She had not told him yet why she wanted to see him, nor did she until they were finished and Jim had pushed his chair back from the table and rolled a smoke.

She asked suddenly, sharp feeling flowing across her face: "How's my baby, Jim?"

He fired the cigarette, tossing the charred match through the door. Except for the way she had greeted him, he might have been any of a dozen men she'd known before she had left Tenmile. Now her lips tightened. She was watching him closely, waiting for his answer, and he knew then why she had come back.

"The kid's fine," he said. "I saw him this morning."

She leaned forward, hands clasped. "Who does he look like, Jim?"

"You. Your eyes and nose, anyhow."

She laughed shakily. "He had them when he was a baby. I . . . I haven't seen him since he was two months old. Can you understand how that is, Jim? Four years, and I haven't seen my baby."

There was misery in her now, honest, sincere misery. He looked away, embarrassed by her show of emotion. He said: "Tough, all right."

"I've done a lot of things that were wrong, Jim, but I don't deserve this. I love Fred, but I guess he doesn't love me or he would not have let me go like he did. He's just as scared of the old man as everybody else."

She bowed her head. "Jim, I just can't let that old devil raise my boy."

"I'll tell you something you won't believe, but I saw how it was this morning. The old man loves the kid."

She shook her head, eyes showing that she did not believe him. "You're just saying that, Jim."

"No. It's true."

She got up and walked to the door. "It doesn't make any difference. I'm his mother. I'm going to have him."

Jim rose and tossed his cigarette stub into the stove. "Gillis figures you'll make a try for him. He wants me to get rid of you . . . offered me a thousand dollars. Said to throw you in jail if I have to."

"That would be like him." She laughed hysterically. "But I'm going to fool him. I am going to take that boy away from him."

"You haven't got a chance, Martha. Not here. The court wouldn't let you."

She ran across the room to him and put her hands on his shoulders. "Jim, listen to me. Don't think about how I treated you. Hate me if you have to, but just think of one thing. Freddy is my boy. He belongs with his mother. You can see that, can't you?"

Her lips were very close to his. She pressed against him, and he was as stirred as any man would have been stirred, but her kisses could not persuade him as they once had. She'd had the rough end of the stick, all right, but he saw her now as just another woman who had run off from her baby.

"You can't change anything, Martha. Don't try."

"I've got to, Jim. That's why I asked you to come here. Don't try to stop me."

"You're talking crazy. First place, you couldn't get him off the Circle G. Or if you did, the old man would get a court order, and I'd have to fetch him back."

"You could let me get away. You're the sheriff." She began to cry. "Jim, Jim, you were always so fine and kind. I thought you'd understand."

She was counting on tears working if her kisses didn't. He shook his head. "You can't take care of him. Anyhow, the old man gives him all he wants."

She was clinging to him now, fingers digging in. "Yes, I can. I've got some money. I'm doing real well in Denver. I'm secretary to a mining man."

She was lying again. She'd had very little schooling when she left Tenmile, and there was a mighty slim chance she'd had any business training in Denver.

He pushed her away, saying: "I can't do anything for you. Maybe I would if the old man was kicking the kid around. But he isn't. And don't forget . . . Fred's his father."

Jim walked to the door. He turned and looked at her. She stood beside the stove, rigid. He asked: "Who's with you?"

"Nobody," she replied.

Another lie. Well, it was plain enough. She had sent for him, she had kissed him, she had cooked a meal for him and shed a few tears, all the time thinking she could persuade him to stand aside while she took the boy. He walked on across the clearing to the shed. Tightening the cinches, he mounted and rode away without looking back.

Later, riding through the aspens with mottled shadows lying across the trail and the clatter of a woodpecker somewhere off to his right, he found himself thinking about it more clearly. He could see how a mother would feel about her child, but he wasn't sure about Martha. She might be prompted by her love for the boy, but again her motive might be revenge. Perhaps she was only trying to strike back at Fred and old man Gillis.

He took a long breath, a worried tension gripping him. Either way, the kid was better off where he was. Anyhow, there wasn't much Martha could do.

It was well in the afternoon when Jim passed the Circle G lane. He glanced toward the ranch, a vague uneasiness working in him that seemed to have no foundation. Jumpy, he guessed, but he couldn't forget someone had been with Martha. If she had been entirely on the level, she would have told him the truth.

A dust cloud rose above the road ahead, and presently he saw Fred Gillis and the Circle G hands returning home. When he came up to them, he reined off the road and nodded. They nodded back in the short insolent way that was typical of Circle G riders. It was a quality the old man had instilled in them, a sort of overbearing insolence, but the thing Jim had always found the most surprising was the fact that of all the men connected with the Circle G, only Fred was mild-mannered and friendly.

"See the old man?" Fred asked.

"Yeah, I was out this morning," Jim said. "I want to talk to you, Fred."

"Sure." Young Gillis reined off the road and motioned for the crew to go on.

Jim waited until the others had ridden on. He thought, with some surprise because he had never considered it that way before, that he should despise Fred Gillis because he'd taken Martha from him. More than that, he resented Circle G's curt insolence; he resented the old man's power and constant effort to run everything in Tenmile County, including the sheriff's office. But nobody hated Fred Gillis. He had his father's big frame and green eyes, but he was easy-going like his mother who had died when Fred was a boy. Jim remembered her, and even then, as young as he had been, he had thought it strange that an old hellion like Gillis could have such a fine wife.

Fred was grinning uneasily. "I suppose Dad told you I heard from Martha."

They turned toward the ranch, riding slowly.

Jim said: "Yeah, he told me. After I talked to him, I saw Martha."

Fred stared at him.

"She's holed up in the Penrose cabin."

Fred took a moment to understand this. "What's she doing there?"

Jim told him, adding: "There's something fishy

about the whole shebang. It's plain she's got a couple men with her, but she denies it. I'm wondering why."

"I wouldn't have a guess," Fred said. "Jim, I've never talked to you about Martha. Always been afraid to. I did you a damned dirty trick, and it's been surprising to me that you didn't beat hell out of me for it."

Jim grinned. "I never figured you were to blame. I knew exactly what she could do to a man when she set her mind to it. I remember I couldn't take her to the dance that night, so she went alone. You just made the mistake of taking her home."

"That's right, but it wasn't really a mistake. You see, I really loved her. Still do." He paused, then added: "She couldn't manage Dad the way she was used to managing men." He was silent a moment, staring across the valley at the Circle G buildings. "I don't like it, Jim. I got her letter a month ago, but didn't answer. Fact is, I didn't even tell Dad until yesterday."

"You won't give the kid up, will you?"

"I couldn't. Just couldn't. Anyhow, she's got no right to him. Or not more than part of the time." He brought his eyes to Jim. "Nobody knows this except Dad and me and the doc, but Dad's got a bad heart. It would kill him if we lost Freddy."

That was the greatest surprise Jim had received on this day of many surprises. He had always thought of old man Gillis as being indestructible.

"Something else I want to tell you now that we're talking about it," Fred went on. "I know how Dad is. I mean, being his son doesn't make me blind, but he's been good to me. Maybe he loved me so much he was jealous of Martha. I dunno. Anyhow, they sure didn't get along. Then she wanted me to go to Denver with her."

He shook his head. "But I couldn't do that. Even for Martha. She left of her own accord, crying her eyes out because we wouldn't let her take the baby. Maybe she thought I'd come later and bring Freddy. I dunno."

They rode in silence for a time, Jim thinking about what Fred had said. They had reached the lane turning off to the ranch when Fred straightened in the saddle. "What the devil, Jim! Look at Pete."

A Circle G rider was coming down the lane in a wild run, cracking steel to his mount at every jump.

"Something's wrong," Jim said, and spurred his roan, reined into the lane with Fred beside him.

The cowboy was waving at them in great sweeping gestures, yelling something, and when they came up to him, Jim made out what he was saying.

"The kid's gone! Old Charley's shot dead!"

They swept past the cowhand who whirled his horse and followed, thundered up the lane to the house, and hit the ground running. Fred beat Jim through the door by a step and went into the old man's bedroom. The cook, Charley Manders, lay on one of the bear rugs in the living room, sightless eyes staring at the ceiling, a shotgun beside him. Jim ran into the bedroom.

Old man Gillis was in bed. One of the Circle G riders was beside him, saying: "I don't know how in hell he did it, but he got out of bed. I found him on the floor over there by the window."

The old man's face was gray, his green eyes filled with a kind of wild fury Jim had never seen in human eyes before. His hands clutched the blanket that had been thrown over him, the knuckles white.

"Two of them," the old man whispered. "Charley . . . fixing a fishing pole for Freddy. One of them gunned him down . . . when he grabbed a shotgun. The other one . . . took Freddy."

Jim leaned over him. "What did they look like?"

"Big. One was red-headed . . . bearded. One wasn't so tall . . . but he was thick. Didn't know I was here, I reckon. I got out of bed . . . watched them ride up High Mesa."

Jim nodded. The riders were Rufe and Blaze Harrigan. He'd seen Reward dodgers on the brothers recently, as tough a pair as ever held up a stage or robbed a bank. Martha must have hired them to kidnap her boy. That was the only guess that made sense.

The old man's eyes were on Jim. "Get him back. I'm cashing in . . . I've got to know Freddy's safe."

"We'll get him," Jim said. "You coming, Fred?"

"Sure, I'm coming."

They saddled fresh horses, working fast. Jim said: "They must have been watching you from the rim. They knew you left with the boys early this morning and then they saw me leave. They probably came down while I was talking to Martha."

White-lipped, Fred said: "Damn her!"

"Hold that," Jim said. "Maybe she didn't figure it would go this way."

They mounted, Fred trembling so that he almost dropped the reins. "Wasn't any other way she could figure it."

They went down the lane on the run and turned into the road, and all the time Jim was thinking they might be too late. He wasn't sure about Martha. But he was about the Harrigans.

Jim had never whipped a horse the way he did on this ride. They swung up the steep trail that took them to High Mesa, Fred saying nothing. Jim sensed that young Gillis wasn't thinking coherently. There would be just one thought in his mind, to get his boy back.

Now, laboring up the switchbacks that took them to the mesa, Jim wondered if they'd get to the cabin in time. This trail was steep and crooked. The Harrigans would have to fight their way through a jumble of scrub oak after they reached the top.

They stopped a moment to let the horses blow. Jim said: "They'd figure you wouldn't get back until night. That's where their luck turned sour. Strikes me there's a good chance we'll get to the cabin about the time they will."

Fred didn't say anything. The corners of his mouth were twitching like a pulse. Then Jim thought about old man Gillis back there in bed, waiting to die. He didn't understand why it had gone this way. He didn't understand it at all, but once he'd heard a preacher talk about folks reaping what they had sowed. Old man Gillis had spent a lifetime sowing meanness. Now the one human being he loved more than he had ever loved anyone was in danger. The Harrigans were the kind who would kill the boy as soon as they'd kill a calf if they had trouble with him.

They went on through the aspens, the sun dropping westward, the mottled shadows still on the trail, the tiny leaves brown and sere under the driving hoofs. There was no question of trying to surprise the Harrigans, of approaching the cabin silently, no question of anything but getting there in time.

The clearing was just ahead then. Jim glimpsed horses. He drew his gun. Two men were in front of the cabin, one with a red beard, the other shorter and as thick of body as the trunk of a great oak.

Fred cried out and pulled his gun.

Jim yelled: “No, Fred! Wait till we see Martha and the boy.”

They came into the clearing, the Harrigans only then knowing they were there. Jim caught a glimpse of the boy, a huddled heap beside the cabin door. Then he saw Martha on her hands and knees, trying to get to him, black hair stringing down her face.

Blaze Harrigan had his gun clear of leather, roaring out a great challenge. He threw a shot at Jim, and missed, for Jim was riding low in his saddle and coming fast. He swung his horse around, knowing this was up to him, for Fred had never been a fighting man and there could be no miracle that would make him one now.

The other Harrigan fired at Fred, knocking him out of his saddle in a rolling fall. Then Jim let go with his first shot and big Blaze Harrigan was thrown back against the cabin wall and his feet slid out from under him and he went down.

It had taken time, that shot, too much time. Rufe Harrigan swung his gun toward Jim. Frantically Jim pronged back the hammer. He pulled the trigger and missed, for his horse was spooked by the sudden gunfire.

Jim spilled off the animal, somehow hanging on to his gun. Rufe Harrigan fired, the slug kicking up dust a foot from Jim's head. The fall knocked the wind out of him. He lay there, paralyzed, able to see and hear, but for what seemed an eternity there was no power of motion in him.

Then it happened, the one thing that could quiet the doubt that had been in Jim's mind from the moment he had told Fred: *Maybe she didn't figure it this way*. Martha was on her feet, blood streaming down her face. She had Blaze Harrigan's gun in her hand and now she swung it squarely across Rufe's head.

Martha wasn't strong enough to give Harrigan a knock-out blow, but she hit him just as he was squeezing off another shot at Jim. It threw his aim off and sent the slug screaming through space. Harrigan struck Martha a back-handed blow, knocking her down, but she had given Jim the time he needed. Flat in the dust, he tilted his gun upward and let go a shot that blasted Rufe Harrigan into eternity.

Jim came to his hands and knees, watching the big man go down. Only when he was sure that both the Harrigans were dead did he tend Fred. He had a shoulder wound and had been knocked cold by his fall, but was not seriously hurt.

He saw Martha on her feet, swaying uncertainly.

Jim walked past her. He picked the boy up. The boy blinked and coughed.

"Sheriff! Where's my daddy?"

"He's all right," Jim said. He steadied Martha and they went to Fred. She knelt.

Martha held Fred's head in her lap, stroking his face and crying. She looked up when she saw Jim's shadow beside her. Fred groaned when his son called to him again.

"He'll be all right," Jim said. Nodding at Freddy, he added: "Both of them."

Fred sat up, managing a smile.

It was strange that at a time like this Jim Waldron would think of old man Gillis, lying in his bed very close to death. Working swiftly, Jim tied both bodies face down across the saddles, and when he was done, he saw the expression Martha and Fred had on their faces, the expression of a man and woman in love.

"Blaze did it," Martha said in a low bitter tone. "Freddy kept crying. Blaze wanted to keep on riding and I wouldn't go. Blaze hit me, and then he hit Freddy."

"Give us the yarn," Jim said sharply. "Tell it straight this time."

She started to protest.

"I'm hightailing it down to tell the old man the kid's safe," Jim said, "but first I aim to get a straight story out of you."

Martha put a hand to her face. "I . . . I . . ."

She looked at Fred then. "I haven't done many things I'm proud of. I married you for your money. Then I found out I loved you and I wanted to give you a son, but the old man . . ."

"I know," Fred said. "I should have gone with you. It'll be different from now on. You'll see."

"I saved all the money I could," Martha went on. "I haven't thought of anything for four years but you and Freddy. I used all I'd saved to hire the Harrigans to steal Freddy for me."

She looked at Jim. "I lied to you, Jim. I worked at all kinds of jobs, from saloons to cleaning to cooking. . . ."

"Somewhere along the line," Jim said, "the Harrigans got another notion, didn't they?"

She nodded. "After they found out the old man was rich, they decided to make him pay to get Freddy back."

"You ought to have known you couldn't trust them," Jim said.

"I couldn't think of anything else to do. I wanted my boy, and I thought maybe me and Fred . . ."

Jim mounted and rode out of the clearing, leading the outlaws' horses behind him.

Later, when Jim stood beside old man Gillis's bed, he couldn't help thinking of what folks said about him being one corner of the universe, and what he'd said himself, about the old man outdoing the devil when it came to downright cussedness. Well, maybe it had been true in a way, but now the old man was dying, and it seemed strange that the greatest happiness Gillis had ever known had come from a four-year-old boy.

Jim couldn't get the old man out of his head when he rode back to town. As long as he lived he would never forget the expression that touched Gillis's craggy face when he told him the boy was safe. The old man was unable to reply, but he had understood. Jim was sure of that.

A lot of lives had been tangled up. The old man's passing would not take the knots out, for too many people had fallen into the habit of blaming their troubles upon old man Gillis when actually they should have blamed their own weaknesses.

Jim knew he had fallen into the same error of thinking as the rest of the Tenmile people. He'd made a big mistake, too, and he was eager to correct it.

His thoughts, freed at last of what he had believed was his love for Martha, came to Betty Miller. He touched up his horse, suddenly eager to see her, to talk to her, to be with her.

Then there was that ten-cow rancher who needed some help.

Shooting for a Fall

Every day old Ben Champion sat on a bench in front of Poke Wilson's Mercantile and whittled. He was a first-class whittler, old Ben was, the best in Juniper Junction. He kept his knife razor-sharp, he used only the best pine sticks, and his shavings were long and feathery and as alike as the matched bays Fred Stanton had just bought in Prineville.

But for some time Ben hadn't been able to get his heart into his work. He was faced with a job of fixing. That meant meddling, and meddling didn't come naturally to Ben.

Nobody in town knew much about Ben except that he was a friendly old codger who liked to pass the time of day with every man, woman, and child in Juniper Junction. That is, all but the town marshal, Trig Akers.

The truth of the matter was that Ben had a smoky past. If he'd wanted to talk about it, he'd have had every kid in town listening all day with their ears hanging out. But that wasn't what he wanted. He'd come here just to sit in the sun for the rest of his days.

Ben had come to Juniper Junction in the spring, rented a house at the edge of town, and when he wasn't whittling, he put in his time puttering around his flower bed. Now, in late August, he had the best snapdragons in town. Every evening he took a bouquet over to Celia Murray, the pretty blonde dressmaker who lived next door. That was how he knew he had to take on this fixing job.

This morning his whittling wasn't good. Maybe his hands were stiff, for it was a mite chilly lately with a hint of fall in the air. Wouldn't be long till he moved inside Poke Wilson's store. Poke wouldn't care as long as Ben stayed out of his way.

For a young fellow, Poke was downright industrious. The fact was, he overdid it. If Poke ever got his nose off the grindstone long enough to look around, he'd see he was losing Celia Murray as sure as the Lord put green apples on a tree. That was half the reason Ben had to meddle. The other half was Trig Akers.

Right now the marshal was standing in front of the Juniper Café, picking his teeth. He always ate a late breakfast, claiming his job kept him up late, but he didn't fool Ben. Akers played poker in Barrelhouse Jones's casino till the small hours, but folks were afraid to call him on it. Akers was just that kind of a hairpin.

Ben didn't see Celia come along the walk until she said: "Good morning, Ben."

He jumped and came close to cutting his thumb off. Celia had a voice that made a meadowlark sound like a crow. She had a way of walking so her skirt swished and showed her ankles, and she had a talent for fitting her dresses so every man in Juniper Junction practically broke his neck just watching her whenever she came downtown.

"Howdy, Miss Celia. Chilly this morning, isn't it?"

"Why, I hadn't noticed." Celia smiled. "Still August, you know."

Whenever Celia smiled at him, Ben wished he was forty years younger. He wouldn't do any meddling, then, you bet. He'd go right to the point. If that Poke Wilson . . .

Ben frowned thoughtfully. Maybe this was a good time to start fixing.

"Sit down." Ben patted the bench beside him. "You aren't in a hurry, are you?"

"Oh yes, I am. Missus Flynn wants a dress finished tonight."

Mrs. Flynn, the liveryman's wife, was nearly as big around as Barrelhouse Jones, a fact which was politely overlooked in Juniper Junction.

Ben leaned forward, whispering: "Sounds like a big order for Poke."

Celia laughed. Ben always liked to hear her laugh. Sounded like the mission bells he used to listen to when he was rodding a town in New Mexico.

Celia said: "*Shhh*. It's a big order for both of us."

"Let her wait. I want to ask you a question."

"Go ahead and ask, but I'm warning you. I haven't got time today to bake a cake for you."

Ben sighed. "Sure had my mouth puckered for one of your cakes. That's isn't my question, though."

"Well, what is it?"

Ben looked down the street. Trig Akers was still standing in front of the café, big and smug as a turkey gobbler. Kind of handsome, too, if you only looked skin deep.

"I've been sitting here and thinking," Ben said, "watching all the folks who go into Poke's store. Got a real good business, Poke has. I thought, well, it's a shame you two kids don't get hitched."

Celia's smile slid off her lips and her eyes began to spark. For a second Ben thought lightning was going to strike right where he sat.

Celia asked sharply: "Did Poke put you up to saying that?"

"You bet he didn't. I just thought . . ."

"Then you think too much. You're an . . . an old busybody."

She flounced into the store, hips swaying and heels clacking on the boards. Well, he'd done it now. An old busybody! He whittled off a long shaving. Heavens to Betsy, why hadn't he kept his mouth shut? He'd pushed her right into Trig Akers's arms.

It wasn't five minutes until Celia stalked out with a big bundle under one arm. She didn't speak to Ben. Just went past him like a snowslide picking up speed. He quit whittling and watched her till she sailed around the corner. Mad or not, she sure did have pretty ankles.

Poke Wilson stuck his head through the door. "Say, what's wrong with her?"

"Stomach trouble," Ben muttered. "That's it. Stomach trouble."

Poke was tall and slender and a little gawky. Alongside Trig Akers he wasn't what you'd call handsome. Some might call him downright ugly. Mouth too long. Ears too thin. But after you got to know him, you didn't think about him being ugly. He had a heart as big as a hayrack and he'd make Celia a good husband.

The way Ben heard it, Poke was engaged to Celia. No ring, but a sort of understanding. Poke had insisted on waiting until his store was out of debt. Then Trig Akers got to shining up to Celia, and now Poke acted as if he was licked.

Poke scratched his nose. "She looked just plain mad at me, Ben. I never heard of her having stomach trouble before."

Ben went on whittling. "Why don't you marry her, Poke?"

"Marry her?" Poke said in a voice that made you want to sit down and cry. "Think she can see a scarecrow like me since Akers came to town?"

Ben squinted down his stick. "Strikes me you aren't using the right medicine. Take her some candy. Rent them bays of Flynn's and take her out for a ride in his new buggy. Get her under the stars and . . ."

"And get my ears knocked off," Poke said in the same unhappy voice. "What do you know about women, anyhow?"

"Not a damned thing," Ben admitted, thinking of the mistake he'd just made with Celia.

"Thought so," Poke said, and walked back into the store.

The morning wore along and Ben started on another stick. Folks came by—Mrs. Flynn under full sail, Doc Socrates Brent, better known as Doc Soc, black bag in hand, very busy, Joe Reem, the blacksmith who had been town marshal until Barrelhouse Jones talked the council into hiring a real gunslinging marshal who could keep the peace when the cowboys kicked the roof off on Saturday nights. Even Barrelhouse finally waddled across the street from his saloon, nodding amiably at Ben as he passed.

Ben mentally admitted Barrelhouse had a point as far as Joe Reem went. Joe just wasn't any hand with a gun. Barrelhouse's casino had been wrecked regularly every Saturday night. His big mirror shot to pieces. The expensive chandeliers he'd freighted in riddled. Poker tables busted. All Joe could do was to wait till the shooting stopped.

So Barrelhouse had got Joe fired, which suited Joe just fine. Then the saloon man had sent for

Akers and the council had hired him. Now Juniper Junction was so peaceful on Saturday nights you couldn't even hear a whispered cuss word. The cowhands were going down the river to Phippsburg. Akers had done too good a job. Barrelhouse didn't have enough business now to pay for the crackers and cheese he laid out for a free lunch, but he was afraid to say anything.

Akers had showed his caliber the first Saturday night he'd packed the star. He'd ordered all the cowhands to give up their guns, and somehow he'd promoted a fight with three Turkey Track hands, and shot all three of them—in the back. One had died.

Yes, sir, Ben told himself, *Akers had sure done a job*. They ought to rename the town Peaceful Junction. Why, it was so bad that if a man had let out a yell on Main Street, the echo was too scared to come into town. But do you think the council said anything about firing him? Not on your grandma's brass-plated tintype. Akers swaggered up and down the street as if he owned the place.

About noon, Trig Akers came along the walk. He gave Ben a short nod, the way a king would recognize his lowest subject. It was the marshal's usual greeting and it always fried Ben's temper. Without much thought on the matter, he said: "Strikes me funny you hang around this one-horse burg, Trig."

Akers looked down at Ben. He was six feet

three and big. Weasel ornery. For a minute Ben thought he was in for some slapping around. Akers cuffed back his black derby, took another bite on his black cigar, and stuck his thumbs through the arm holes of his chipmunk vest.

"Meaning what, friend?" Akers asked.

The lawman's voice sounded like a knot going through a buzz saw. When he used the tone, folks jumped. Kind of funny, if you thought about it. When he was around Celia, he was honey-sweet. Fine manners like that English lord who owned the Quarter Circle Z north of town. He had Celia fooled, all right.

"I like it quiet," Akers said. "I fixed it that way. Remember?"

"I remember, all right." Ben knew he'd set his salary, too—intimidating the council into a sum three times the amount Reem had drawn.

Ben got up and went home. Usually he had dinner at the café, and then he'd get back to his whittling. He'd buy a sack of horehound and when the kids got home from fishing they'd hang around until the candy was gone and tell him about the big one that got away. But today Ben was in no mood to hear about the big one. He had a different kind of whittling job to do. He was going to whittle Trig Akers down to size.

Ben built a fire and cooked dinner, all the time thinking about Akers. After he'd cleaned up the dishes, he took his gun belt out of his trunk, strapped it on, and tried his draw. Too slow. Just too damned slow.

He had seen Akers cut down those Turkey Track boys. It had been murder. Plain unvarnished murder. In Ben's book Akers needed a hanging the same as any trigger-happy gunslick did, but a badge covered up a lot of sins.

Ben worked in his flower bed a while, still thinking. It wasn't that he cared so much about Juniper Junction. The townspeople had got themselves into this mess. It was a case of grabbing the wrong bull by the tail and not knowing how to let go. But Celia was something else. And that fool Poke Wilson was so busy wrapping up whatnots and sundries that he kept right on neglecting Celia.

The more Ben thought about it, the more he became convinced that he had to do the job with a gun. That was Trig Akers's chosen tool. If Ben could hit on the right notion, he'd run Akers out of town and at the same time show Celia what the fellow was. But it wasn't just a case of buckling on his gun and going after Akers. He'd get a window in his skull and no good would come of it, either.

Ben watered his flower bed, hoed it, and got the water going again, keeping his brain working. Men of Akers's caliber all ran pretty much to a pattern. They were vain and proud, they liked to brag, and they never missed a chance to squeeze a weaker man. Ben was willing to bet his bottom dollar that in a showdown Akers would pan out just like the others Ben had known.

Actually Akers wasn't particularly fast or accurate with a gun. That is, compared to gun artists Ben had seen in Ogallala and Abilene and Dodge. In his day Ben had been as good as the best. He could still shoot straight, but he just didn't have the speed. At sixty-five a man could not expect his muscles to respond with the fluid grace they had at thirty-five.

The trick was to tap one of Akers's failings. He had enough of them. Pride. Vanity. Confidence. Love of power. Ben gave thought to each, trying to think of a practical way to use one of those weaknesses. Finally, in late afternoon, he caught hold of an idea that showed promise.

Ben cut a bouquet of snapdragons and took them to Celia. When he knocked on her back door, she called around a mouthful of pins: "Come in."

Ben opened the screen and went into her kitchen. "I fetched some posies over."

She didn't say anything, and he wondered if she was over her mad yet. He found a fruit jar, pumped water into it, and fixed the flowers, taking more time than he needed. Celia was working in a small room off her kitchen where she did dressmaking. When Ben couldn't think of anything more to do with the flowers, he carried them into her work room and set the jar on the end of the sewing machine.

"Pretty," Celia said, her mouth still full of pins.

The room was cluttered with scissors, pins, pieces of patterns, and the flowered print she had bought for Mrs. Flynn's dress.

Ben sat down and cleared his throat. "I want to talk turkey."

She took the pins out of her mouth. "If Poke Wilson's the turkey, he's a bird I don't want to hear about."

Ben looked aggrieved. "Why, I didn't have a notion of talking about Poke."

"Well, what's on your mind? I'm busy."

"The gent I want to talk to you about is Trig Akers. He's no good, Celia."

For an instant he thought lightning was going to strike again. The clouds rolled in fast, but before she let go, he added: "I've seen plenty of sidewinders like Akers."

She stared at him for a long moment, not saying a word. Then she turned and began pinning a section of pattern to the cloth. She kept on working while the seconds ticked away, and finally Ben couldn't stand it any longer.

"I tell you, he's no good."

"How do you know?" she demanded.

"I know the breed. Celia, I know you don't want

to hear about Poke, but I've got one question. What happened with you two?"

"I don't want to marry a store," she said. "He told me, wait a year, so we waited a year. I was willing. I know he's a good man. But he still works sixteen hours a day, and he paid off the mortgage three months ago."

"I reckon Poke isn't much on being romantical." Ben stared out the window. "I lost the girl I loved the same way. Maybe that's the reason I'm butting into your business, Celia."

The hard lines of anger left her face. "I'm sorry, Ben."

"I came here to whittle and eat my three squares a day," Ben went on, "but I found out something. I reckon I've got to earn the right to do my whittling, so I aim to take care of Akers."

She looked at him sharply. "Don't talk foolish, Ben. Trig wouldn't harm anyone except in the line of duty."

Ben rose. "You'll see."

He walked to the door, stepping carefully around the pieces of print she had cut out.

She said: "Ben, there is something else. I shouldn't think about it, but I can't help it. Poke's afraid of Trig. I . . . I just can't marry a man who's a coward."

He turned to look at her. She sat with the clutter all around, motionless, the misery that was in her showing on her face. This, he guessed, was what had really held her and Poke apart. Trig Akers, by hints here and there, had planted the seed in her mind.

"Poke isn't a coward," Ben said.

She shrugged.

"Folks have to do what they're suited for," Ben went on, "and Poke is no hand with a gun. Just like Sam Flynn knows horses, but he'd sure pay hell passing out pills to sick folks like Doc Soc does."

He motioned to the dummy that stood next to the window. "Or me pinning a dress on that thing. But courage is something else. Poke's got his share, all right. Don't you believe everything Trig tells you."

Ben walked out, leaving the girl staring after him. He went downtown, passing Akers who gave him his contemptuous half nod.

Ben stepped into the mercantile. Poke was in the back, opening up cases of canned goods. He called: "I'll be right out, Ben!"

Ben moved along the counter toward him. Poke stood and wiped sweat off his face.

"Hot, isn't it?"

"Hadn't thought about it." Ben sat on a sack of sugar. "Keep on working. I'll tell you what you're going to do."

Poke grinned. "Kind of bossy, aren't you?"

"Bossy as hell. I'm fixing to get rid of Akers."

Poke stared. "You drunk, Ben?"

"Listen. You're putting up a hundred dollars prize money for a shooting contest. Me against Akers. You'll do the judging and timing. Winner has to get at least one bull's eye to qualify. If we tie, which we won't, you'll figure points on speed and accuracy."

Poke frowned. "I don't know if that's such a good idea. Besides, I don't have a hundred dollars to spare."

Ben reached into his pocket and pulled out five gold coins. "Here's the prize. Now, I'm going home to paint the target. You spread word around town. Nine o'clock in the morning in the vacant lot on the other side of the hotel."

Poke took the money, still frowning. "I don't savvy."

"You will. Just one thing, son. This may be a dangerous job for you."

"I'm not afraid of that pistol-packing marshal," he said. "But I don't see what this is going to buy us. You can't beat him."

"You just come by and pick up the target after dark. Don't let on to nobody that I've got a hand in this."

Ben walked out, leaving Poke staring after him.

Poke did a good job of getting the word out. Every inhabitant of Juniper Junction was on hand by nine o'clock the next morning, men, women, and children.

When Ben appeared, someone yelled: "You figure this is a whittling job, old-timer?"

Ben grinned. "Sort of."

Trig Akers came up, beaming like a full moon. "Easy money."

"Reckon you can use it," Ben said.

Akers scowled. "Yeah, I can use it. But there's one thing I don't savvy. How come this counter-jumper's throwing away a hundred dollars?"

"Maybe he's not," Ben replied. "You know Celia's his girl, don't you?"

Akers cuffed back his Stetson. "What's that got to do with it?"

"You'll see," Ben replied.

The target was nailed to an upright at the alley end of the lot. It was covered with a canvas, and now Poke called: "Pull the cover off, Sam!"

Poke scraped a boot through the dirt next to the walk. "Toe this line. I'll hold the watch, and I'll judge the accuracy of the shooting. If neither man makes a bull's eye, the contest is over, and I'll keep the money."

Flynn jerked the canvas off the target and the instant it came into view, Akers yelled.

"What kind fool trick is this? You need a spyglass to see that bull's eye."

Ben said: "I can see it."

"You're both going by the same rules," Poke said. "You in or out?"

Akers swore. Ben threw a quick glance at Celia nearby. She looked puzzled and more than a little bit worried.

Akers was swelling up, getting madder by the minute and acting as if he'd just as soon use his gun on Poke as the target.

"You're a cheap tinhorn, Wilson. I want no part of this."

"Some excuse for a marshal, aren't you?" Poke said. "Guess old Ben wins."

There was some low talk from the town folks gathered around. Akers scraped his feet in the dirt, looking from Barrelhouse Jones on down to Doc Soc.

Ben said: "He's scared off, Poke."

"Just a big wind," Poke agreed.

Akers whirled to face him. Poke glared at him, not backing up a step.

"I'm ready," Ben said.

Poke pulled his watch out of his pocket. "Go ahead, Ben."

Ben drew, very slowly, and emptied his gun. It was a pitiful showing. When the hammering echoes died, not a single bullet had hit the target. One of Mrs. Flynn's roosters across the alley let out a squawk, and a limb dropped out of a cottonwood tree high overhead.

Everybody but Ben and Celia laughed.

"Better stick to whittling, Ben," someone said.

"Looks like it," Ben said. He turned to the

marshal. "But I doubt this back-shooter can do any better."

"I sure as hell will," Akers said, and stepped to the line.

Ben reloaded his gun and smoothly dropped it into his holster. Poke was looking at his watch.

"Any time, Akers."

The marshal squinted. Then he drew his gun and fired, fast, one shot rolling out after another, the target quivering with the impact of each slug.

"Take a look, counter-jumper," he said when the gun was empty. "I guess I got one in the bull's eye, all right."

Poke shook his head. "No, you missed the bull's eye."

Bawling an oath, Akers started for the target in a lumbering run. He grabbed Sam Flynn by the shoulder and yanked him aside. He stooped to stare at the target, and wheeled around.

"I said you were a cheap tinhorn, Wilson." He jabbed a finger at a bullet hole. "What do you call that?"

Ben had painted a very small bull's eye in the center of the target and had purposely left a smudge below it. One bullet had cut through that smudge, but the bull's eye had not been touched.

Poke said: "I call it a miss."

Ben waved them aside, his hand sweeping downward. He drew his Colt and fired one shot—through the small bull's eye.

Akers got very red in the face then. He moved closer to Poke, breathing hard. "You're a crook and a liar, Wilson. You can't make a fool out of me. . . ."

For just a moment Akers stared at Poke as if he found this thing that had happened to him hard to believe. Then he grabbed for his gun, which was exactly what Ben had counted on him doing. Akers took aim at Poke Wilson.

Ben's next bullet caught Aker's gun hand. The man howled, his revolver dropping to the ground.

Ben moved slowly toward Akers. "You're a murderer. You have no right to wear the star . . . not here, not anywhere."

He motioned to Barrelhouse Jones and Doc Soc and the rest of the council, all huddled like so many sheep against the hotel wall.

"If you had any gumption, you'd have fired him a long time ago. Now as soon as Doc Soc fixes Akers up, he'd better make himself scarce in this town." He paused. "You know, maybe me and Joe Reem could handle the star between us. If Joe's willing."

"Sure!" Joe called out. "I just reckon we could."

There were some other things going on, too.

Like Poke embracing Celia. They held one another as if making up for lost time. Ben grinned when he heard Poke say: "Will you marry me, Celia? Today? No sense waiting."

It's Hell To Be a Hero

Nobody in the town of San Rafael considered Ed Casey a hero, not even Ed Casey himself. He was an ordinary man, a lawyer in his late twenties, sandy-haired and blue-eyed, and possessed of a good pair of shoulders. Single, he was mild-mannered, and respected for his integrity.

Then the Potter gang knocked over Eli Scoggins's bank, and Casey's way of life was forever changed.

It started the day before hunting season opened. Casey left his office shortly after twelve and stepped into Abbot's Hardware to get the .30-30 he had left there to be worked on. He bought a package of shells and loaded the rifle, thinking he'd walk across the creek and take a few shots to see if the sights were true.

Lou Abbot joshed him a little about how many bucks he expected to get. Casey was the best shot in San Rafael, and when he went out with a party of townsmen he usually got as many as the others added together. Casey said he'd be satisfied with six, paid Abbot, and left the store.

Just as Casey stepped on the boardwalk, two men ran out of the bank, one carrying a heavily weighted gunny sack. A third man held their horses in the street. The instant they hit saddles,

Fred Bent, Scoggins's teller, let out a squall that the bank had been robbed. One of the outlaws put a bullet through the window, and Bent let out another squall that had a different tone.

Casey acted purely on instinct. He let go with his first shot before the outlaws had traveled ten feet, knocking the lead man out of his saddle. There was a lot of dust then, the other two cracking steel to their mounts at every jump. Casey missed his second shot because of the dust, but he tallied number two with his third bullet. The remaining outlaw, the one with the gunny sack, made the corner and was out of sight.

Casey wheeled into the store and charged along the counter, slamming into Lou Abbot and piling him up on a keg of nails. Abbot yelped and came upright. Casey raced through the back door to the alley. The third bank robber was departing for open country when Casey let go with another shot. The man threw up his hands and plunged out of the saddle, the gunny sack disappearing into the sagebrush.

There was plenty of excitement after that. Everybody was in the street yelling questions and answers that were less than half-truths. Doc Miller took a look at Fred Bent and said: "Get him over to my office. He's hit pretty hard."

Eli Scoggins, the bank owner, sat on the floor, his narrow face lowered to his knees. He rocked back and forth, moaning. The sheriff, Pete Ennis, appeared from somewhere, and began bawling orders that achieved nothing. By the time folks caught on to what had happened, Casey was back with the gunny sack.

"Here you are, Eli." Casey dropped the sack beside the banker. "You didn't lose a nickel."

Scoggins and Casey had had one thing in common for years—their low opinion of each other. Now Scoggins sat there and blinked at Casey as if he didn't see him at all. Shock, Casey thought. It was the first time he had ever seen the banker unable to talk.

There was a lot of hand-shaking and back-slapping, and a deal of talk about Casey being a hero and how much the town owed him. The sheriff came in and announced that all three Potters were dead, and it was a good thing on account of it saved the state hanging money.

"There was a big reward out for them murdering *hombres*," Ennis said. "Five thousand, I think. You'll get it all, Ed."

Five thousand! Casey blinked. He'd never seen that much money in his life.

Then Lou Abbot yelled: "I guess Eli will add something to it, Ed."

Scoggins came awake in a hurry. He grabbed the gunny sack and jumped up. "The hell I will. Casey gets the reward. That's good wages for one day."

"Damned skinflint," Abbot growled to himself.

Casey saw Lola Horn then and he got through the crowd to her. Lola was the town teacher and the only reason Casey was glad he was chairman of the school board.

Now she laid a hand on his arm. "It was wonderful, Ed. Looks as if you've been unappreciated around here."

He grinned. "I know one place where I've been unappreciated."

It was Casey's opinion she was the prettiest woman in San Rafael.

She smiled. "Perhaps you could change that, Ed."

They walked along the street toward the schoolhouse. Lola was lovely, Casey thought again as he gazed at her, with her cricket-black hair and dark eyes, and a disconcerting way of keeping her distance from single men in town.

Now there was no trace of the chill manner. Casey walked in silence, wondering about it. Lola's hand was still on his arm, and she held her head proudly as if she wanted everyone to notice who she was with.

For weeks Casey had been trying to work up enough nerve to propose, but he'd been afraid to risk it. Now he had a hunch she'd say yes. The time to strike was when the iron was hot, but doubts took possession of him.

Maybe she'd heard Ennis say there was a reward coming, and he sure didn't want a woman marrying him for his money—a consideration which had not been a cause of worry before.

It was nearly one when they reached the schoolhouse. The yard was filled with children, too many for one teacher. San Rafael needed a two-teacher school, but it was a reform Casey had been unable to achieve because of Scoggins's opposition. An idea took root in his mind as he paused outside the door. Scoggins owed him now.

"Come inside," Lola said.

She closed the door behind them. She put both hands on his arms and looked up at him. "Ed, I know I haven't been here long, but I think I know these people. They have very short memories."

He didn't know what she meant, and this was not the time to go into it. Her lips came together. He leaned down and kissed her. It seemed like the thing to do, something he'd wanted to do for a long time except that he'd never had the nerve.

He wasn't disappointed. It was a nice kiss with her arms around his neck, a kiss that set his heart to pounding.

"I'll see you tonight?" he asked.

"Of course, Ed."

As he walked back to town, he wondered why she'd let him kiss her. He had figured she'd slap his ears off if he tried it. Then came a suspicion he didn't like. Maybe it was because he'd become a hero. Some women were like that, he'd heard. He couldn't believe Lola was, but she had definitely changed her attitude toward him.

Still, he thought glumly, he loved her and figured he'd better speak his piece while she was in the mood.

Casey stopped at Doc Miller's office and learned Fred Bent would live, but he'd be on his back for a long time. Bent was the one good thing about the bank. It would be like Scroggins to fire him when he didn't come to work in the morning.

Casey crossed the street to the bank. Scroggins had been a millstone around San Rafael's neck for years and no one seemed willing to do anything about it. He was cool and scheming, and had a talent for keeping his political fences mended. There was no doubt the sheriff was his man—a very handy situation when Scoggins stepped outside the law to beat down a business competitor.

Scoggins had been able to use his financial power to get a stranglehold on every business in the county except the Yankee Boy Mine. The one person who had successfully defied him was Julia Larson, the mine owner.

Now that Casey thought about Julia, an idea lingering in his mind flowered.

There was no one in the bank when Casey went in except Scoggins himself, in the vault putting the money away. Casey went through the gate at the end of the rail and stood watching Scoggins fondling the coins as if they were the most precious things on earth.

"I want to talk to you, Scoggins."

Surprised, he whirled around, dropping a handful of gold eagles on the floor. They jingled musically and rolled away in a half dozen directions.

"What do you mean, sneaking up on me like that?"

"I want to talk to you."

No one used that tone of voice on Eli Scoggins. Not even Julia Larson. He stepped out of the vault, scowling. "I'm not paying you a reward, Casey."

"I don't expect any."

"I'm not throwing any business your way, either. When I need a lawyer, I'll use a man who's dry behind the ears."

Anger rose in Casey. "I don't want any business from you."

Scoggins sat down at his desk and leaned back in the swivel chair. "What in hell do you want?"

"Fred's got a wife and six kids."

"So?"

"What are you going to do to help him while he's laid up?"

"Nothing. He'll be back to work in a day or two."

"No, he won't. He's got a slug in his chest. Doc says he'll be laid up for weeks."

"If Bent had kept his damned mouth shut, he wouldn't have gotten himself shot up."

Casey eyed him. "Maybe you wanted your bank robbed."

Scoggins jumped up and motioned to the door, his hand trembling in rage. "Damn you, Casey. Get out!"

"Not till I find out a couple things. Are you going to pay Fred's salary until he's able to come back here?"

"No."

"Another thing. The school needs an addition."

"I've told you ten times . . . I won't stand for that."

"The school will get more crowded with the Yankee Boy taking on more men. New families will be moving in."

Scoggins pounded a fist on the desk. "I'm not blind, Casey. You figure I'll bow down and scrape to you because some damned fools called you a hero. Well, you're no hero to me. You're just a shyster who happened to be handy with a Winchester when my bank was held up. I've licked you on this school business before, and I'll do it again. Now, will you get out?"

"Yeah," Casey said. "There's only so much skunk smell I can stand at one time."

He walked out, feeling the pressure of the banker's eyes on him. Maybe he was acting the fool. Folks got along better in San Rafael if they didn't buck Scoggins. The banker made it tough for anyone who got in his way. That was where Casey took his hat off to Julia Larson.

Most people in San Rafael didn't like Julia.

Some even said she wasn't a good woman, maybe because she was doing a man's job in handling the Yankee Boy Mine. Or perhaps it was because she had a way with men that made other woman jealous. That was Casey's private opinion, but one no woman he knew would corroborate. In any case, she was fighter, and Casey respected fighters.

Lou Abbot was in the back of the store talking to half a dozen townsmen when Casey walked in. Abbot stopped, saw who it was, and let out a whoop. "Speak of the devil!"

There was more talk about Casey being the town's hero and saving everybody's money, and putting San Rafael on the map. Then Casey couldn't stand it any longer.

"That's enough of this palaver, boys. I'm no hero. You know it as well as I do."

"It takes sand in a man's craw . . . ," Abbot began.

"Hell," Casey broke in, "you'd have done the same thing if you had been in my boots."

"I sure wouldn't have shot as straight."

They laughed. Then Casey said: "Scoggins agrees I'm not a hero. He says I'm just a shyster who happened to be handy with a Winchester."

There was no laughter then. They looked at each other and then they looked at the floor. Abbot reached into the keg at his feet for a handful of nails. "You damned near punctured me when you shoved me down on these, Ed."

Still no one laughed. Casey said: "It's Scoggins I'd like to puncture, and I've got an idea how to do it."

"Aw, let's forget Scoggins," Abe Rucker said. He was the newspaper editor, but as far as he was concerned, Eli Scoggins's activities were beyond the reach of the press. "Go ahead and tell him, Lou."

"Well, we're damned ashamed of Scoggins," Abbot said bluntly. "Bucking civic improvements because they'll raise taxes is one thing, but the way he took what you done is something else."

"Thought we were going to forget Scoggins," Casey said.

"We can't, and Abe knows it. Anyhow, you did something that was a benefit to all of us, so we're fixing to have a feed tonight to show our appreciation. Maybe have a medal struck off."

The idea that had been working in Casey's mind now spurted into full bloom. "That's mighty thoughtful of you boys. Is Scoggins invited?"

There was an awkward moment of silence before Abbot said: "He'll be there if we have to drag him. Besides, his wife wouldn't miss a social event."

"About that medal. Wouldn't it be better if you got up a subscription list? I don't aim to use the money for myself, but it fits into my idea for trimming Scoggins down."

They looked at each other, the kind of look a bunch of rabbits might give each other when they were considering going after the fox. There was some head-scratching and ear-pulling and a good deal of hesitation.

"Look," Casey said, "we all feel the same way about Scoggins. It just happens that right now I'm in position to go after him. Give me some ammunition, and I'll do the job."

"All right," Rucker agreed reluctantly. "I might be able to find some room in the paper."

"One more thing," Casey said. "Is this going to be for women?"

Abbot nodded. "Sure. Lola can sit beside you."

Casey grinned. "Now, that's right generous, with Abe feeling about Lola like he does."

They laughed again, all but Rucker who looked down his long nose and muttered something about lawyers.

They were still laughing, all feeling good again until Casey said: "Let's invite Julia Larson."

He might as well have dangled a skeleton in front of them. The laughing stopped. There was some more head-scratching and shifting around before Abbot said: "Damn it, Ed, have you gone clear off your nut? You know what that woman is?"

"I know she's smart enough to make money and manage a payroll," Casey said. "I've heard the gossip. Maybe she does wear her skirts too short and she tears around at crazy times of night and she runs a business without asking some man to do it, but nobody knows if any of the rest of it is true."

"You know how women feel about her," Abbot muttered.

"Then let the rest of the women stay home," Casey said.

"You can't do it, Ed."

"Ask her, Lou," Casey insisted. "I aim to beat Eli down a peg, and having the one person at the table tonight who has stopped him the way Julia has would just about fix things."

Abbot threw the handful of nails back into the keg. "All right, Ed. I don't know what you're thinking, but I'll invite her. It's a damned fool mistake. You'll see."

Casey left his office early that afternoon, but there was no escaping the halo fate had hung on him. People stopped him on the street to shake hands. School children stood motionless, staring solemnly. Then he caught the buzz of talk.

"Got all three Potters."

"Shot them dead."

"Bravest man in San Rafael."

"Bet he gets Duke Dorsey next time that outlaw rides into town."

That made Casey squirm. It was a new thought, and he hoped nobody else got the notion. Duke

Dorsey would kill anyone for a price. He was the fastest man with a gun in the county, and now that Casey thought about it, he was the kind who might show up just to challenge him. That would be the end of Ed Casey. He was no hand with a revolver.

Mrs. Davis, Casey's landlady, met him at the door, beaming with pride.

"Look, Missus Davis," he said, "I've boarded here ever since I put my shingle up. Did you ever figure I was a hero?"

His words wiped the smile off her face. "Well, to be right honest, Ed, I guess none of us knew. But I think it's wonderful. We all do. Why, there's talk of making you mayor."

Casey groaned, and went up to his room. By the time he had taken a bath, shaved, and got into his best suit, it was time to go after Lola. He started out through the back, intending to go down a side street, when Mrs. Davis called: "Ed! Wait a minute, Ed. I hitched up the buggy for you. Nothing's too good for our hero."

"If you don't quit this hero stuff . . ." Casey stopped when he saw Mrs. Davis's face.

"I thought you'd like to take Lola for a ride after the shindig," she said.

Mrs. Davis owned a pair of matched bays and the newest buggy in San Rafael with the reddest wheels. Casey thanked her.

He got in and headed down Main, gritting

his teeth and deciding a hero had no business taking a side street. The strange part of the whole business was that Mrs. Davis never let anyone drive her bays.

Lola was ready when Casey got to her place. She was something to make a man look twice. She wore a blue silk dress that rustled when she walked, a blue bonnet on her black hair, and she carried a blue parasol.

Casey thought about that kiss in the schoolhouse, so he asked: "Let's take a ride. They won't start until we get there."

"I guess they won't," she said.

He took the creek road out of town, contemplating the gloom-shadowed life of a hero. Then he reached the cottonwood grove and put his mind to more pleasant things. He slid an arm around Lola. Nothing happened except that she looked up at him. He kissed her.

It was a kiss to remember. When she finally drew back, she asked: "How long have I known you, Ed?"

He fumbled around for words. "Ever since you got here. I guess we'd better get back."

The dinner came off as expected except that Julia didn't show up. Casey asked Abbot, who shrugged in silent reply. Casey had a hunch Mrs. Abbot had stopped it.

The local Circle of the Royal Women chapter of the Throne of St. George put the meal on. Scoggins was there with Mrs. Scoggins, a small sharp-tongued woman who ruled the Scoggins home as effectively as he ruled the business life of the county.

After ice cream and cake there was a good deal of speech-making about Casey's heroism that kept him fidgeting and red-faced. Then some songs and some more speeches, including a touching tribute from Abe Rucker. If there had been a hole in the floor, Casey would have crawled into it. Then Abbot called on Casey.

Rising, he began: "A lawyer should be an orator, but I don't make any more claims along that line than I do to being a hero. I appreciate all this tonight." He put a finger under his collar and tried to stretch it, suddenly aware that there were tears in Lola's eyes. "Folks, I just did what had to be done, and I'm glad I was there to do it."

They cheered. Casey waited for quiet, and went on: "We all know what a bank means to a community. Credit is the life blood of business." He paused and took a drink. "I don't need to tell you about the place Mister Scoggins and his bank hold in this community, but I do want to say something that will interest all of you. I understand from the sheriff that a reward of five thousand dollars is coming to me. I intend to turn it over to the community to add a room to the schoolhouse and to hire another teacher. I hope there will be enough left over to build a gymnasium."

They gave Casey a tremendous ovation. Scoggins clapped lightly, twice, green eyes suspicious as he waited for the rest of what Casey had to say.

"I regret that some cultural advantages are lacking," Casey went on. "As you know, we need a library. I am afraid, however, that my contribution will not be enough, so I hereby challenge Mister Scoggins to come to our assistance, matching dollar for dollar what I give."

Silence. Mrs. Scoggins was the first to recover. She prodded her husband with a sharp elbow.

Scoggins was very pale when he gripped the table and pulled himself upright. "I'll do it . . . we've got to encourage culture." He sat down and wiped a hand across his brow.

No one cheered. Everyone but Casey was too shocked to believe what they had heard.

Abbot said: "Well, Ed, here's another surprise. We wanted to show our appreciation, so we took up a purse for you." He handed a heavy bag of money to Casey. "There's two thousand dollars for you, contributed by the businessmen of San Rafael."

Casey rose again. He paused while he gathered his thoughts.

"Folks, this is mighty generous of you. I'd like

your permission to add this money to the reward. With Mister Scoggins doubling it, you will have fourteen thousand, enough to give us the finest library in the county . . . along with enlarging the school and adding a gym."

More cheering, but not so loud. Everybody had heard too much. It was like looking at a plate of candy after filling up on cake. There was dancing afterward, but the Scogginses excused themselves and went home.

When Casey had a chance, he asked Abbot: "Why isn't Julia here?"

"She's smart, Ed. She wouldn't come. Anyhow, you don't need her. Eli can't back out now."

Casey grinned. "He'll try."

Casey drove directly to Lola's boarding house after the dance. He helped her down, and she took his arm as they walked up the path to the house. She had been strangely quiet after they left the lodge hall. Now she stood with her back to the door and looked at him.

"It was a generous thing you did tonight, Ed," she said, "and the way you handled Scoggins was miraculous, but there's something else that's more important and I want you to know it. It's wonderful to have an example like you in a community that has had too much Scoggins."

"Not as wonderful as having you for a teacher," he said. He drew a deep breath. "Lola."

"Yes?"

"Lola . . . will you . . . marry me?"

She lifted her lips to his, murmuring: "Of course, Ed."

He kissed her, knowing beyond all doubt this was what he wanted.

"You've got to know," he said, "I'm no part of a hero."

"Oh, Ed, it's you I love. Just be who you are." Then she shivered in his arms. "I'm afraid, Ed."

"Of what?"

She did not answer for a long moment. "People's memories are so short."

Casey drove back to Mrs. Davis's, telling himself he should be the happiest man in town. He was going to have the prettiest wife in San Rafael. Lola was respected and liked by everyone. Abe Rucker would say Ed Casey was a fool for luck. He was. He knew he was. That was the thing that bothered him.

Lola hadn't known she'd loved him until he gunned down the Potters. After a while the glamour would wear thin. Where would he be with Lola then?

He stabled the bays, seeing a light in the parlor and thinking Mrs. Davis had left it there for him. But when he came in, he saw Mrs. Davis sitting on the edge of her chair and Eli Scoggins in the loveseat over in the corner, his thin face as sour as clabbered milk.

Casey controlled his surprise. “Howdy, Eli. That was a fine thing you did tonight.”

Scoggins made a noise in his throat and sat as if he were paralyzed, green eyes as sharp and as wicked as chipped glass.

Mrs. Davis said uneasily: “Mister Scoggins has been waiting to see you for an hour.”

Casey dropped into a chair. “I noticed you left the shindig early. I was afraid you were sick.”

Scoggins made another noise in his throat. He turned to Mrs. Davis. “I want to talk to Casey. Alone.” He added: “And no eavesdropping.”

Mrs. Davis rose, red-faced. “Eli, you ought to be ashamed.”

Casey spoke after she sailed out of the parlor. “You should be ashamed, Eli. What do you think she’s been sitting up for?”

“I am not here to exchange pleasantries,” he said. He paused. “Casey, you surprise me.”

“I’ve been surprised a few times myself today.”

“I thought at noon when you played hero that it was a case of being in the right place at the right time. You have practiced law in San Rafael three years, but without spectacular success. I will say people like you well enough, especially around deer season.”

Casey eyed the banker, wondering what was coming next.

“I had classed you with Abbot and Rucker and

the rest," he went on. "Now I see I was wrong. You caught my weakness as accurately as you shot the Potters. I cannot stand ridicule or public disgrace, even if it costs me seven thousand dollars. There is another queer thing about what you did tonight. I can afford the loss of seven thousand dollars, but you can't. I daresay you haven't made that much since you hung your lawyer shingle out."

"Let's say I have principles, Eli."

"There's only one basic principle beneath all human actions, Casey. We do things or don't do them according to how much they benefit us. The extra teacher and the gym and library don't mean a damned thing to you except that they'll make people notice you and thereby bring more business to you. Today luck was beating you on the head. Everybody has noticed you. You'll have more business than you want. And you've got Lola Horn. So we can forget all of this civic improvement nonsense."

"Afraid not, Eli. I said I had principles. I meant it."

"Oh hell," Scoggins said in disgust. "That's a public show. This is between you and me. We can get out of this if we work together." He added: "I'll make it worth your while."

Casey felt like laughing in his face. "You're wasting your time."

"There are other considerations besides the

financial ones," he said. "There's talk of making you mayor. I would go further. Say a seat in the legislature."

"Not interested." Casey rose. "Deer season opens tomorrow, Eli. I've got to get some sleep."

Scoggins came to his feet. "I never threaten a man, Casey, but your attitude leaves me with only one course of action." He paused. "I know how to destroy you. All the ammunition I need is right here."

"You scare me, Eli. Good night."

Scoggins rose, picked up his hat from the walnut table, and walked out.

Despite tough words, a vague uneasiness burned in Casey. He'd had his choice of peace or war, and he'd picked war. Maybe he was a fool. In a showdown men like Lou Abbot and Abe Rucker would give him no help.

Casey stepped into his room, struck a match, and lighted the lamp on his bureau.

"You keep late hours, Mister Ed Casey."

He wheeled, the lamp chimney in one hand, the burning match in the other. Julia Larson was sitting on the bed, laughing silently. The match burned his fingers. He cursed and dropped it, stepping on it immediately as he thought of what Mrs. Davis would say if she found a hole in her carpet.

First he slipped the chimney into place. Then he locked the door. "What are you doing here?"

“Do you have to lock that door to keep Missus Davis out?” she asked.

“She just might sail in if she heard a woman’s voice in here,” he answered.

“I’m not worried about my reputation,” she said, smiling. “Maybe you are about yours.”

“Maybe I am,” he said. “Do you usually go around getting into men’s rooms at night?”

“Not often,” she replied. She added: “Just when they’re town heroes.”

He dropped into a chair and filled his pipe. He had known Julia Larson only casually. She had given him some legal business, and he had danced with her a time or two. She was a very striking woman, blonde and a little plump, but not too much so. Her blonde hair was rumpled as if she had been lying down while waiting for him. Her pale green dress was low-cut, her skirt too short by San Rafael standards.

She rose and shook her dress into place, and when she sat down again, she drew her skirt higher.

He asked: “How’d you get in?”

“Window,” she said.

He said: “From now on I’ll have to lock it to keep beautiful women out.”

“You won’t have to worry about this one,” she said. “I didn’t suppose you were so straight-laced.”

“I got myself engaged tonight.”

“Engaged? Not that black-haired teacher?”

"That's right."

She shook her head in disgust. "Ed, I thought better of you than that."

He struck a match and sucked the flame into the pipe bowl. "Jealous?"

"Sure," she said with a laugh. "You're a big man."

He liked the way she laughed. She rocked on the edge of the bed, hands clasped around her knees.

"What did you come for?" he asked.

"Business." Her full red lips tightened as she studied him. "Ed, I want to thank you for inviting me to the shindig tonight, but it's like I told Abbot. I don't belong to San Rafael's version of society. I want something else out of life, and I'm going after it."

"What?"

"Wealth and independence," she said. "And I want to hammer Scoggins." She asked: "What was he doing here tonight?"

"He wanted me on his side."

She laughed again. "I don't blame him. I want you on my side, too."

"How did you know he was here?"

"Saw him go in before I climbed in through your window." She asked: "Did you say yes?"

"Nope."

"That makes you my kind of man, Ed. That's why I'm here."

Julia rose and moved toward him. He started to rise, but she motioned for him to keep his seat. She stood before him, looking down and breathing a little hard. Lola had never affected him this way. It was like receiving one electric jolt from Julia after another.

"A lot of people wonder how I've been able to hold up against Scoggins," Julia said. "Mostly it's because I have financial backing outside. The Yankee Boy is a good mine. I've got enough ore blocked out to keep me going for years. My trouble right now is, I've bitten off more than I can chew. Last week I bought all the claims on the hill. I own it all, now."

She moved back. "Scoggins would give his eyeteeth to get his hands on my property. He just may do it, too. Those crazy prospectors who owned the claims I bought demanded cash. I had fifteen thousand dollars brought in secretly on the stage." She paused. "I can't prove it, but I think Eli Scoggins sent for the Potter brothers."

Casey stared at her, pulling on his pipe. It just might have been that way. He remembered Scoggins saying that if Fred Bent had kept his mouth shut, he wouldn't have been shot. And when Casey had suggested Scoggins wanted his bank robbed, the banker had flashed anger.

"It would have looked good," Julia went on, "Scoggins saying my money was handy and in the hurry the Potters didn't take anything else.

No one would ever know he divided it up with the outlaws."

"But they didn't get it," Casey said. "So you're all right."

"No, I'm not. I've paid for the claims, but now old Poley Gibbs who owns the toll road down the mountain has jumped his rates. Most of my ore is low grade, so I operate on a pretty small margin. I suppose Scoggins put Poley up to it. Anyhow, the only thing I can do is buy Poley out. Ten thousand, he says. Cash."

"Can you raise it?"

"Sure, but it's got to be here tomorrow. Scoggins won't loan it, so I've got to bring the money myself. I'm afraid to do it. Pete Ennis won't give me any protection. Ed, if I don't have the money tomorrow, Poley swears he'll make a deal with Scoggins. Then I'm finished."

Casey knew Poley Gibbs by sight, a tough, loud-mouthed old man who spent most of his time drinking in San Rafael saloons.

"What can I do?" Casey asked.

"You mean, you're on my side?"

"Sure."

"What will Lola say?"

"I don't know."

She moved closer, dropped down on his lap, and put her arms around his neck. "I'm driving an ore wagon to the bank at Cotter's Junction tomorrow. I want you to ride shotgun."

"Julia, I'm a lawyer."

"No, Ed. You're the town hero who shot three outlaws as neat as if you'd been cutting cake. News like that goes out over the owlhoot trail fast. With you on the seat beside me, I won't have any trouble. Will you do it?"

He was uneasy, not from the prospect of danger, but wondering about Lola. But he said: "Sure."

She kissed him and jumped up. "We're leaving at six." Crossing the room to the window, she added: "Don't worry. I won't tell Lola."

Casey got up at five, dressed, and wrote a note telling Mrs. Davis he wouldn't be around for breakfast. He left the house, taking his Winchester, had breakfast at the Top Notch Café, and got to the stage depot at five minutes before six. Julia, clad in a man's shirt and Levi's, was pacing nervously around the big wagon.

"You had me worried, Ed," she said as he came up. "I was afraid you'd get to thinking about Lola and go back on our deal."

He said with some sharpness: "I don't go back on a deal."

"Let's roll," she said, and climbed to the high seat.

It was said around San Rafael that Julia Larson could do anything a man could. Now, watching her handle the ribbons, Casey agreed. They wheeled into Main Street and five minutes later were out of town and starting down the long grade to the railhead at Cotter's Junction.

Lola cast a sidelong glance at him. "You sure Lola's the woman for you, Ed?"

He nodded. "Don't you like her?"

"You know how it is with me," she answered. "Nobody in San Rafael invites me into their homes. Lola will fit that pattern. She'll give teas and parties, and she'll be a social asset to you." She added: "If you want to live like that."

"Guess I do," he said.

"I would have agreed up until yesterday noon," she said. "Now I think you're fooling yourself. You're made to live tough. Maybe you'll die young, but not before you've had a hell of a good time."

"I'm not that way. I haven't changed just because . . ."

She laughed. "You're really fooling yourself now. Up until yesterday you were a lamb like Abe Rucker and Lou Abbot. Now you're a hell-roarer and you'll never be the same again."

He didn't believe it. Circumstances had pitched him into a position where he could challenge Eli Scoggins. He would have done the same any time in the past.

"You're wrong, Julia. I haven't changed."

She gave him a quick penetrating glance. "When we get back to San Rafael, you'll find out. Either you'll bow and scrape like the rest of them, or you'll keep on being a hell-roarer until Scoggins is licked." She stared down the twisting road, her face suddenly bleak. "I set out to be a hell-roarer and I can't back up. Know why I'm blackballed?"

"No."

"It's Missus Scoggins's tongue. Eli's idea, of course. He thought that was the way to get me out, but I'm stubborn. So I've done without the things most women think are important. No husband and no home and no kids. I've had to fight off the men I didn't want, and the men I like treat me like poison."

"If you went somewhere else . . ."

"I won't, Ed. I'm not made that way." Her lips tightened. "When a woman debases her pride, she hasn't much left, but that's what I'm going to do now."

Casey looked at her.

"If you ever decide Lola isn't the woman for you," she went on, "I'd like to try to fill the bill."

This was something he hadn't counted on. He stared ahead, knowing he had to say something and failing to find the right words. He finally said: "Thanks, Julia."

"Now you forget it," she said with forced lightness. She added: "Unless the time comes to remember."

There was no more talk until they reached

Cotter's Junction. The heavy box was passed up and slid under the seat. Two men on horseback watched. Before Julia climbed back up to the seat, she said loudly to the agent: "What do you think of my guard, Phil?"

The agent squinted up at them. "Who is he?"

"Ed Casey."

"The fellow who shot up the Potters in San Rafael?" he asked.

"Yep!"

On the road back, Julia laughed and said softly: "That pair watching us will think twice now before they start anything."

Casey looked back. They were not followed. He watched every turn in the road, every tree and every boulder, Winchester held on the ready. They reached town before noon without trouble.

They wheeled down Main to the bank, chain traces jingling, dust rolling up behind them. Julia drew a long breath. "We're here, Ed, but I don't think I'd have made it if it hadn't been for you. If there's ever anything I can do to help you out, let me know."

"Forget it," Casey said.

There was a crowd in front of the bank, Abbot and Rucker and Sheriff Pete Ennis, and a few others. Casey stepped down and walked over to Abbot. "I figured you'd be out after your buck this morning."

"Not today," he said sullenly.

Something was wrong. He looked around the half circle, feeling their hostility. Scoggins hurried out and the box was carried inside. Poley Gibbs was on hand, acting disappointed and saying he hadn't thought Julia could raise the *dinero*.

After she had gone inside with Gibbs and Scoggins, Casey asked: "What's the matter with you boys? This looks like a wake."

"It is," Rucker said. "The wake of a hero."

"I don't get it," Casey said.

"You ought to get a rope," Rucker said. "Yesterday you're walking high and handsome and you propose to Lola. Word is, she said yes . . . because she doesn't know what you are. She knows now."

Casey grabbed a handful of Rucker's shirt front. "You'd better keep talking, Abe."

"I'll talk, all right. You couldn't wait, could you? You promise Lola, and that same night you have this woman in your room."

It soaked in then. He knew what Eli had meant with that comment about destroying him. He had seen Julia, too.

Casey hit Abe, knocking him off the walk into the street. "Put that in your paper."

"That didn't buy you anything," Lou Abbot said. "You're finished in this town. You can't buy us. We don't want the money you were giving away last night."

"You sure as hell don't have to take it," Casey said. "You don't even know the truth."

"You're denying Julia came to your room, Ed?" Ennis demanded.

"I'm denying nothing," he said.

"I happen to love Lola," Rucker said, "and I don't aim to see her treated this way."

"That's right," Ennis said. "We'd run you out of town if you had more than five minutes to live."

"What're you gents talking about now?" Casey demanded. "A lynching?"

"We're talking about Duke Dorsey," he replied. "Go get your gun. He's waiting for you in the Idle Hour saloon."

Julia had come out of the bank in time to hear what Ennis said. She pushed past Abbot. "Don't do it, Ed. This is Scoggins's work."

"I reckon it is," Casey agreed, "but these boys seem to favor the idea. Yesterday I was the first citizen. Now Eli is."

Julia said: "That's the way the men of San Rafael are."

"Two of a kind," Ennis said with a sneer. "She's your woman, all right, Casey."

Anger built a fire in him. He hit Ennis, battered him back across the walk, and knocked him headlong into the bank. He turned to the others. "If you had any sense you'd see that you're playing Scoggins's game."

Ennis was on his feet, one eye swelling. "You're hell with your fists, Casey, but too yellow to face Dorsey."

"You're hell for shooting a bunch of running men, too," Rucker added, "but you haven't got what it takes to face Dorsey."

"Have you?" Julia asked.

"Shut up . . ." Rucker bit back another word he would have called her.

"Or you, Sheriff?"

"He isn't after me," Ennis answered.

"But you'll sit still and let him murder a man," Julia said angrily. She swung to face Casey. "You aim to do it, don't you?" she asked.

Casey's gaze swung around the bunched men, his face bone-hard. Yesterday he had been a hero; today he was a tramp.

"There's a sort of code, Julia, like in the days of old when men dueled. There isn't another man here who'd do what this bunch expects me to do."

"Then what difference does it make what they think?" she demanded.

"None," Casey said. "I don't know any reason why I should be killed because these cowards call me a coward."

Without another word he swung away from them and slanted across the street. He passed the front of the Idle Hour saloon and turned the corner. He remembered Lola. She had said people's memories were short. To hell with the bunch of them. Scoggins had done a perfect job. He'd proved he understood these men better than Ed Casey had. He had fixed it so they would make a pariah out of him, the way his wife had shunned Julia.

School was out. Kids were moving away from the schoolhouse. Lola would be along in a minute. He turned down a side street and waited. Soon he saw her coming in her graceful stride. She lifted a hand to him and waved, hurrying her steps.

Casey took off his hat and held it at his side. "Have you heard the gossip about me?"

The smile froze on her lips. "Why do you ask?"

"I've got to know."

Her eyes searched his. "Yes, I heard. Does it make any difference?"

"There is one thing that makes all the difference. Do you believe it?"

"Yes. I believe Julia was in your room. Abe Rucker is a truthful man. But I won't believe you did anything wrong unless you tell me yourself."

A great breath came out of him. In that moment he knew that only Lola's opinion was worth anything, that the rest of San Rafael meant nothing by comparison. He had Lola's love, and that was enough.

"I never heard anything in my life that meant more to me than what you just said." He took her hand. "Whatever happens, believe two things. I did not do anything wrong. And I love you."

He let go of her hand and wheeled away, walking rapidly to the alley. He turned there and came into the Idle Hour through the rear door.

There was no one in the saloon but the barkeep behind the mahogany bar and Duke Dorsey on the customer side. He was a tall, long-necked man with a leathery face and a pair of blue eyes that were on Casey from the moment he entered.

"You're Dorsey?"

"That's right," the gunman answered.

"I hear you're gunning for me," Casey said, cocking the Winchester.

Dorsey edged away from the bar. "Where's your Forty-Five?"

"I don't own one. This will do."

Dorsey looked shocked. "Go get a real gun."

"This will do," he repeated. He added: "You're a fool for taking Scoggins's money to kill a man you never saw before."

"A thousand dollars," Dorsey said, "makes a good day's wages."

"All right. Earn your money."

"Not with you holding that Winchester on me. Go get a handgun and fight like a man."

Casey moved one step to the side and put the Winchester on the bar. "Now it's as far from my hand as that Forty-Five is from yours. Make your play."

"The hell I will," Dorsey said, and turned away, heading for the door.

Dorsey took two steps, halted, and swung back, drawing his gun. Casey had expected treachery and had grabbed the big rifle. He fired once, just ahead of the Colt .45. Dorsey's face twisted. He dropped his gun, grabbed at his shirt front, and fell.

Casey ran past the dead man into Main Street. The crowd was moving slowly toward the Idle Hour, led by Rucker and Ennis. They stopped and stared.

Doc Miller broke the silence. "Did he hit you, Ed?"

"No," Casey replied. He added to Rucker: "Tough luck."

Casey went past them to the bank. Then Lola was at his side. He didn't know where she had come from. He only knew she was there, holding his arm and trembling as she clung to him.

"I'm all right," he said. "I've got business with Scoggins. You go on now."

"I'll stay with you, Ed."

He grinned. She walked beside him to the bank. The crowd followed at a distance. Casey glimpsed Julia coming out of the hotel, angling toward them.

Casey found the banker at his desk. He stepped through the gate at the end of the railing. Scoggins saw him and rose.

"Good scheme, Eli, but it backfired. Dorsey's dead. Now you've got me to contend with."

The banker's mouth sagged open. "This doesn't concern me."

"You're wrong, Eli. Dorsey said you paid him a thousand dollars to kill me."

"He's lying."

"Barkeep heard it all. You're done in this town."

"Keep threatening Eli!" Ennis called out behind him, "and you'll find yourself behind bars."

"No, you won't," Julia said. She came through the crowd and stood beside Lola. "It's time somebody took care of Scoggins, and I'm picking Ed Casey to do it."

Some of the townsmen started toward Casey. He turned, his Winchester at the ready. "Stay there, Pete."

Julia turned to the townsmen. "There's something you boys need to know. A while back Scoggins used the bank's money to speculate on mine properties. He lost, and I quietly helped him out to keep the bank from going under. Now I own a chunk of this place, a big chunk." She smiled. "And you can be sure I'll straighten Eli out."

Scoggins wiped a hand across his face, looked at Casey, then at the men out front. They were obviously shocked to learn of the misuse of funds. Pete Ennis was no help now.

Julia turned to Scoggins. "Well?"

"All right, Julia," he said, "all right."

"From now on this bank will be operated in good faith," she announced. "With honesty."

Casey strode to the sheriff. "Resign, Pete. Resign, or I'll yank that star off your shirt myself."

Without a word, he pulled it off his shirt, threw it at Casey, and stomped out.

Rucker gave a last look at Lola, and followed.

"Well, Ed," Julia said, "this bank partnership will take some legal paperwork. Can you do the job?"

"As soon as I take Lola back to school," he said with a smile.

Julia turned to her. "I made a mistake about you. I thought you were all milk and toast. You know, silk and ribbons and foofaraw. But you're a hell-roarer, like me and Ed."

Puzzled, Lola said: "I don't understand."

"Ed will tell you," Julia said, holding out her hand. "He's a good man."

Lola took her hand. "I've got to get back," Lola said, and turned to Casey.

They walked into the street, Lola holding her head high, a hand on Casey's arm. Lou Abbot was waiting outside with Doc Miller and some others.

Abbot asked: "When are we going deer hunting, Ed?"

That was the way they were. When a man was on top, they were with him, and right now Casey was up there. But he couldn't forget.

He said curtly: "Not this fall, Lou." Then went on with Lola.

When they were out of earshot, Casey said: "You changed yesterday after the Potter business. I'm not a hero. You've got to remember that. After everything settles down . . . I mean . . ." He floundered, searching for words.

Lola said: "You're trying to say that I suddenly became too forward after you made yourself San Rafael's number one citizen."

"No, I mean . . . well, you had been kind of offish."

"You might remember, Mister Ed Casey, that you are the chairman of the school board. Perhaps you weren't aware of it, but you always acted very official. Second, after the shootings, I knew you'd need some support." She added: "And as far as the rest of the single men of this town are concerned, I don't want any of them."

Ed Casey stopped and turned to face her. "I never thought of it that way. Will you accept my apology?"

"I'll forgive you," she said, adding: "There's one way you can fix it."

He leaned closer and kissed her there on the street where all could see them.

The Tongue-Tied Cowboy

They had held the Pothook cattle here at Dead Horse Spring for three days, and the buyer, Sam Badger, hadn't shown up.

Bill Price had a hunch he wouldn't, for Badger was the kind who respected neither God nor man. Crossing Ute land, he had consistently defied treaty rights, sneered at their traditions, trampled their pride into Colorado dust. Now with twilight marking the end of the third day of waiting, it was Bill's guess that Badger had finally met his end at the hands of warriors.

If Mel Jarvis had been a million miles away, Bill wouldn't have minded the waiting, for, as usual, Lissa Kane had come along. Every summer for the last three years, Bill had helped drive a small herd of three-year-olds from the Blue Mountains up here to the western shoulder of the La Sal Range where Badger met them and made his deal with old Soogan Kane, the owner of the Pothook.

This year, however, everything was different. Soogan was in bed with a broken leg. Rustlers had been active, so most of the Pothook hands had been kept at home to keep track of livestock. To make it complete, Soogan owed a note to the bank and was depending on this herd to bring in enough cash to pay it off.

Bad luck, according to Bill, always came in batches. Sam Badger's failure to show up was in this batch. Jarvis being along was more of the same, and that was a chunk he could lay at Lissa's door, a fact which made him mad every time he thought about it.

A week before old Soogan had called Bill in. "Four days from now I've got to have a hundred head of three-year-olds at Dead Horse Spring. We're short-handed, so I'm sending you and Lissa and Mel. You're running the outfit and you'll do the dickering with Badger."

Bill rolled a smoke, not meeting Soogan's eyes. He didn't argue about Jarvis going, but he was dead sure it was a mistake to send him. He'd had a hunch from the first Jarvis was a crook, but it would take more than a hunch to change Soogan Kane's mind.

Now Sam Badger was a different proposition. Everybody knew he'd steal the gold right out of your teeth if you held your mouth open, so he was treated accordingly. Every summer for three years now Badger had trailed the Pothook herd he'd bought across the La Sals and on through Paradox Valley, which was part of the Ute reservation.

So far Badger had made it safely. He delivered his herd to one of the San Juan mining camps, but Soogan allowed that sooner or later the man would have trouble.

Plumb foolish, Soogan claimed, to take chances when Badger could follow a longer route and go around the reservation. But it saved time to follow the valley, and Badger was the kind who figured one white man was as good as Mancos Jim and his whole band of warriors.

"You got anybody else except Jarvis?" Bill asked finally.

"Don't cotton to Mel, do you?" Soogan laughed. "Jealous on account of him beating you out on Lissa?"

"Whether I am or not, it isn't good business to let Lissa go, her being moon-eyed over that dude like she is."

"I couldn't keep her here if I wanted to," Soogan said, "and you know it. Anyhow, I'm not worried. I know Lissa."

Bill recalled how Mel Jarvis had ridden in a month ago, singing "Clementine" in that tenor voice of his, dressed as if headed for a Saturday night dance. He sported silver foofaraw on his chaps, gun belt, and saddle, a gold-plated Colt, wore a green silk shirt and a cream-colored Stetson that must have set him back a month's wages.

Bill had to admit he was jealous. What was more, his suspicion of Jarvis was just a hunch. He never had cottoned to a man who called himself a cowhand and dressed like a danged dude. To top everything off, Jarvis had snow-white teeth and a smile that was enough to curdle a man's supper, not to mention his habit of keeping his hair longer than necessary.

Lissa was sweet on him the first minute she saw him ride in. Bill knew that because he was standing with her at the trough. Jarvis stopped singing, flashed his smile, and lifted his fine hat.

"You must be Lissa Kane. They told me you were the prettiest girl in Utah, and I can see they were right."

Lissa's mouth popped open. Then her blue eyes began to shine. Bill saw that, and started to sizzle. He'd worked for Pothook for three years, and he had loved Lissa every day of those years. He'd taken her to dances and on rides up into the timber, but he'd never been able to work up enough gumption to ask her to marry him.

Ordinarily Soogan would have kicked a fancied dude off Pothook range, but Lissa was on the side of this one. Soogan hired him. It made Bill sick, watching her go mushy over Jarvis. She even started wearing her party dress evenings when she went walking with him.

Then there was that first Saturday night. Bill had hitched up the buggy to take Lissa to the dance the way he always did, but just as he drove up to the house, Lissa came out with Jarvis.

"I'm taking her, pretty boy," Bill said. "Get."

"Not tonight you aren't," Lissa said. "You didn't even ask me."

"But we always . . ."

"Thanks for hitching up," Jarvis said politely. "Now move out of the way."

That did it. Bill jumped down and took a swing at Jarvis's grinning mouth, intent on knocking one of his white teeth loose, but the target didn't stay there. In the next three minutes Bill took the quickest licking had ever taken in his life. He tried again two more times the next week, but it always turned out the same. Jarvis was as hard to hit as a spring breeze, but he packed a wallop in either fist that was like the kick of a Missouri mule.

Bill knew as well as anybody that all his trouble with Jarvis didn't make the man a crook. Still, it seemed mighty funny that he'd ride in asking for a job at thirty a month and beans. He just didn't look like that kind.

The only way to prove anything to Soogan Kane was to get real evidence, and three days of waiting for Sam Badger had not produced one clue.

But it did prove one thing. Soogan didn't know Lissa as well as he thought he did. She stayed in camp, humming to herself and smiling a little and acting as if she knew something that made her mighty happy. It looked to Bill as if she was fixing to run off with Jarvis, and that was the worst thing Bill could think of.

Every evening had followed the same pattern. Bill hunkered down on one side of the fire, smoking. Jarvis sang. Right now he was in the middle of “Sweet Bunch of Violets”. In a minute or two he’d start on “Gathering the Myrtle with Mary”. Lissa was lying back on her elbows, eyes almost closed as she listened. Bill could just see her head and shoulders and the curve of her breasts from where he sat. *Pretty,* Bill thought, *mighty pretty*.

There had been a strange poignant ache inside him right from the day Jarvis had first showed up. Lissa was twenty, young enough to be impressionable and old enough to think she knew what she wanted. It wasn’t fair to Bill, with his flat nose and brown hair and liberal coating of freckles, to have to compete for a girl’s love with a dude like Mel Jarvis. But the way it turned out, he hadn’t given Jarvis much competition.

Whatever happened from here on, Bill wanted Lissa to be happy, but he knew as well as he knew anything that Jarvis wasn’t the man for the job. Still, there didn’t seem to be much he could do about it, for Lissa had a lot of her father’s stubbornness once she made up her mind. Bill was trying to think of something and Jarvis was starting “Gathering the Myrtle with

Mary" when they heard a horse coming down the mountain.

Bill jumped at the fire, saying—"Shut up, Jarvis."—as he swung a boot through the coals.

Lissa began: "What's the matter . . . ?"

But Jarvis pulled her back into the shadows, whispering: "Someone's coming."

"Get back into the rocks," Bill said softly.

"I'm staying here," Lissa said.

"Better move back," Jarvis urged. "You're too pretty to get cut up by a stray slug."

She went then. Lissa would do anything Jarvis asked, Bill thought, but if he opened his mouth, she rammed a boot down his throat.

They waited, hearing the horse plunge down the trail at a reckless pace. Bill had his Winchester in his hands, and Jarvis had pulled his gold-plated six-gun. A moment later Bill glimpsed the horse coming out of the cedars. The rider was tall and skinny, but the light was too pale to show his face. He swung around the water hole, calling: "Soogan! You around?"

It was Laredo, one of Sam Badger's men. "Over here!" Bill called out. "Soogan's home with a busted leg. We brought the beef."

Laredo laughed. "You can herd 'em back. Sam won't be buying no more beef."

Bill threw an armful of cedar limbs on the coals. They flamed up as Laredo led his sweaty-gummed horse toward the fire. "Got any coffee?"

Bill motioned to the pot. “Help yourself.”

Lardeo saw Lissa then. “Howdy, ma’am,” he said. His gaze brushed Jarvis and swung to Bill. “You running the outfit?”

“Yeah,” Bill replied. “What happened to Sam?”

Laredo filled a tin cup with coffee. “You can guess. Mancos Jim’s band is in the valley, madder’n blazes because they’re being moved out next week. Sam got a late start from Telluride, so he was traveling fast. Fast and careless. He’s dead. So’s two of his men.”

He drank the coffee and threw the cup down in a sudden wild motion. “They’d have got me, too, if I’d been with ’em. My horse went lame and I fell behind. Nothing I could do.”

“Sam should have waited,” Bill said. “That deadline’s only a week off.”

Laredo laughed again. “Ever hear of Sam waiting five minutes on account of Utes?” He wheeled toward his horse. “I’m going. I aim to ride and keep on riding till I forget what Sam looked like with his hair gone.” Laredo swung into the saddle. “Tell Soogan he lost a pile of *dinero*. Sam figured on offering seventy dollars a head. Men are swarming into Telluride by the thousands, every one hungry for beef.” He spurred his tired horse and rode into darkness.

Jarvis cleared his throat. “This is up to you, Price.”

"What is?"

"I keep thinking about Soogan and that note he owes. . . ." He shook his head. "No, it would be too dangerous."

"What is it, Mel?" Lissa asked.

"I was just thinking," he went on, "if this Badger fellow was willing to pay seventy dollars, the cattle must be worth more than that in Telluride . . . a lot more. Why don't we drive on through and make that sale ourselves?"

"No," Bill said. "The Utes are losing their homeland. They've been buzzing like hornets ever since the Meeker Massacre."

"But Mancos Jim has probably gone over the plateau by now," Lissa said.

"No."

"Bill!" she said angrily. "We have to try it. It's the only way to save Pothook."

He shook his head. "Not if we die."

"We'll push this herd fast," she said. She demanded: "Are you with us?"

Bill looked at Jarvis. "I ought to bust your neck for starting this wild idea."

"Don't you lay a hand on him!" Lissa said.

Jarvis laughed. "He's tried that."

Bill knew what Soogan would say. Lissa was more important to the old man than Pothook. Even if Bill knew he could count on Jarvis in case of trouble, which he didn't, Lissa's life was at stake.

"Lissa, this is a crazy idea," he said. "We aren't going to . . ."

The starry sky suddenly fell on him, and Bill pitched forward on his face.

He was out for a long time. When he came to, the moon was far down in the west, the sky a star-filled glitter above him. He got to his feet, head aching. The earth began to spin. His knees gave out and the ground came up to meet him.

It was full daylight when Bill revived the second time. He crawled to the water hole, drank, and doused his face. He lay there for a time, feeling the beat of his headache. Even now in the early morning, the summer sun hammered the desert.

The only shade came from the grotesquely-shaped sandstone rocks, honed into all sorts of spires and arches by the erosive wind. He crawled back among the rocks and lay there, his mind slowly digging into his consciousness for memory.

He still had his gun. They had not taken his brown saddle horse, and some food had been left behind. The herd was gone. He rose, grabbing at a projection of rock to steady himself until the dizziness passed. Then he lurched back to the place where he had lain when he had recovered consciousness, and saw Lissa's note.

Go home and tell Dad what we've done. Laredo got hungry and came back. We've got three riders, so we'll make out fine.

Lissa

Bill made a fire and cooked breakfast, trying to make some sense out of what had happened. Laredo must have been the one who knocked him out, for both Lissa and Jarvis had been in front of him, but for Laredo to have come back out of hunger did not sound right. The man had been almost hysterical from fear when he left here.

He finished eating, caught up his horse, and saddled. Still he could make no sense out of this except that Laredo was play-acting. That probably meant Sam Badger was alive, and Mancos Jim and his band of warriors might not be within a hundred miles of Paradox Valley.

Bill turned his horse upslope. His head still hurt, but he felt better. At least, he told himself, he could shoot straight. The first thing he'd do when he met up with Mel Jarvis and Laredo would be to start shooting.

An hour later Bill was in the pines. He rounded a twist in the trail, and almost ran into Laredo. Both grabbed guns and fired. Laredo must have been the most surprised, for his shot missed by a foot. Bill's bullet caught the tall man in the chest and knocked him out of the saddle. Bill rode slowly toward him, cocked gun on him.

For a moment Bill thought Laredo was dead, but when he swung down and knelt in the thick blanket of pine needles, Laredo's eyes flickered open.

"Badger sent me back to kill you," he said. "Wants to leave your body beside the girl so folks will think savages done it. Better hurry . . ." He tried to finish, but death blotted out his words.

Bill swung back into the saddle and went on up the trail, his anger growing to rage. Sam Badger aimed to steal the herd, and Jarvis had been in on the scheme. But it was still guesswork. Even if Bill got down the other side in time, Badger might not have tipped his hand yet. Lissa would never believe Jarvis had any part of it.

He held to a steady pace, often stepping down and running beside his horse to rest him, and all the time one thought lay in the back of his mind like a chill blade: *I might not make it in time.*

The hot sun was swinging westward, its light sharp upon the long descending sweep of the cedar- and pinon-covered slopes behind him. Then he was in the quaking aspens, tiny leaves turning in the hot breeze, and within the hour he was over the top and swinging down the trail that dropped rapidly into Paradox Valley.

Hour after hour, with his fear for Lissa's safety on his mind, he went on at a reckless pace. Below stretched the great trough in the earth that was

Paradox, red stone cliffs rising on both sides, the walls chiseled by the forces of nature.

Bill figured he was closing the distance. Every moment he expected to glimpse the drag rider or Badger himself. He kept his gun handy, eyes searching the valley for signs of cattle on the move. Then, almost at the bottom, he reached a sharp ledge just above the valley floor. He reined up. The herd spread out before him, and panic struck him. Ute warriors had pulled up a hundred yards from the foot of the trail, and the leader, Mancos Jim, was palavering with Mel Jarvis.

It seemed to Bill that he could hear the pounding of his heart. His lungs refused to work. In that one sweeping glance he could not see Lissa or Badger or any of his men. Just Jarvis, sitting straight-backed in his fancy saddle, and Mancos Jim with a dozen warriors fanned out behind him.

But then, directly below, Bill suddenly saw them. Lissa sat on the ground with her hands and feet tied, while Sam Badger and two of his men hunkered behind a sandstone upthrust.

The Indians could not see these men, but Badger had found a crack in the stone that gave him a view of the meeting between Jarvis and the Ute leader.

If Mancos Jim discovered Badger, it would mean the end of all of them. Bill couldn't guess what Jarvis was telling the Utes, but for the moment their attention was fixed on him. So was Badger's, and that gave Bill his chance to reach the bottom.

Turning back onto the trail, he swung down the last loop. He pulled up behind the cover of a tall rock. Jerking his Winchester from the boot, he stepped down and edged forward. What he saw now brought a flood of relief—the Utes had turned and were headed out across the valley.

Mel Jarvis rode back toward the sandstone upthrust.

Badger poked his shaggy head out. "What'd you tell 'em?"

"Stay out of sight, you fool," Jarvis said.

Badger swore, but dropped back. A moment later Jarvis swung in behind the upthrust. Bill did not stop to consider the odds, for this was his chance. He ducked around the rock and lunged toward the sandstone barrier that hid Badger and the others.

For twenty yards he was in the open. If any of them had been watching, they'd have cut him down, but he reached the great upthrust and stopped, panting. He drew deep breaths and then heard Badger's voice.

"Don't be a fool, Jarvis. What does the girl mean to you?"

"I'm no woman killer. I won't stand for this. . . ."

"You're a little late," Badger said. "You knew the deal."

"I didn't know all of it," Jarvis said. "Stealing cows is one thing. This is something else."

Bill moved around the upthrust and leveled his Winchester at them. "That's right, Jarvis. This is something else. Raise your hands. All of you."

Badger swore again. He stood still. The pair behind him weren't reaching skyward. Their hands swept guns from their holsters. Bill fired, once, twice, and again, aware that Mel Jarvis had drawn his gold six-gun and cut down Badger as he reached for his gun.

Bill's first bullet caught the nearest outlaw in the head. The second gouged out a long slice of skin, and the third hit the other outlaw high in the chest. He swung to Jarvis, but the man had holstered his revolver.

"For once I'm glad to see you, Price."

Still not fully trusting him, Bill stepped sideward until he reached Lissa. He dropped to his knees, pulled his knife out one-handed, and slashed the ropes that bound her. Right then he might as well have dropped his gun because Lissa was crying and kissing him, her arms around his neck so tight that she almost choked him.

Bill might have imagined it, but it seemed to him like she acted like a woman who had almost lost the man she loved. Anyhow, it was mighty pleasant, and he did set his gun down to hold her with both arms.

Jarvis brought horses up and, lifting the dead

men into the saddles, tied them there and led them back around the upthrust so they would be out of Lissa's sight.

Then he returned and his voice was brittle hard when he said to Bill: "I love Lissa, but it's your pot if you've got sense enough to pull it in. How a man can be as blind as you are, or maybe just plain stupid, is beyond me."

"What're you getting at?" Bill demanded.

"Ask her." Jarvis jabbed a thumb at Lissa. "I'm riding."

"Before you go," Bill said, "tell me what got into Badger?"

"He lost his shirt in a deal this spring," Jarvis said. "With cattle prices sky high, he figured on stealing the Pothook herd. He didn't know Soogan wouldn't be there, and sent Laredo into our camp to spin that yarn about Badger being scalped. I was supposed to suggest going on to Telluride. It worked with Lissa, but not with you. Laredo had sneaked back and laid his gun barrel across your head. We pulled out right away and we've been shoving the herd ever since." Jarvis paused before adding: "Badger paid me to get a job with Pothook, but I couldn't stomach it. Not after knowing Lissa. No reason why you two can't take this herd on to Telluride now. You can get back to Pothook in time to pay off that note. Mancos Jim won't come back. He's going on over the Uncompahgre

Plateau to Fort Crawford, just as the treaty says."

"What did you tell him?" Bill asked.

Jarvis grinned. "Told him these were my steers, and Badger wasn't with me. He believed me."

Jarvis walked back to the horses and a moment later Bill heard him ride away. Bill sat there looking at Lissa and she looked at him. All of a sudden it seemed that everything that had happened was a long way behind them and here he was alone with a woman he'd loved for three years.

"I . . . well, uh, I wonder what he meant by saying I was blind. Or stupid."

"You're both," she said. "If a man can't propose in three years, he must be."

"But you've been crazy about Jarvis."

"If you had a lick of sense, you'd have seen that all I was doing was trying to make you get up and do something. You just took me for granted."

"I was trying to get some money saved," he said lamely.

"You could have told me you loved me. You were a coward every time we came home from a dance. And I don't want to hear anything more about money."

"So I was a coward every time I brought you home from a dance, was I? Well, uh . . . I'm a changed man."

"I don't believe you."

But soon she did. He proved it to her.

From Hell to Leadville

Johnny Becker was young, too young to ramrod the South Arkansas-Bowstring line of the Becker & Estey Stage Company. But if you were Hank Becker's only son, you had to start someday, that day being the one Hank picked. Johnny was old enough to be in love, old enough to die if he had to, and Hank thought he was old enough to be superintendent.

At twenty-three Johnny knew it wasn't always the years that gave a man age. He'd grown up knowing about stagecoaches because old Hank had run stages out of Denver from the days of the first gold strikes, but knowing about them wasn't enough. Johnny could unlimber a gun and shoot the buttons off a man's vest in less time than a good many gents could who lived by the gun, but that wasn't enough, either.

Johnny paced the floor of his office in long, nervous strides, a slender, blue-eyed man, sandy hair as rumpled as if a comb had not touched it since he'd slept. Doubts prodded him, doubts of his strength, his talents, his understanding. It took a vast fund of all those qualities to run a stage line. Old Hank had it. Twenty-odd years of experience had given it to him. Or perhaps he had been born with it.

Sitting down in his swivel chair, Johnny built a smoke and lighted it. He knew he had not been born with it. Impelled by the undefined uneasiness that had been growing in him from the day Hank dropped this job into his lap, he got up again and went to the window. That was when he saw Duff Darley leave the Silver Star. The saloon man turned toward the stage depot.

He saw Darley pause in front of Kimroe's barbershop, wipe a match alive across the new pine front, and light the thin cigar he held between his teeth. He came on to Johnny's office then, walking in the short-paced stride that was characteristic of him.

"How are you, Becker?" Darley asked in his cool, impersonal voice.

"Still kicking."

Johnny didn't ask him to sit down. He didn't like the man. Darley was too ambitious, a dapper, dark man with a trimmed mustache and green eyes as expressionless as twin emeralds. He owned the Silver Star, Bowstring's finest saloon, and he had a part in a dozen businesses in and around this mining camp.

There was no telling where Darley's throbbing ambition would take him next. Johnny knew him well enough to be certain that a cunning web was always being spun in the depths of his mind. Now Darley's eyes swept the office and came to rest on the litter that covered Johnny's desk.

"Just got out of college, didn't you?"

"That's right."

He paused. "Red Kimmel shot a man in the Silver Star the other night. Self-defense, of course. Red's pretty fast on the draw." Darley fingered the ash from his cigar. "A mining camp is different than a college town in the East, isn't it?"

"What are you getting at, Darley?"

"I know your old man, kid . . . maybe better than you do. He put you in here, wondering whether you'd pan out solid color." He added: "I've got a proposition to offer you. Interested?"

"No."

"Listen, anyway. Bowstring will be a good town, Becker. Not just a boom camp that will be a ghost town tomorrow. I aim to grow with it. I'll go from here to Denver. I'll be out of the saloon business then. I'm branching out now. Own a sawmill up Tenmile. I've got a part of the Golden Lady mine. Next month I'll set up a stamp mill. You listening?"

"I hear you talking."

"Most all the freight that goes north to the mines is hauled by my outfit. My next jump is the stage business. One line between here and South Arkansas is enough. Two will make trouble."

"And you think Dad and Estey will sell?"

"I think Estey is a bookkeeper who will do whatever your dad tells him to. Tell him the mines are petering out, and you've got a sucker on the hook. He's been smart enough to get out of other camps when peak days were gone. I'll make a good offer, Becker, to convince your dad."

"Get out."

Darley tossed his cigar into the street. He stood perfectly still, smiling.

"I've been watching you, too, Johnny. Someday you'll be smart and tough like old Hank, but you aren't now. You've got to learn. Hank hasn't been so smart and tough all of his life, either. He made a big mistake in Central City. It hurt him, but he learned. The difference is, you won't get a chance to learn. One mistake, and you're done."

Johnny eyed him.

"Before you kick me out, Becker, I've got a few more cards to lay on the table. You know damned well you're in over your head. So far you've had easy sailing. What'll you do when it gets tough?"

Darley was calling it right, so right that he must have been reading Johnny Becker's mind. The uneasiness seeped in again, but anger was there, too, like a red fog sweeping across his brain. He wanted to wipe that smug expression off Darley's face.

"I'll show you how tough things can get right here," Johnny said, "if you don't clear out."

Darley's laugh was soft, but as insulting as a slap. "There's a sort of dignity in running a stage line that a saloon never gives a man. Look at old Hank. Tough as they come, but he cuts a wide swath in Denver. I'll be there in his place in another five years. King of the Colorado stage lines. That'll be me. I'm giving you a chance your dad won't. Put this deal over for me, and I'll hand you ten thousand dollars." He paused. "Turn it down, and I'll make your line lose money so quick you'll have old Hank over here from Denver in his fine surrey as fast as his horse can bring him. You know what that'll mean."

"No."

"Don't tell me I've got it figured wrong, kid. Back East you can be civilized. You can be afraid, but you can hide it. Not here, Becker. This is a wilderness. No law except the one you carry in a holster. Don't figure on the marshal for any help and don't figure on any rules when the fighting starts. The tough make it. The others wind up in Boothill."

The red haze of anger took control of Johnny then. He crossed the office in two quick strides, his fist lashing out. He hit Darley on the chin, knocking him through the open doorway and down on the plank walk. Darley rolled and came up with a Derringer in his hand.

"I didn't think you had the guts to do it," he said. He eyed Johnny. Then he returned the little gun to a holster on his belt. "You just made a bad mistake, Becker."

Turning, Darley walked back to the Silver Star

in his careful, short-paced stride. Johnny stood in the doorway, shoulder pressed against the jamb while he rubbed his skinned knuckles. Maybe he had made a mistake, but he knew one thing. Old Hank Becker would approve of what he'd just done. If that meant anything.

When Johnny turned toward his desk, he saw old Hodge Hogan standing in the doorway to the inner office. Hogan had been with Becker & Estey from the first. He was a white-haired, stooped man, all hide and bone, tough and as loyal as a man could be. He was a timekeeper now, and that was the wrong job for him. When Johnny learned the old man had transferred from Leadville only a week before he had come to Bowstring, he'd jumped to the conclusion that Hogan had been placed here to spy on him and report back to the home office.

"Darley ain't one to take a crack on the jaw," Hogan said.

"You think I made a mistake, too?"

"Didn't say that. I never heard what the dispute was about. I just know what Darley will do now."

"What?"

"Sic Red Kimmel on you."

Johnny sat down at his desk and picked up a pen. Hogan was curious, and stood there watching. Well, he could just keep on being curious. Hank Becker wouldn't find out about Darley's offer through Hogan.

The old man stared at Johnny for a while, then went back to his own office. Johnny laid down the pen when he heard the door close. He rolled a smoke, took a single drag on it, and tossed it out the door. It was bad enough for his father to drop him here without a word of instruction or advice. It was worse to send Hodge Hogan to spy on him.

Less than a week after Johnny had returned to Denver from college, Hank Becker had bundled him into his fancy surrey, the outfit he always used on inspection trips.

"We'll take a trip over Marshal Pass to Bowstring," Hank had said. "Just added that line last year after Otto Mears got his toll road finished."

They stopped at every stage stand between South Arkansas and Bowstring, and when they reached it, Hank called the men together. He introduced Johnny all around. Then he said: "Johnny's the new boss, boys."

The father shook the son's hand. Wishing him luck, he climbed into his surrey and headed back for the pass. Johnny's clothing and other personal items would be sent via stagecoach.

Johnny had expected to drive stage as he had the summer before, not to be dropped into a boom camp with responsibility like this. What Darley had said was right. One mistake would be his last. Anger had ebbed out of Johnny now, leaving only the cold gray ashes of doubt. He was scared, and Darley had sensed it. How many others had?

Johnny cocked his feet up on the desk. He tried to analyze his own fears, to grip the cause of the uneasiness that had drawn his nerves fiddle-string tight. He didn't fear Darley, or even Kimmel. It wasn't that. He brought his feet to the floor and paced the length of the room and back.

He'd never tackled a job he couldn't handle. But on the other hand he'd never had a big one thrown at him before. That was it. His previous jobs had been driving a stage or breaking horses or running a stage stand. Little jobs. It was the magnitude of this one that scared him.

There were stage stands every twelve miles between South Arkansas and Bowstring. Thirty head of horses were kept at each of them, and two attendants. He had the responsibility to hire and fire, to see that hay and grain and food were distributed, to get tough when the need arose.

For the first time in days Johnny laughed, the tension in him easing. If the job was too big, he'd fail, and a man had to fail to learn. There were a million other jobs he could get. He'd find another. Darley had said Hank had made a bad mistake in Central City, but Johnny had never heard his father say anything about it. He was a man who liked to talk about success.

Johnny turned back to his desk. There was plenty of bookwork to do. He dipped his pen. Then he heard a man's boot heel on the floor. He looked up. Red Kimmel stood in the doorway, a sardonic grin on his face.

"Take it easy, Becker. No fast moves. That's what always scares me. Fast moves."

"I told your boss to take his deal and go to hell," Johnny said. "You need to hear it again?"

Johnny's gun was in his desk drawer. He wondered if Kimmel planned to shoot him where he sat. He could, for Johnny didn't have time to jerk the drawer open and grab his Colt.

"I'm not hard to convince," Kimmel said.

The gunman built a smoke, taking his time while the seconds dragged by, head cocked to one side, pale blue eyes fixed on Johnny. There was always an air of unsubdued energy about the man, as if he was likely to go into action at any moment. A long knife scar curving along his left cheek added a sinister quality to his appearance and made it impossible to read him because it gave an upward slant to one end of his mouth as if he were smiling.

"What do you want?" Johnny asked.

"Got some news Duff figured would interest you," he replied.

"News?"

"We're starting our own stage line in a month or so."

Johnny shrugged. "It's a free country. I won't try to stop him."

"Guess you're a little smarter than we figured,"

Kimmel said. "But I doubt you're smart enough to get hay for your stock."

"What are you talking about?"

"We contracted for Nesbitt's hay," he said. "The whole crop."

Johnny stared at him. This was the kind of move he should have foreseen and countered, but it had never occurred to him that Nesbitt would sell to anybody but Becker & Estey. There had been no argument last year about price. Nesbitt knew his market was waiting for him this year, and Johnny had not seen the need for a formal contract.

"What are you telling me for?" Johnny demanded.

Red Kimmel was neither a diplomat nor an errand boy. He was Darley's killer. No more, no less, with Duff Darley doing his thinking for him.

"Duff just thought you'd want to know," Kimmel said.

Kimmel wheeled out of the doorway and walked away. Johnny had no time to figure out a solution then, for two stages wheeled in from South Arkansas and he was busy until evening. Work was the one way he had been able to keep his sanity. It was the quiet time when he sat down at his desk to do his bookkeeping that he felt butterflies in his innards. Or when he went to bed and sleep avoided him.

Johnny was finishing his supper in the café

when Hodge Hogan took the stool next to him. "What'd Kimmel want this afternoon?"

He pushed his plate back, apple pie half eaten. "Just a friendly visit," he said, and left before Hogan could question him.

Walking up the ramp into the depot, Johnny wondered if Darley had sent Kimmel to start a fight, hoping a wild claim about the hay crop would prod Johnny into a foolish move—going for his gun, for example.

Whether that was the case or not, Johnny knew what he had to do this evening. He had to ride out to the Nesbitt place and get a contract nailed down.

It took a few moments for him to write out a purchasing contract on Becker & Estey letterhead and sign it. He put it in his pocket and went to the livery. There, saddling the white gelding he used for personal trips, he took the west road out of town.

Matt Nesbitt had settled on the creek before the first strike was made. He'd had nothing in mind except that he saw a future as a stockman. Then, with the first trickle of gold seekers over the pass, he had realized that hay was his bonanza. It had been no great trick to clear the sagebrush off, dam the creek, and flood several hundred acres of the best hay land a man could find. Last year every ton he could spare went to the stage company.

Johnny had heard his dad say a dozen times: "Very few prospectors or miners make anything. Other gents take it away from them. Transportation is as good a way as any, and it's honest work."

Transportation had made Hank Becker a millionaire. Farming would make Matt Nesbitt wealthy in a few years. He had only a log cabin now set back against the hill in a grove of cottonwoods, but he had plans for a bigger house in another year. "My wife's lived in cabins and dugouts all her life. She's going to have something better," he would say.

Johnny found Nesbitt at the dam, turning water back into the creek. The sun had dropped behind the western hills and dusk was steadily deepening in the valley. Nesbitt didn't look up until Johnny reined to a stop beside him.

Even then Nesbitt threw a couple of shovels of mud on the bank of the creek before he thrust his shovel into the dirt and slowly looked up. "Howdy, Johnny."

A premonition of disaster slid down Johnny's spine. This wasn't like Matt Nesbitt. He was a lanky, loose-jointed man, stooped a little with the years of hard work that had been his lot, a friendly man who had always greeted Johnny with cordiality. Now he shifted his weight and looked up at him without quite meeting his eyes.

Johnny swung down and produced the contract.

"I thought it would be good business to sign a contract for your hay. We paid forty dollars a ton last year, and I'm here to offer that price again."

Nesbitt cleared his throat and kicked aimlessly at a clod of muddy soil. "Sorry, Johnny, but I can't let you have the hay this year. Duff Darley offered fifty dollars, and I took it."

Johnny drew a deep breath. Red Kimmel hadn't been lying. Either Darley figured on starting a new line, or he thought his monopoly on the hay crop would force the sale of Becker & Estey.

Johnny slid the contract back into his pocket. "You could have asked me. Or are you too money-hungry?"

"You don't need to talk that away," he said. "It was just good business."

"Sure, good business for you, if he ever pays you that much," he said. "It would be good business for me to burn the crop, but that doesn't mean I'd do it."

Nesbitt moved angrily toward him. He stepped too close to the edge of the ditch. Mud on the bank caved in, and he slid down the side, sprawling into six inches of water. He kicked and floundered and swore. When he got to his feet, he shook his fist at Johnny.

"Darley told me you're a kid who got into a job that's too big, and I believe him. If your old man hadn't been Hank Becker, you'd never be super of this line."

"So you threw in with Darley," Johnny said. "And now you're covered with mud."

"I reckon you've said enough," Nesbitt said. "Ride out."

Johnny turned and walked to his horse. Mounting, he rode away. He had not handled that confrontation well, and wondered what his dad would have done in the same situation.

It was dark when Johnny returned to the stage terminal. He turned his gelding over to a Becker & Estey hostler. Then he stood on the wooden platform, watching two Concords being maneuvered into place. Two coaches made the run from South Arkansas every day, and a night run back. Often they went east empty, but they were always packed when they rolled west to Bowstring.

There was something about staging that got into a man's blood. This nightly scene was as commonplace to Johnny as pulling on his boots in the morning, yet he always thrilled to it. Becker & Estey made a point of putting on a show. "Good for business," old Hank maintained. The horses were white, the decorative paint bright on the coach, brass fittings glinting in the lantern light.

Hostlers were hooking up the six-horse string. Chain and rings made metallic music. Then the drivers and shotgun guards were on the high seats. Brakes were kicked off. Whips cracked with the sharpness of gunshots, and the Concords rolled up the street.

For the first time in his life Johnny Becker watched this scene and found no enjoyment in it. He was the end man in a game of crack-the-whip. There was a strange detached feeling in him as if he had just seen a drama that would never be repeated quite the same way for him. These stages could belong to Duff Darley someday; this could be Duff Darley's terminal because Johnny had not seen far enough ahead to checkmate his move.

Johnny strode along the platform to his office. He touched a match to the hanging lamp, slipped the chimney into place, his mind surging with dark thoughts. He picked up his revolver and looked at it.

Hodge Hogan came in. "What're you fixing to do, son?"

That was the snapping point. He put the gun down and cursed, a bitter wild rush of words bursting out of him.

Hogan didn't react. He waited until Johnny ran down, then he sat in the chair beside the desk.

"Sometimes a man gets loaded up till he's got to go off," Hogan said. "Then he can think straight. I've done just about everything in the stage-coaching business except this time-keeper job. Me and figures don't jibe. I'd give anything to get out of here. Just anywhere to feel the wind on my face again."

Johnny ran a hand down his jaw. "But you've got to stay here so my dad will know what I'm doing. That it, Hodge?"

"Hell no, son." Then he laughed. "Now I begin to see some things. You've treated me like a dirty shirt ever since you took over. That's the reason, isn't it? You thought Hank put me down here to play nursemaid for you."

"Didn't he?"

"No. Hank don't play that way. Far as this job goes, you're not his son. You're the super, and you're on your own. Hank's the kind who drops you into water over your head. You learn to swim sudden-like. Or you drown."

"Hodge," Johnny said, "I'm drowning."

"Let's have it, kid. Come on. It'll do you good to talk."

He leaned forward in the swivel chair as he told Hogan about Darley's visit, Red Kimmel's news, and finally the situation with Matt Nesbitt.

Hogan listened closely. "I reckon you've done right well, considering."

"Done well," Johnny repeated, shaking his head slowly.

"Hold on, now," Hogan said. "Don't get down on yourself. I happen to know where we can get some hay. Let Matt Nesbitt sell to Darley. At fifty dollars, that saloon man will lose money."

"If he doesn't pull this off," Johnny said, "he'll try something else."

"There's always a way to block a punch if you see it coming," Hogan said. "You can count on one thing. There'll be no double-crossing in our outfit. Every man jack of 'em has worked for Becker and Estey for years. You won't find none of them selling out to Darley."

Johnny felt a glimmer of hope. "Where's this hay crop?"

"On the mesa south of town," he replied. "Finest wild grass up there you've ever seen. Higher than a horse's belly. We'll have to make a road to get our wagons on top, but it can be done."

"And you're the man to do it," Johnny said.

Hogan's eyes lighted with the fire of anticipation. "I'd sure like a crack at it. I'll show Hank Becker I ain't finished."

"Then go to it. Get all the men you need. This will be expensive, but we won't be licked by Duff Darley."

Johnny left the office, knowing what he had to do. Darley figured Johnny Becker wouldn't do any swimming when the water was over his head. He'd figured this hay deal would crack him down the middle. All right. Duff Darley was going to learn tonight that it hadn't worked.

Bowstring's main street was alive with sound and light and music. Ore wagons and trailers rumbled past. There were carriages and surreys and men on horseback. The plank walks were filled with miners, all intent on finding release from the hours of darkness and labor and danger that were their days.

Johnny threaded his way through the crowd, heard the barker calling the games of Darley's Silver Star, and moved with traffic into the big saloon. An ornately carved mahogany bar ran the length of the room, a bar Darley claimed was the largest west of the Continental Divide.

The bar was packed three and four deep. The gaming tables on the other side of the room were thronged, and the space in the room reserved for dancing was so crowded the dancers barely moved to the waltz the orchestra was playing.

Johnny, eyes sweeping the room for a glimpse of Darley, wondered why the man would want to leave this business for anything as prosaic as running a stagecoach business. Then Johnny answered his own question. Darley would make his pile of gold. Then he'd seek power and social position. He would have neither as a saloon man.

A percentage girl, her face bright with rouge, dress low cut and revealing, plucked at Johnny's arm. "Dance with me again?"

He knew the girl. Juliet, she called herself. He had danced with her a few times.

Johnny grinned. "No time right now."

"You're sure?"

He nodded. "Why don't you get out of this hell hole? You don't belong here."

"A woman has to eat."

"Reckon so." He looked around. "Where will I find the big boss?"

Her hand tightened on his arm. "He's riding high lately, Johnny. Don't make trouble."

"If there's trouble, it'll be his making. Where is he?"

She didn't answer for a moment, her eyes mirroring concern. He didn't know whether it was intuition on her part, or if she had heard Darley talk, but she clearly knew something was up.

"You won't get a fair fight here, Johnny. I know the way they work it. Come back in the morning."

"I see him."

Johnny plowed through the crowd, ignoring the curses of miners. Darley did not know he was there until he reached the saloon man's elbow.

"It didn't work, Darley."

Duff Darley swung around to face him, surprise showing in his green eyes. "What are you talking about, kid?"

There were some big men at the table—mine owners, businessmen, a couple of Eastern capitalists, the kind whose respect Darley coveted. Like any man reaching above him, he played a smart game of dignity and self-importance. Now he treated Johnny as if he were a child, and Johnny, sensing his game, laughed in his face.

"You're a tinhorn, Darley," he said, "running games of chance rigged for suckers. Better stay in shallow water. You don't swim any better than I do."

Darley's eyes narrowed. "If you're drunk, Becker, and looking for trouble, you'll find it here."

"No trouble," Johnny said. "I just wanted to return the favor Kimmel gave me this afternoon. Your hay deal will cost you more than it will us. We'll cut and bale our own."

Johnny turned and moved into the crowd. He had crossed the room and moved through the door when he heard a curse. A gun fired, and he went down, hearing Juliet's scream fade away.

There were wild, fever-cursed days for Johnny Becker, days that he clung to life with a stubbornness that had something of Hank Becker in it. Juliet stayed with him day and night. Hogan told Johnny she'd quit her job to nurse him.

Red Kimmel was not arrested even though witnesses had seen him shoot Johnny from behind. No surprise there. The marshal was Darley's man.

Johnny's talk was the wild talk of delirium, of hay and station schedules and Hank Becker.

Juliet tried to assure him everything was all right. Every day hay wagons rumbled down the steep north slope of the mesa and mingled with the great ore wagons and burro trains that clogged the street, and every day the stacks behind the stage terminal grew.

"We've got Darley whipped!" Hogan crowed one night when he was in town. "He contracted for all of Nesbitt's hay, and this year Nesbitt's got more hay than you ever saw. At fifty dollars a ton it'll bust Darley."

"Who's running our stages?" Johnny asked. "Got to be somebody down there while you're working the hay."

"I got Juliet to keep time," Hogan said. "Hell, that wasn't a job for me. She keeps things running smooth. We got a good crew. Hasn't been one stage late since you got shot."

"Guess the outfit doesn't need a superintendent," Johnny said with a grin.

"Now you stay in bed until the doc says you can get up," Hogan said. He added: "You know Johnny, women are critters I never had no truck with, so I don't understand them, but that Juliet girl is something different than you'd expect to come out of a dance hall. She's done a job of looking after you while keeping the office in order."

After Hogan had gone Juliet came back into the room. He gazed at her. She was pale compared to her saloon days with red rouge on her cheeks. She wore a gingham dress, and somehow she was plainer and prettier now.

He was like Hogan. He didn't know why she had given up her job to help him. Unlike Hogan, he asked her.

She didn't answer for a moment, busying herself folding a sheet of paper and slipping it next to the lamp chimney so the shadow would be on Johnny's face instead of the flame's glare.

"Hogan says you saved my life. I'm grateful to you."

"I'm glad for that," she said.

"Tell me about yourself."

"Back home folks said I was wild and bad. My mother was a washerwoman, my father the town drunk. I ran away. I thought it would be different out here, but there weren't any jobs except the kind Darley gives."

He thought about his own upbringing, his college studies, and his expectations. Her life was vastly different, but he sensed her dreams were as large as his. She did not fear risks. There had been some security for her in Darley's Silver Star, but she had given it up to keep the spark of life in him, a man who meant nothing to her.

"Doc says I'll be able to work next week," he said. "What are you going to do then?"

"A woman can always make a living out here," she said dully.

"What would you like to do?"

She rose and walked to the window. "Funny thing," she said, "but I always had an idea I wanted to cook. I thought that where there were so many men, there would be room for a restaurant, but when I got out here, I found out it takes money to make money. I just didn't have it."

Johnny thought about that. "I need a dinner stop this side of the pass. I haven't had time to get one started. Would you be interested in taking over that job? It's no restaurant, but it's a start."

Her face brightened. "I couldn't think of anything better. All I've ever hoped for was a chance, just a chance."

Johnny lay awake long after Juliet had gone to bed, thinking about her and about himself. A chance! He'd had one, all right. Hank Becker had shoved it at him and rammed it down his throat, and now with Hogan's help it was going to be all right. Duff Darley was licked. Red Kimmel would be dealt with when the time came.

Johnny went back to work the next Monday. Except for the haystacks and the miracle of his desk being cleared, it was as if he hadn't been away. He was there on the ramp when the stages came in from South Arkansas. He was there when they rolled out in the evening, and pride was in him.

The next night Hodge Hogan, down from the mesa, talked about Juliet.

"Somebody had to do my job," Hogan said, "and that girl is smart. She's down on Darley, so I figured we could trust her to keep our business private. Hope I was right."

"Me, too," Johnny said.

"I heard about Nesbitt."

"Heard what?"

"Darley ain't hauled much because we've still got the stage business." He laughed. "Maybe Nesbitt's got it through his head he bet on the wrong horse."

"Yeah. Maybe." Johnny was remembering Nesbitt had said he was just a kid who got into a job too big for him.

"All the time I was flat on my back," Johnny said, "Darley didn't make a move. I figured he'd send Kimmel to finish the job."

"Darley's the kind who wants folks thinking right about him," Hogan said.

Johnny nodded, remembering Darley's words when he'd said he would not always be known as a saloon man. "I figure he'll try something that'll make me look bad."

"Your dad's due in tomorrow to see you," Hogan said. "Maybe Darley knows that."

"Maybe," Johnny said.

"Uh, I need to tell you something," Hogan said, "now that you've got your strength back mostly."

“What is it?”

“Well, we cut every blade of grass on the mesa,” he said, “but we haven’t got enough to make it through the winter.”

“But you said . . .”

“I know what I said. I kept hoping it would pile up faster than it did, but the grass just wasn’t there. Looks like we’ll have to get some hay from Nesbitt.”

“Does Darley know about this?”

“Don’t reckon he does . . . unless Juliet told him.”

Then Duff Darley wasn’t licked and Hank Becker would be here tomorrow. Johnny had been living in a fool’s paradise. He’d been thinking all the time that he could sit pat and force Darley to make the first move. All the time it had been Darley who was sitting in the driver’s seat. Now it was the tag end of summer, too late to haul enough hay from the east side of the pass, even if hay could be bought.

Outside, one of Johnny’s hostlers pulled a lathered horse to a stop and ran up the ramp to the office. “Somebody fired one of Nesbitt’s stacks! They’re blaming you, Johnny, and they’re coming after you.”

“The hell!” bellowed Hogan. “If that crooked marshal gets you into custody, Johnny, you’ll never get out alive.”

“We won’t let them take him,” the hostler said.

"Most of the boys are downtown. I'll round them up."

"See that you've got plenty of ammunition, Johnny!" Hogan said, moving fast to his office. "I'll get my Winchester."

Johnny stepped out to the ramp, alone, with the sharp insight that comes to a man at such a time. He wondered if Darley knew Hogan had not cut enough hay, if he'd planted Juliet in the office to find out.

Johnny checked his gun and slid it back into the holster. He moved down the ramp toward the street. In the distance he could see the glow of burning hay, and now he heard the pounding hoofs of a dozen horses. He waited there until the riders roared down the street and pulled to a dust-rolling stop.

"I'm arresting you, Becker," the marshal called out, "for arson! Surrender peaceable."

Darley was there beside the marshal. Red Kimmel was on the other side. Matt Nesbitt was there, too and the others were Nesbitt's hay hands, not gunmen. If Johnny chose to fight, he could discount Nesbitt's crew. It would be Kimmel, Darley, and the marshal, and even that made the odds too long, for only Hogan was here, back on the ramp with his Winchester. The hostler had not yet returned with the stable crew.

"I've got a couple things to say, Marshal," Johnny said. "I didn't fire the stack. This is one of Darley's tricks. And, Matt, I didn't think you were low enough to back one of Darley's plays."

"I ain't forgot," Nesbit replied, "that you said it would be good business to burn my hay to keep Darley from getting it."

Johnny nodded. "I spoke in anger, Matt. I admit that. You told me I was too young for this job, and when I said that, maybe I was." He paused. "But I'm telling you, I didn't burn you out."

The marshal said: "Two of Matt's crew saw you out there."

"I was in my office," Johnny replied, "all evening."

"That's a mite thin," he replied.

Darley had foreseen everything, Johnny thought now. If he resisted arrest, they could gun him down—legally. If he went to jail, he'd have no chance of coming out.

"You're finished," Darley said. "Might as well go peaceably with the marshal."

When Johnny made no move, the marshal said: "We're wasting time, Becker. You'll stand trial, fair and square. Put down your gun . . . or you'll see ours."

Even with Hogan up there on the ramp, Johnny knew they stood little chance. He might cut a man or two out of their saddles, but the odds against him were too great. If even only a few other men drew their guns and fired, Johnny and Hodge would go down.

"I'm not guilty," he said, "but if you aim to take me away like a steer to slaughter, you'll pay a price. . . ."

"Wait!"

He turned to see Juliet run up the ramp toward him. "Johnny didn't fire that hay! It was Darley's scheme. I know that for a fact. After Red Kimmel shot Johnny in the back, Darley sent me here to spy on the whole Becker and Estey operation."

"Hear that, gents?" Hogan bellowed. "One of Darley's own girls backs Johnny."

Kimmel muttered: "Not for long."

Johnny saw the gunman reach for his revolver. His first shot pitched the man out of his saddle in a rolling fall, his horse whirling and bucking down the street.

There was a sudden chaos of pitching horses and firing guns, orange flames licking into the gloom. Echoes bounced against the false fronts of nearby buildings and rolled down the street in a slowly dying reverberation of sound.

Hodge Hogan cut the marshal out of his saddle with his first shot. The lawman's head jerked back with the impact of the slug and he fell like a sack of wheat. Nesbitt, never a fighting man, grabbed for his gun, and found all he could do was fight to stay in the saddle when his horse reared.

Strangely enough, it was Duff Darley who got first chance at Johnny, but he was as useless as

Matt Nesbitt, for he depended on hired guns, and Kimmel's failed him. He fired twice, sending both bullets into the wall inches from Johnny's head. Johnny shoved Juliet to the floor of the ramp, turned, and laced a bullet through Darley's chest. He rolled out of the saddle and fell to the ground beside his plunging horse, a dying man pounded by driving hoofs.

Becker & Estey hostlers came running up the street. Their shouts took the fight out of Nesbitt and his farm hands. The air was strong with the smell of dust and powder smoke, and in the silence Hogan's squall of triumph rolled across the street to muffle the last dying echo of the guns.

Johnny helped Juliet to her feet. "Sorry I was rough on you. I figured one of Darley's bullets was meant for you."

"Johnny, I'm the one who is sorry. You must hate me."

He shook his head. "You saved my life. I don't hate you. I want you to have that chance you're looking for."

She smiled up at him.

Hogan's voice came from behind them. "Reckon the old man'll be proud. Right proud."

The Deputy with a Past

Jim Harlan woke with the early morning sunlight cutting sharply across the foot of his bed. It might have been the light that had awakened him or perhaps the bird singing in the lilac bush just outside the window. Or it might have been the worry that had tied knots in his stomach for a week.

For a long time Harlan lay staring at the ceiling as the deepening light washed shadows out of the room. The bird's song seemed to grow distant and die. Harlan's fists clenched at his sides. There had been a time when he had wondered how much of life was real and how much was nightmare, but that had been before he'd come to Amity and Sheriff Ben Norris had trained him and then given him the deputy's star.

Now it seemed to him that life was nothing but a nightmare; he hoped he would wake up and find that everything was all right. He threw back his blanket and swung his feet to the floor, knowing he would not wake from this nightmare.

Harlan dressed and, going to the kitchen, lighted a fire and set the coffee pot on the front of the stove. He went into the woodshed and cut an armful of pine, and returned to the kitchen. He ate a breakfast of bacon and eggs. Then he stacked dishes neatly on the kitchen table, buckled his gun belt around his waist, and left the house.

For three months now Ben Norris had been bedridden and to all intents and purposes Jim Harlan had been sheriff for those three months. It meant that for the first time in his life he was respected and trusted by the right kind of people, the people who had always been on the other side of the fence. Now he was on their side, and it was a good feeling, a feeling he didn't want to lose. And there was Ann Norris.

It had been Harlan's habit to stop at the sheriff's house every morning on the way to town to ask if there was anything he could do for Norris, and to see Ann. He didn't want to stop this morning, but it was expected of him and since he had come to Amity he had learned to do the things that were expected.

Ann met him at the door and kissed him as she always did, very tenderly, and patted his cheek. He looked down at her, hating himself and what he had been, and hating Blackie Critz. It would be worth killing a man to keep this woman, especially if the man was Critz, but one of the first things Ben Norris had pounded into him was the principle that a good lawman never kills for personal reasons.

"How's Ben?"

"No different. He ate his breakfast." She put her hands on Harlan's arms. "Jim, it's just a month."

"Is it? Guess I've been forgetting to count the days."

"Well, I'd better remind you how it will be. No more bachelor cooking for Jim Harlan. No more darning of socks. You'll be in clover, mister."

He nodded. "Clover up to my neck. I don't deserve it, honey. You know that."

"No, I don't."

His somber expression puzzled her, and because he could not answer the question that her eyes held, he turned away and walked into Norris's bedroom.

"How are you, Ben?"

Ben Norris was fifty, a big-framed man grown gaunt from suffering. A bullet through his back had paralyzed him from the waist down. Now he was dying and he knew it, but still he remained cheerful, joshing Harlan with the easy humor of a man who sees nothing but good times ahead.

This morning Norris was not cheerful and he did not smile. He motioned toward the door. "Shut it, Jim."

Harlan obeyed, feeling the urgency that was in the lawman, and came back to his bedside.

"Sit down, son. I've got to talk. I've been putting it off, but Doc was in last night. He figures I've just about got my string wound up."

"Any doc can make a mistake. . . ."

Norris held up his hand. "Let's take off our rosy glasses, Jim. If this is my time, that's it." He looked at Harlan, gray eyes speculative. "Jim, you've learned fast, and you're a good lawman. Soon as I'm gone, they'll appoint you sheriff, I reckon, and next year you'll get elected."

Harlan dropped into the chair and sat forward, Stetson held awkwardly by the brim. He stared at the floor. He wanted to say: "I'm a fake, Ben. My past has caught up with me. . . ." But he couldn't say the words.

"You'll make out," Ben said. "Just remember it's your job to protect the sheep and the lambs. They're not much on protecting themselves. The heck of it is you've always got a few wolves hanging around." He ran his tongue over dry lips. "I'm talking about Russ Bain."

"He doesn't fool me," Harlan said. He wondered if Norris had somehow heard about Blackie Critz, and about Fred Yarby who had forted up in his office for a week.

"Just thought I'd mention him," Norris said. "That isn't what I had in mind, anyhow. I'm thinking about Ann. You know how I feel about her, and I'm glad you came along when you did. I know you'll take care of her. Afraid I'm not leaving her much. Just this house and a few hundred dollars in the bank. Don't reckon you've got much, either."

"Not much money," Harlan agreed.

"At your age," he went on, "I owned a horse, a change of clothes, and a handgun." He added:

"She doesn't expect more than your love, Jim."

Harlan looked at the gaunt face. "She's got that."

He got up and turned to the window so Norris would not see his lips trembling. He stared at the lawn outside, alternately light and dark with the shifting pattern of sunlight and shadow from the big cottonwood tree in front of the house.

"Ben, I've had a rough background. I wasn't worth . . ."

Norris cut him off. "Jim, a man's worth what he makes out of himself. Don't ever forget that."

Harlan turned to him, grinning a little. "Seems like I've heard that before."

"Well, I won't be around forever to keep reminding you. Do your job the way you see it. Many was the time I was tempted to throw my star away and walk out, but I never did, and I'm glad I didn't . . . even though things didn't turn out . . ."

Harlan looked down at the gray face, the skin pulled tightly across the cheek bones. "I'll remember, Ben." He walked to the door. He put his hand on the knob, and looked back. "Ben, a lawman can't do anything to stop trouble before it comes, can he?"

"Depends."

"I mean, go out and arrest a man before he does something."

"No, you can't do that." He added: "I've often wished I could, though."

He found Ann washing dishes in the kitchen, and shook his head when she offered coffee. He stood looking at her, filled with his love for her, wanting to be fair and not knowing how. He couldn't just walk out, and he couldn't tell her the truth. It was the nightmare again. He felt as if he were in a dark room and the walls were pressing in around him, smothering him, and there was no escape.

"I'll go over and tidy your place up," she said. "Haven't been there for a couple days."

"You don't need to. Better stay with Ben."

She cast a glance at him. He didn't need to tell her Norris was weaker. She dried her hands and crossed the kitchen. He kissed her, holding her for a moment.

She said: "That was crazy talk a while ago, Jim. About not deserving me. I think you're the biggest man in the world."

"Don't ever think anything else," he said, and left the house.

It was still early when he came into the business block of town. Old Barney Cleek was swamping the Belle Union out. He called: "Howdy, Jim."

Jim said: "Howdy, Barney." Then he moved on.

Barney was an old cowhand, beat up and unable to ride anymore, so he was down to this. But Barney was as righteous as a deacon. He'd be one of the first to tear the star off Harlan's shirt if he knew.

Russ Bain's bank was two doors down from the saloon. Blackie Critz loitered in front of the stairs that led to offices above the bank. Now he gave Harlan a thin grin, cigarette dangling from the corner of his mouth, blue smoke shadowing his lean face.

"How are you, Deputy?" he asked.

"All right. Why?"

"Just wondering." Critz shifted his weight, back against the doorjamb. "Kind of fun, isn't it, playing big?"

"Not much fun. When are you and your wolf pack leaving Amity?"

"Leaving?" Critz's black eyebrows lifted. "We're not leaving. This here climate is salubrious."

"You've been here a week. Kind of tiresome, isn't it?"

Critz shook his head. He had always reminded Harlan of a cat, but never more so than now, a cat with a mouse held lightly in his claws.

"Not tiresome," he replied. "There's three of us. We take shifts. Frog's due in a few minutes. Then I'll go to bed."

"Reckon I'll have to take you in for vagrancy."

Critz laughed easily. "I'm not real worried. And you know why."

Harlan swung away. He walked on, slanting

across the street to his office. His shadow danced before him, long now with the sun still low in the east. The shadow was always there—behind him, in front of him, beside him, short or long. He was never free from it.

He went into his office and sat down at his desk. There was nothing to do but wait, and waiting was not easy for Jim Harlan.

This day was no different from the past seven. There were twenty nester families on Poverty Mesa. They had come a month or so before in covered wagons, driving a few head of stock before them. Now their cabins dotted the mesa, some of the sod had been turned, and so far Russ Bain had done nothing but visit each family and serve a blunt warning that they had better move on.

They were the sheep, these nesters, according to Ben Norris, along with the townsmen and a few small ranchers who clung tenaciously to their land in the foothills. Bain wanted the nesters out because Poverty Mesa was misnamed. The soil was rich and deep, and with a reservoir at the upper end there would be ample water for fifty families, not just the twenty there now. More population meant more business for the townsmen, but Harlan knew that none would lift a hand to help either Fred Yarby or the settlers.

Yarby had come the previous fall on a hunting trip. He had returned in the spring and set up a real estate office and advertised as a land locator. Bain had given him a warning, but like the settlers, he had disregarded it.

In the past Bain's warning had been enough, or so Harlan had been told. It had not been enough for Yarby. He had located the settlers, assuring them that Bain's bark was only that, but in the end he had lacked the courage he needed. Bain had brought Critz and his men in. Critz had told Yarby he'd better be packing a gun when he left his office, so Yarby hadn't left. That had been a week ago.

At noon Harlan ate dinner in the hotel dining room, and when he came back, he passed the bank building. Frog Delaney was at the foot of the stairs, the same position Blackie Critz had held early that morning. He was a stocky man with a great head anchored on a short neck that gave him the appearance of having no neck at all. Now he grinned at Harlan in derision.

"Feeling pretty tough today, Deputy?"

"Tough enough," Harlan replied, "to come after anyone who shoots at Yarby."

Delaney pulled a cigar out of his pocket. "Figure you can take on three of us?"

"We'll see," Harlan said, and went on across the street to his office, the noon-high sun throwing a short shadow that dogged his heels.

More waiting while nerves tightened, waiting for something to happen that should never happen. A man can build a dam and hold a stream back for a time, but sooner or later it will rise high enough to spill over, and when it did, hell would break loose. They all knew it would come soon. Ben Norris must have heard. Ann knew, although she had never given voice to her worries.

The afternoon dragged by. Curly Mize took Delaney's place. Yarby still had not stirred from his office. He slept on a cot and had his meals brought up, but this was the eighth day. No man could stand being cooped up in that tiny room forever.

Harlan walked around his office. He started to read, but put the book down. He smoked more cigarettes than he should. He sat down at his desk and tried to think of something he could do. No ideas, no plan came to him. Then with the sun almost down, Russ Bain came in.

Bain was power and wealth and prestige. He was in his early forties, slender and good-looking, smooth of manners. As far as Harlan knew, he had never tangled with Ben Norris, but there had been no occasion for it. Bain's position had never been challenged before. He owned the bank, the biggest store in town and the RB, a big spread with a massive ranch house on the upper end of Poverty Flat and more cattle than all the rest of the stockmen in the county.

" 'Evening, Jim," Bain said, and sat down across from Harlan's desk. "How's things going?"

“Fine.” Harlan flipped his cigarette butt through the open door. “So far.”

“Ben’s pretty bad, isn’t he?”

“Pretty bad. Been to see him?”

Bain’s pale blue eyes squeezed almost shut. “I dropped in yesterday afternoon. Made me sick to see him. He’s always been a big, robust man.”

“Got shot doing his job,” Harlan said. “But who cares now except me and Ann?”

“Now, that isn’t the right slant to take,” Bain said as if pained by Harlan’s bitter words. “Everybody likes Ben. Chances are we’ll build a monument to him.”

Harlan cuffed back his Stetson. “Now isn’t that a fine way to say thanks? Wait till he’s dead, and then build a monument.”

“Got a better idea?”

“Darned right. Don’t give him any trouble.”

Bain laughed shortly. “You’re talking wild, Jim. Nobody’s fixing to give Ben trouble.”

Harlan leaned forward. “Who do you figure you’re fooling?”

“Nobody.” Bain took a cigar from his pocket and bit off the end. “Speaking of thanks, Jim, I want you to know we’re all happy Ben’s got a good deputy to take over for him. For years he didn’t have any deputy at all. As the town grew, he had a couple who didn’t pan out. Then you showed up, and Ben took a shine to you.” Bain fired his cigar and blew out a long plume of smoke. "I might say that most of us were skeptical, not knowing a thing about you. Didn't even know where you'd come from. Did we?"

Bain rolled the cigar between his fingers. Harlan, eyes on the banker's bland face, thought of Ben Norris saying that Russ Bain was a wolf licking his chops and pretending to be a fat woolly sheep like the rest. He looked like a sheep, all right, courteous and mild-mannered. In the year Harlan had been here in Amity, he had never known Bain to lose his temper or even raise his voice in anger.

"Ben's a good judge of human nature," Bain went on, "and he was right in deputizing you. After he passes on, we'll want you to stay on the job . . . regular salary, of course."

Harlan thought he knew what was coming, and by his silence gave Bain more rope.

"Good sheriffs are hard to get." Bain made a small gesture. "Oh, we can always find someone to wear the star, but a sheriff needs to be more than that. You'll marry Ann and settle down in Ben's house. You'll pay taxes and raise a family and go to church. You'll be part of the community just as Ben's been, and you'll want to see things happen that are good for a stock-raising community."

Harlan said: "I'm not one to beat around the bush, Russ. What you want is for me to shut my eyes while Blackie Critz guns down Yarby. Or maybe take a short trip out of town."

Bain laughed. "You're a forthright man, Jim. As a matter of fact, the fishing is very good about now, and the aspens are beautiful with their leaves as yellow as gold." He jangled coins in his pocket. "You just might find a trip about now to be interesting. As well as profitable."

It was in the open now. Harlan knew what Ben Norris would have done in this situation, but there was one other thing Ben Norris would not have faced.

"Suppose I don't take that trip, Russ. Suppose Yarby is shot down, and I put Blackie in a cell. What happens then?"

Bain's face was grave. "I think you know, Jim. I don't believe Ann would marry a man who had served time in the Canyon City pen for bank robbery, and I am very sure the voters would not favor keeping such a man in office. I don't like to be this blunt about the matter, but you force me to call a spade a spade." He added: "In other words, you have a fine future here if you want it."

Harlan leaned back. He had been sure what Bain would say, although the banker had phrased it a little more pointedly than he had expected. He was trapped just as he had known he was from the day Blackie Critz had ridden into town. This week was a reprieve, nothing more. Now

Bain was sure Yarby was ready to break, or he would not be here.

There was a long moment of silence with Bain patiently pulling on his cigar. It was in Harlan's mind to tell him where he could go. That's what Ben Norris would have done.

But Harlan thought of the drifting years after he had left prison, hard years. Then he thought of Ann. She loved him. That was the one thing he could count on, but he would not ask her to ride out with him. This was her home. Riding the grub line with an ex-con was not for her.

So Jim Harlan waited while dusk moved in upon the town and here and there lamplights came to life. Bain smoked his cigar down, tossed the stub into the street, and kept on waiting. Now, with the time of decision at hand, Harlan did not know what to do any more than he had through the past week when he had foreseen the coming of this moment.

The town seemed very silent. Then steps sounded on the walk, the quick tap of a woman's heels. Harlan rose, thinking it was Ann, but the young woman who came in was a waitress from the hotel, the one who had been taking Fred Yarby's meals to him.

"Mister Yarby wants to see you, Jim."

"Thanks," Harlan said, and the woman turned and walked out.

Bain said: "You might have an interesting visit

with him, Jim. I've talked to him a few times. He can't seem to savvy a basic fact . . . if he was out of town, those poor, ignorant squatters on the mesa would leave."

"Maybe that is just what he does savvy."

Bain shrugged. "I never know what goes on in a mind like his." He paused. "And if I was in your boots, I'd have no trouble making up my mind."

Harlan left the office. Blackie Critz was back on duty when he reached the bank's outside staircase.

"Figured you'd be out of town by now, Jim. Russ Bain was saying you like trout fishing, and the fishing's real good this time of year."

Harlan moved past Critz and had started up the stairs when the gunman said: "Jim."

He stopped and turned to him.

"Remember when we were in stony lonesome," Critz went on. "We used to talk about things like this. We made one mistake, you and me, just like a lot of youngsters do. Knocking over a bank wasn't the answer. Working with the big boys is. Don't make another mistake, Jim."

"I'm trying not to," Jim said, and went up the stairs.

Yarby's office looked out over the street. There was no light in the room, and when Harlan knocked on the door, the locator failed to answer.

Quick fear washed through Harlan. He knocked again.

"Yarby. This is Jim Harlan."

Then he heard the man cross the room. The door opened.

"Wasn't sure that girl would tell you," Yarby said, "with Bain having his finger on everything like he has."

Harlan stepped inside. Yarby closed and locked the door behind him.

Harlan said: "Light a lamp."

"Just a minute." Yarby walked across the room to the windows and pulled the blinds down. Then he struck a match and held the flame to the wick, saying: "I'm not taking any chances."

Harlan had not seen him since he had locked himself in his office. Now he was shocked by the man's appearance. He had always been neatly dressed, but he was anything but neat now. He had not shaved and his clothes were rumpled and he smelled of sweat. As he slipped the chimney back onto the lamp, his hand trembled so that he had trouble getting it into place.

"I figured you and Ben Norris were on the level, Jim. Ben's laid up, but I thought you were the kind that wouldn't scare."

Suddenly angry, Harlan asked: "What're you driving at?"

"Don't try ducking out of it," Yarby said.

"Looks like Bain got to you, or you'd run those killers out of town."

"They haven't broken any laws," Harlan said. "Why don't you stomp your own snakes?"

"I don't want to die, Jim. I've got a job to do. Without me, those nesters are finished. You're smart enough to know that."

"And you were smart enough to see what was coming," Harlan said. "Don't try putting the blame on anyone else. It isn't my job to step into a private ruckus."

"Private!" Yarby exclaimed. "It's your job to keep order, isn't it?"

For a moment Harlan stared at the land locator. In this country a man had to stand on his own two legs, and Jim Harlan had never been one to scream for help the way Yarby was now.

"Look, Fred. Far as I know Blackie Critz isn't wanted by the law. So until he breaks a law, there's nothing I can do." He turned to the door.

"Wait, Jim!" Reaching out, his trembling hands clutched the desk. "I've done a good thing for the county by bringing these folks in and I deserve protection. You've got to give it to me."

"Real righteous, aren't you? Were you thinking about doing a good thing, or just taking the fee you got for every parcel of land?"

"Doesn't make any difference," he said.

"They're here. When I'm gone, they'll go. It's bigger than you or me, Jim. It's families and homes."

Yarby lifted his hands and rubbed them against his beard-stubbled jaw. "If you don't get rid of those killers, you'll have a bloodbath on your hands."

Harlan studied him. "There's just one thing I can do, Fred. I'll tell Critz what will happen to him if he doesn't give you a fair fight. But I don't reckon he'll scare."

Harlan unlocked the door and went out. Before he reached the stairs, he heard the lock snap back into place.

Blackie Critz was still at the foot of the stairs. "Well, I suppose Yarby wants you to get him out of town."

"No. He wants me to run *you* out."

Critz laughed. "Doesn't he know you're going fishing?"

"I'm not going fishing," Harlan said. He added: "Yarby won't fight. Shoot him, and you'll hang."

Critz said nothing for a long moment. "I thought you had more sense, Jim. I didn't aim to tell folks what I know about you, but it looks like I'll have to."

Harlan had fought his indecision for a week, but after Russ Bain had come to his office the indecision was gone. He wasn't sure why, but he knew one thing. If he bowed to Russ Bain now, he would always bow. And he'd lose Ann's love and respect.

"If I made the law," Harlan said, "I'd take care of you like a coyote in the chicken coop. Just don't forget what I said."

"Big talk," he said. "Better tell Russ you're not taking that trip."

"I aim to," Harlan replied, but when he got back to the office, Bain was gone.

Harlan ate supper in the hotel dining room. Tonight the food was tasteless. In one way he felt better now that his mind was made up. In another way he felt half sick. He finished his meal, paid for it, and went outside, thinking he ought to go to Ann and tell her. Ben, too. But he couldn't. They believed in him, and he could not bring himself to destroy that faith.

It was almost time for the evening stage that connected with the narrow gauge at Black Mountain summit. It was one of the things Ben had taught him.

"Know who's coming and going," he had said. "At times you can smell trouble just by seeing who gets off and who gets on."

Tonight Harlan got more than a smell of trouble. The lone passenger got out, a tall, agate-eyed man with a yellow mustache and two guns on his hips. Harlan remained in evening shadows while the stranger stood in the patch of lamplight from the hotel lobby. When his valise was handed down, he moved inside, boot heels clacking sharply.

Harlan returned to his office. He rolled a cigarette and fired it, half expecting Russ Bain to drop in again. He thought about the stranger. There was no need of Bain sending for another gunman, but he couldn't think of anyone else who would.

He heard steps outside, and turned to the door.

The stranger stood there, thumbs hooked in his belt. "You the sheriff?"

"Deputy. The sheriff's home . . . sick."

"So you're running the sheriff's office?"

"Trying to."

"I'm Bill Fiske."

The name meant nothing to Harlan. "Howdy."

"Know where'll I find Fred Yarby?"

Surprised, Harlan hesitated. "Why?"

"Deputy, that's my business."

Harlan considered telling this man how things were, but decided against it. "Over the bank. Room Ten."

Fiske eyed him. "Keep out of things, Deputy, if you want to stay healthy." He turned and walked away, boot heels sounding on the boardwalk.

Harlan waited for a time, then blew out the lamp and headed toward the bank building.

A gun sounded from an office there, the report thunder-loud in Amity's evening silence.

Harlan had never thought that Fred Yarby was

man enough to take a gun and fight Blackie Critz, or either of his men. Now he wondered if Yarby had been murdered. He ran to the bank and took the stairs two at time, gun in hand. He stopped in the doorway of Yarby's office, for what he saw seemed to confirm his suspicions.

Yarby lay on his back beneath the window, a bullet hole in his forehead. Fiske stood within ten feet of him, staring at the body, a gun dangling from his limp right hand. Critz, Frog Delaney, and Curly Mize were in the room, too, their guns on Fiske.

"We got the goods on him, Jim. He was standing over the body when we came in."

"I didn't do it," Fiske said. He cast a desperate look at Harlan. "He was dead when I got here."

"Liar," Critz said. "You did the job, and we're hanging you for it, mister. We don't stand for this in Amity."

Harlan said: "What kind of talk is that, Blackie? You're the one who threatened to kill him."

"In a fair fight," Critz replied. "Not murder."

Fiske turned to Harlan. "Fred was my friend. He sent for me a week ago. Said he needed help."

Harlan looked at all them. He said to Fiske: "I'm taking you in until I find out who's lying. Come on."

For a moment Critz's eyes locked with Harlan's.

Fiske said: "I saw who did it. A slick dude . . ."

Then the roof fell in on Jim Harlan. He tumbled to the floor and lay still.

When Harlan came to, he had a foggy moment trying to think where he was and remember what had happened. He recognized the sharp smell of antiseptics and he saw Doc Patterson standing beside the cot. He was in the medico's office down the hall from Yarby's room.

Harlan sat up. "What happened?"

Patterson said: "Take it easy, Jim, and lay back. Somebody hit you hard."

Harlan saw the rest of them: Joe Beeler, the blacksmith, Abe Rawson who ran the hotel, and a dozen other townsmen who had spent a good many years bowing to Russ Bain. These were the men Ben Norris had called the sheep and the lambs. They stared at him uneasily. Then Harlan remembered, and got to his feet.

"Doc, what happened?"

"Yarby's dead. Found you on the floor in his office. That's all I know."

"Where's Blackie Critz? And that man . . . Fiske? Didn't you see the rest of them?"

Patterson shook his head. "Abe got here ahead of me."

"I saw three toughs with masks on," Abe said. "They had a fellow under their guns. A tall fellow."

Harlan swore. "They aimed to hang him." He

lunged past Doc toward the door, hand dropping to his hip. His gun was there. Someone had shoved it back into his holster. He hurried down the hall to the stairs, surprised, the townsmen followed.

There was a big cottonwood back of the livery stable that was known as the hanging tree because years ago a band of horse thieves had their necks stretched from its limbs. Harlan raced toward it. He did not know how long he had been out. He sprinted across the vacant lot beside the stable, reached the alley, and saw a lanky body hanging from a limb of that tree—Fiske.

Doc Patterson and the others caught up with him. "Cut him down! He may still be alive!"

Harlan ran into the stable for his horse. He'd have a hard time catching Critz and his men if they'd left town. Fiske had said something about a slick dude who had gunned down Yarby. That would be Russ Bain. But if Fiske was dead and Critz and his bunch had fled, Harlan had no chance of nailing Bain for the murder.

Harlan ran along the runway just as two men stepped out of a stall. In the murky light from an overhead lantern, he recognized Frog Delaney and Curly Mize. They halted and pulled their guns.

Harlan got Delaney with the first shot, slamming the man flat into the litter of the stable floor. Mize fired a bullet at Harlan, but he must have been rattled by Harlan's unexpected appearance and hurried his shot. The slug whispered past Harlan's head. Harlan's second shot knocked Mize's right leg out from under him and he went down within five feet of Delaney.

Harlan moved down the runway, keeping them covered. Mize sat up, cursing. Delaney had a slug in his shoulder. He rolled over and tried to get up, right hand reaching for his dropped gun.

"Don't try it, Frog," Harlan said. "You're under arrest."

Delaney's hand dropped. He fell back, grimacing in pain. Harlan scooped up both guns.

"Where's Blackie?"

"Get . . . get a doc," Mize said.

"You'll talk or you'll lie there and bleed to death," Harlan said. "Where's Blackie?"

Rawson and Beeler had come in from the alley, Rawson calling: "Fiske wasn't dead. These fellows were just letting him strangle."

"Where's Blackie?" Harlan said again.

"Go look for him," Mize said.

"I reckon a couple coyotes who'd string a man up that way ought to bleed to death," Harlan said.

Delaney had wadded up his bandanna and he slid it under his shirt. He fell back and on his side.

"It was Bain's idea, Jim," he said. "Blackie

wanted to shoot him up there in the office and be done with it."

"Shut up, Frog!" Mize said.

"I ain't bleeding to death to cover up for Bain," he said. He went on: "Blackie's at his house getting the pay-off. We was supposed to fetch the horses."

"Who killed Yarby?"

"Bain," Delaney said. "He slugged you from behind. Told us to string up Fiske and get out of town. We spotted him as a gunman, and figured Yarby had sent for help."

Harlan handed their guns to Rawson and Beeler. "I'm going after Critz and Bain."

Mize said: "Jim, I don't reckon these folks want an ex-con like you packing the star, do they?"

Here it was at last. Harlan didn't look at Rawson and Beeler. He heard the blacksmith exhale.

"That true, Jim?"

Harlan stood motionless. All the worry that had been in him for eight days left an aching emptiness. Well, these folks would either take him the way he was—Ann and Ben and Doc and Abe and the rest—or send him on his way. He remembered words from Ben Norris: *Look ahead, Jim. You can't change what's behind. Don't bust your heart trying.*

Jim Harlan had not known before what to do. But he knew now.

"That's right, Abe," he said, thumbing fresh

rounds into the cylinder of his revolver. “Take care of these boys, will you?”

Harlan hurried down the runway and into the street. He heard someone call for the doc.

“Wait, Jim!” Rawson said. “We’ll give you a hand.”

But Harlan didn’t wait. He ran to Russ Bain’s house on the next corner, harboring no illusions about his future in Amity, but knowing this job must be finished.

Russ Bain’s big house was set behind a metal fence, Russ Bain who had run roughshod over everybody in the county, Russ Bain who had been able to exact obedience from most folks by a nod of his head. Anybody else except Ben Norris would have gone on the fishing trip and come back with a pocketful of Bain’s gold—and Jim Harlan.

Bain’s front door stood open, the yellow lamplight falling across the well-kept lawn. Harlan saw Bain alone in his living room, reading. It was an inviting scene, and Harlan knew at once it wasn’t right. Blackie Critz was around somewhere. They’d heard the shooting and guessed something was wrong. Harlan drew his gun. He stepped around the splash of light, eased across the porch, and went into the house without knocking.

Bain looked up from his book. “Hello, Jim. What was that shooting about?”

The banker sat on the far side of the big oak table that held the lamp. The book was clutched in his left hand and from where Harlan stood he could not see his right.

"Bain, I'm arresting you for the murder of Fred Yarby. Stand up, slowly."

Bain didn't stir. "You're talking pretty wild, son. Did you forget what I said about your future here?"

"You're the one who has no future in Amity," Harlan said. "You figured Yarby would break, didn't you? Then you'd drive out the nesters from the mesa, and take over their land." He added: "It didn't work."

"Son, you simply do not have a case against me," he said. "I'm respected in this town. You won't be, when word of your past gets around."

"Get up," he repeated. "Delaney and Mize are on their way to jail. Delaney says you killed Yarby. He's not one to hang for your crime."

Harlan had eased away from the front door. There was another door at the far end of the room, opening to a bedroom, Harlan guessed. Blackie was probably waiting back there, his presence bolstering Bain's confidence.

For a moment Harlan hesitated, wondering how he was going to get Bain out of that chair without shooting him. Bain must have seen the hesitation, and took it for weakness.

"It's not too late for you to leave town," Bain

said. "You can leave now with enough money to live on for a good long while. Take the offer, Jim. I think you know you haven't got a chance to pull this off."

Harlan heard someone cross the front porch. He couldn't take his eyes off Bain and the door at the end of the room—but at once he feared Blackie was coming.

"On your feet, Bain," Harlan said.

A man stepped into the doorway. "Better do what he says, Russ."

It was Abe Rawson. In a quick glance, Harlan saw a gun in the man's hand.

In the next instant Blackie Critz lunged out of the back bedroom, his gun thundering. A slug ripped into the wall behind Harlan. Before he squeezed off another shot, Harlan fired. Hit dead center in the chest, Blackie fell.

Rawson fired as Bain came out of his chair. The banker stiffened, his gun falling from slack fingers. Then he fell across the table.

Relief was in Jim Harlan. He went slack against the wall, sweating now. He had to fight to keep his knees from buckling.

"Thanks, Abe," Harlan said. "I didn't know you'd help me."

The townsman nodded. "Maybe if we'd helped Ben, he'd never have been gunned down like he was."

Other townsmen crowded into the house,

Beeler and the rest who'd been in Doc Patterson's office. Harlan holstered his gun and left the house, ignoring questions called out to him. He moved along the walk to the sheriff's house, not wanting to do this anymore than he had wanted to this morning.

There was a light in the living room, and Ann opened the door before he knocked. Harlan saw she had been crying. She came close, put her hands on his arms, and bit her lip a moment before she could speak.

"You're . . . you're all right?"

"Sure," he said. "Ann, I need to talk to you. You and Ben."

"He's been hoping you'd come," she said. She turned, picked up the lamp, and led the way into her father's bedroom. "Dad, Jim's here."

Harlan stood beside the bed, looking down at this man he had learned to respect and love.

"Tell me how it went," Ben said.

Harlan gave him a shortened account. Norris held out a claw-like hand, and Harlan grasped it.

"Glad I lived long enough to hear that," he said. "Fine job, son."

"Ben, I need to tell you about my past . . . ," Harlan began.

Norris lifted his hand again. "Hell, I know all that. Bain told me, hoping I'd fire you."

Harlan heard the man draw a deep breath. "That's what I mean by looking ahead, Jim. We all make mistakes. Don't bust your heart trying to change what's behind." He paused before adding: "You've made me a happy man today, Jim. Now, you two go on. Let me sleep."

Harlan left the bedroom, and Ann closed the door behind him. She put the lamp on the table. She faced him and whispered his name. He saw the love and trust in her eyes.

"I knew, Jim," she said softly. "I wanted to tell you it didn't make any difference to me, but Dad said you had to fight it out yourself." She smiled. "Everyone knows you're a good man. And I want you to know you'll always be the biggest man in the world to me."

He kissed her, holding her close. Afterward he said: "I can start counting the days again."

Judge Peterson's Colt Law

Judge Pete Peterson sat slack in his seat in the passenger car, a half-smoked cigar gripped between his teeth. On his way to Aspen Gulch, he was thinking sourly of Lon Herrick who ran the camp with the kind of iron hand that feudal lords had used in medieval times. They had said *off with the prisoner's head* with as little fear of contradiction as Herrick had when he'd say to Peterson: "Give this man ten years."

It wasn't that Peterson liked Herrick or the way he ran the camp. Nor was he afraid of him. It was simply a case of Herrick always having cast-iron proof against any man he brought into court. The proof might have been contrived, but who could dispute it? A judge had to rule according to evidence presented in court.

Peterson probably held the strangest record of any judge in Colorado. He'd served a term in the penitentiary at Canyon City for robbing a bank. After that he'd gone straight. He'd carried a marshal's star, studied law at night, and wound up as a judge.

Now in his late forties, Pete Peterson packed a Colt wherever he went, interpreted the law as best he could, and despised Lon Herrick with a passionate fury. But hating Herrick wasn't enough to change anything. The man was as firmly entrenched as he had been the day Peterson took office.

The train had come to a complete stop before the shooting started. There were three reports, evenly spaced, and then a man's yell: "Come back here, girl! Come back, and you won't get hurt! We don't want you running to Peterson!"

That was enough to bring him out of his seat. He plunged down the aisle past a sprinkle of miners in the coach and two girls bound for Lon Herrick's Gold Palace. None offered Peterson a hand. Some slouched in their seats, others dropped flat, and all were scared.

Peterson lumbered out of the car and down the steps, hammer back on his Colt .45. It was a dark night with only a thin wedge of a moon and a few stars in the strip of sky that showed above the steep-walled Canyon.

Peterson halted. He couldn't see anybody, not even the trainmen, but he heard running steps along the tracks. Then a gunman cut loose again from the aspens across the creek, and for the first time in years Pete Peterson heard the *zing* of a bullet meant for him.

The girl was there beside him then, sobbing for breath. Peterson snapped: "Inside!" He then pushed her up the steps. He began firing, slowly and methodically, laying his bullets two feet apart. Unless the gunman was forted up behind something better than a skinny aspen, he ran a good chance of getting tagged.

Reloading, Peterson held his fire. The steam engine gave a snort and a rush of steam. The shooter in the aspens was either dead or retreating to cover in the forest.

The train began to move and Peterson swung up. He went into the vestibule. He waited until he was sure the gunman was too far away to make more trouble, and then came down the aisle to the young woman's seat. He dropped down beside her.

The miners and dance-hall girls in the back of the car were in their seats now, still scared and staring at Peterson with the respect that timid people have for daring ones.

She wasn't more than twenty, he saw now, blue-eyed and dark-haired with a turned-up nose and full-lipped mouth that was trembling a little. Still breathing hard from her run, her cheeks were pink. She was downright pretty. Peterson had never married. The way he saw it, his past forbade that, but he admired a beautiful woman as much as any man.

"Seems like I heard that man hollering he didn't want you to see Peterson. What was all that about?"

"Must have been one of Herrick's men." The woman took a deep breath. "I'm Sharon Ross, your honor. I hired a livery rig to bring me down to the junction so I could talk to you before you got to town. Herrick must have found out what I meant to do." She took another deep breath. "Guess I've been talking too much. I've told Herrick what kind of crook he is. Told him I knew you wouldn't let Ernie hang." She added: "You're the only man who can bring justice to Aspen Gulch, your honor."

"Court isn't in session," he said, "so I'm not 'your honor' right now. I'm plain Pete Peterson." He stretched his thick-muscled legs in front of him and leaned his head back. "So your name's Sharon Ross. Related to Sam Ross by any chance?"

"He was my father," she said. "I've heard him talk about you. He said he never knew another man who had gone all the way down and then came back to do the good you have. That's why I knew you'd help me."

So this was Sam Ross's daughter. Peterson snapped a match to life and lighted a cigar. He pulled hard before he said anything. Sam had been his saddle pal when he'd ridden with the Wild Bunch, but he'd got clear after that bank job, and Peterson was the one who went to the pen. Later Ross tried his hand at prospecting, and made the first Aspen Gulch strike. He was in the big money when Peterson was released, and was waiting when he walked out a free man.

"No use staying outside the law," Sam Ross

had said. "There are enough loopholes inside to let you do anything you want."

"I'm going straight," Peterson had said. "You can be a crook inside the law as well as outside, but you'll wind up behind the walls of stony lonesome either way. I'm not going back."

"I've got a proposition for a smart gent," Ross had said. "Mining stock. Financiers eat it up in the East. I've got a good start. I'm married to the prettiest, blue-eyed girl you ever saw."

All through the years it had rankled Peterson that he had spent his youth behind bars while Sam had been free to spend his money, to live with his wife and baby girl. Peterson wanted none of the man's schemes.

Sam Ross had been too smart, just as Peterson knew he was. He'd died in the Canyon City penitentiary, and his wife passed away a year later.

Now Peterson took the cigar out of his mouth. He felt the young woman's keen eyes on him. She had a decent look about her, not the hard-eyed gaze in the rouged faces of dance-hall girls. He didn't know why she'd tried to see him before Herrick did, and he'd never heard of this Ernie she mentioned, but the whole thing had a smell he didn't like.

"I didn't know you were in the gulch," he said.

The young woman shrugged. "I have a millinery shop. I'm engaged to Ernie Patton."

She went on: "Judge, they're going to hang him. They claim he murdered Hank Snead. He didn't. He isn't that kind. It's another one of Herrick's crooked deals. Probably he killed Snead himself."

"What happened?"

"Ernie and Snead were in a poker game. Snead was drunk and accused Ernie of cheating. They had a fight, and Ernie licked him. Snead said he'd get Ernie, but that night Snead was found in the alley with a bullet hole in his back. The marshal has a signed confession, but they must have got it by beating him."

"Have you talked to him?"

"They won't let me."

The train moved slowly up the steep grade to Aspen Gulch. The switchbacks here were named Herrick Loops. If anything in this region had been unnamed when Herrick arrived, he had seen to it that his moniker received another memorial.

"What do you think I can do?"

"You're a great man," Sharon said. "Dad told me you were not afraid of anything. Everybody in the gulch is afraid of Herrick. Everybody except Ernie. I think that's why they framed him. He stood up. He has a ranch down the Canyon, and sells beef to miners for half what Herrick's store charges."

"I have to caution you," he said, "that if there

is hanging evidence against Ernie, I can't do anything."

"But it isn't real evidence," she said. "It's a frame. You'll see when you get into court. You'll see." She added: "Dad always said you were the smartest man he ever knew."

They were almost to the top of the mountain now, the engine throbbing with the exertion of the final pull. In another three minutes they'd be in Aspen Gulch. Peterson stood and pulled his valise down from the rack above the seat. It was Dad this and Dad that.

"I guess I'm not that smart," Peterson said to her. "There's only so much a judge can do."

"But you know what it is to be accused of a crime and go to prison," she said. "I know you've helped innocent men before."

He balanced the valise on his lap. "Hope you're not expecting a miracle."

The train clanked and bumped to a stop. Peterson stood and moved down the aisle to the open gate, stepping down from the coach. This was the only daily train from Durango. As usual, half the folks in camp turned out to see it come in.

Someone yelled: "Howdy, Judge!"

Another asked: "How's your shooting eye?"

"I can take the head off a gnat at fifty feet," he said, keeping a straight face when they laughed.

He had lost track of Sharon Ross. Alone, he

shoved through the crowd and strode around the depot to the street. There was the usual lurid light falling across the street from flares in front of the saloons, and the familiar chant of the barkers as they paced back and forth on the plank walk. All of the saloons were Herrick's. The hotel, the stores, and the shacks that rented for twice what they should belonged to Herrick. This was his town—lock, stock, and barrel. And Peterson reckoned Ernie Patton would hang here as sure as night followed day, if Herrick wanted it that way.

Pete Peterson took a room in the hotel. He washed in the cracked basin, combed his hair in front of a mirror that threw back a wavy image. The hotel bed was a dirty one, considering its price, he thought sourly as he went down the stairs to the dining room. Supper was greasy, unseasoned.

Lon Herrick came in when he was spooning sugar into his third cup of coffee.

"Howdy, Judge," Herrick said, sliding into the chair across the table while signaling the waitress for coffee. He was a slender and satin-smooth man with dark eyes.

"Good trip in?"

"Should have stayed in the coach for the night."

"Now, now, Judge, it isn't that bad here."

"Herrick, you've browbeaten enough people in Aspen Gulch to have them believing that."

"Something must have grated you," Herrick said.

"A young woman named Sharon Ross boarded at the junction. She told me about Ernie Patton. One of your men shot at her when she was getting on, a man telling her not to see me."

"That's a lie," Herrick said. "I didn't send anybody to stop her. I don't care if she sees you or not."

Peterson finished his coffee. If anyone was lying, it was Herrick, he figured. Sharon Ross had not fired a gun at herself, that was for sure.

"Patton's guilty," Herrick went on. "You can't change the facts. That's what I came to see you about, Judge. It was a grudge killing, and I've got to support my men. Patton shot down one of my dealers, Hank Snead, and you're going to instruct the jury to hang him."

"I hear he was selling beef here," Peterson said, "to bust your monopoly."

Herrick shrugged. "Suppose you could say that. I don't like unfair competition. But that's not what we're hanging him for."

"What makes you so certain he will hang?"

"Signed confession," he replied. "When you see it, Judge, you'll know it's the real thing."

Pete Peterson stood and left the dining room. Usually he had a drink before he retired, more to talk with mining men than to drink, but not this night. He was not in a mood for talk with any of the dozens of men he knew by name in this camp. In his darkened room he sat by the window overlooking a street gay with sound and light, packed by pleasure-hungry miners.

He thought about Herrick and then about Ernie Patton and Sharon Ross. Then, in a way it hadn't since the day he'd left the pen, the image of Sam Ross's smug face pressed into his mind

Before he went to bed, Peterson made his decision. He'd keep his hands out of things tomorrow. He'd bent the law more than once to bring to justice an accused man because, as Sharon had said, he knew what it was to stand accused. This time the jury would decide the case. Maybe Ernie Patton was framed—and maybe not—but either way it was the decision of twelve jurors.

In the morning he walked along the street, empty and quiet now. He could see shacks scattered haphazardly among the aspens. Someday, he thought, maybe miners would be in a position to demand something better while their labors made mine owners rich. Until that day came, they had two choices—take what you get, or leave camp.

A crowd gathered in the saloon used for a courtroom. Miners and miners' wives, all of them dour-faced and resentful of what was sure to come. Sharon Ross was there, sitting in the back, red-eyed.

When they brought Ernie Patton in, Peterson saw bruises on his face. Maybe Sharon was right, he thought. They beat the tar out of him to force him to sign a sheet of paper.

Patton's lawyer was shrill-voiced. The other one sat quietly, talking only to go through the legal motions. Herrick was in the front row of benches, his eyes on Peterson, as if daring him to challenge testimony or evidence.

The two lawmen, Tex Wade, the marshal, and Monk Miles, the night man, lounged by the door. They were a pair—gunmen hired by Herrick, predatory and brutal men who were well paid to take orders. Peterson thought about his resolve of last night.

The first part of the trial went smoothly. Peterson sat on the platform, a cold cigar tucked into the corner of his mouth, his Colt on the desk in front of him. He never had used his gun while court was in session, but he'd found a revolver was better than a gavel to call for order in a mining camp.

They picked a jury, the banty defense lawyer making no objections. He seemed as conscious of Herrick's presence as anybody else in the room. Patton sat still, one eye too bruised to open, the other fixed on the judge.

Peterson chewed on the cigar end, rapped for order with the gun butt, and reminded folks he'd clear the courtroom in case of trouble.

Then when the last juror was seated, it happened. Sharon Ross rose and stepped into the aisle. “Your honor, before my dad died, he said his greatest mistake was in not taking your advice the day you left prison . . . to be honest, always.” She pointed to the jury box. “But Dad was wrong, wasn’t he? You must have sold out to Lon Herrick, or you’d never let a bunch of rabbits like this decide a man’s life.”

Peterson hammered the gun butt on the desk, at once thinking about her words. He had never seen himself as the lucky one. He’d made his mistake, paid dearly for it, and now he held the respect of men, all of whom knew his background. Sam Ross had died in prison, died without his family and hated by the folks he had cheated.

“I’ll have no more demonstrations like that,” Peterson said to her. “Clear the courtroom.” He drew a look of betrayal from Sharon when he added: “Herrick, you stay.”

Wade and Miles moved the crowd out, and took up their positions at the back again. When the doors were closed, Peterson looked at Herrick.

“Laws are made to protect us from injustice, greed, and the power of ruthless men who claw their way to high places. Sharon Ross was right about this jury, wasn’t she? It is a foregone conclusion they’ll bring back a verdict of guilty, and I’d have to sentence this man to death by hanging.”

The state’s attorney stood. “Your honor, this is unorthodox . . .”

"I know it is," Peterson interrupted, "so shut up."

Herrick began: "Peterson, I'll see you . . ."

"Herrick, I'll tell you a few things about law," he cut him off. "There is a right to live in peace with your fellow men. It existed long before the United States Constitution was drawn up and adopted, and long before the state of Colorado ever passed a statute. Ernie Patton is guilty of challenging you in the marketplace, nothing more."

Herrick was on his feet, right hand slipping under his tailed coat. "You're making a farce out of this case."

Peterson lifted his gun. "I'll see that justice is done." He nodded to the accused. "Those so-called lawmen beat a confession out of you, Patton, didn't they?"

"Yes, sir. Herrick was there. He watched the marshal and deputy hit me with axe handles. I'd be in a pine box right now if I hadn't signed that fake confession."

"Let me see the document," Peterson said.

The prosecuting attorney handed up a sheet of paper. Peterson read a simple admission that the undersigned had shot Hank Snead in the back. Patton's signature was in jerky, half-formed letters.

"Come here," Peterson ordered.

When Ernie Patton approached the bench,

Peterson dipped a pen into the ink well and handed it to him. "Sign your name. Right here on the bottom of this confession."

After he signed it, Peterson studied the two. Then he picked up his revolver. "Case dismissed for want of evidence," he said. "This first signature was obviously obtained under duress and therefore is not acceptable as evidence."

He eyed Herrick, knowing the gunmen would do nothing without a signal from him. The moment stretched to the breaking point. Lon Herrick was smashed. Peterson had thrown defiance into his teeth. Herrick had two choices. Let it go and see his little kingdom kicked out from under him, or fight.

Herrick tilted his head toward the gunmen. In the back of the room Miles and Wade exchanged a glance, and went for their guns. Lawyers and clerks slid out of their chairs to lie flat on the floor. So did Ernie Patton.

Guns roared, the sound of the explosions flung from wall to wall. Powder smoke rolled upward as gun flame stabbed the morning light. Peterson took Wade with his first bullet, squarely between the eyes. Miles got in a shot, but the slug did no more than raise a welt along the side of Peterson's freshly shaved face.

Moving sideways, Peterson fired twice more. The first caught Miles in the side, the second higher, knocking him off his feet.

He dove away from Herrick's bullet, rolled, and came up firing. Three slugs sent Herrick reeling backward. He fell and lay still.

Peterson stood, his gaze moving from the lawyers to the members of the jury, all of them lying on the floor. "Any argument, gentlemen?"

Outside, Sharon watched and waited. Then Peterson saw her run to Ernie Patton. When she saw him, she broke away. She ran to him and hugged him.

As a bachelor who privately longed for the embrace of a woman, he said: "Miss Ross, I didn't know this was in the bargain."

"More than that," she said. "Ernie and I decided if you got him out of this fix, we'd marry and name our first son Pete Patton."

Judge Pete Peterson grinned. He watched them walk away arm in arm, thinking it was time he kept his eye out for a good woman.

The Breaking of Sam McKay

They rode out of Granite City at noon, the golden-haired woman who had left her youth behind and the slender, blue-eyed kid with the brace of guns tied low on his hips. They topped the hump west of Granite Creek and, angling southwest, came into the pines. By sundown they reached the divide and looked down into Blackbow basin.

"Your inheritance, Neil," the woman said. "All of it but that broken country along the south edge of the basin and the town of Jericho."

The boy stepped down, thinking of how he had a right to the name of McKay, but instead called himself Neil Larkin. "We'll eat here," he said.

She looked at him, a small smile touching her lips. "I thought you'd be more pleased by it."

He built a fire, holding his silence until flames curled around the deadfall pine limbs. Then he stood and cuffed his Stetson back over wavy brown hair. "Why should I, Ma? It's just another piece of range run by another *hombre*."

She sat wearily. "Sam McKay is a tougher *hombre* than you've seen before. You don't take after him in looks, but you're a lot like him."

He sliced bacon into the frying pan. "You've fooled yourself about a lot of things, Ma. Like thinking he'd send help when Pa died. I'll never forget that letter you got from him." He slid the pan into the fire and stood. "I don't want any part of this layout."

She stared across the basin that stretched westward, darkening now as purple shadow filtered across it. She didn't understand her son any better now than when he'd killed his first man. Fourteen then, he'd made himself the hero of the Colorado mining camp they were living in, for the man was a murderer and much feared.

But it was a point that made little difference to Magda McKay. She had never understood the violence that was all around them. She knew only that Neil looked like his father, with none of Phil McKay's softness in him. He was rawhide tough at fourteen, the same as Sam must have been at that age. That was the year Neil's father had died, and he'd made his own way ever since.

They ate hurriedly, wanting to get down off the bench before it was fully dark, and were in the saddle again as the sun dropped behind a ridge of the Blue Mountains. They would have made it if Neil hadn't glimpsed the cattle ahead of them and pulled in behind a rock upthrust. Motioning to his mother to be silent, he stepped down.

"What's wrong?" she asked softly.

"Maybe nothing, but you'd better get down. We'll stay here a spell."

She obeyed, knowing her son had a feeling

about things of this kind, and his instincts were seldom wrong.

The cattle were being moved at an angle up the steep slope. Neil, belly flat atop the boulder, watched the cowhands. Three riders, one riding point, came directly below Neil, so close that even in the thin light he saw a square face and short, wiry mustache.

There were about fifty head, all in good shape and bearing the Wagon Wheel brand. At current beef prices in Granite City these steers represented a sizeable piece of money. But why were they being moved this time of evening? His suspicion grew as he watched them, and he fought his urge to follow. He had no reason to interfere with anyone smart enough to rob Sam McKay. He slid down and waited beside his mother until the sounds of cattle and three horses died out.

"What's going on?" she asked.

"Some Wagon Wheel steers being moved to another pasture, I guess," he answered. "I thought it was better if they didn't see us." He added: "I figure we'll surprise the old devil."

It was completely dark before they reached the basin floor. They rode slowly until they left the pines and the lights that marked the town of Jericho came into view. It was another hour before they reached the settlement—a dozen scattered dwellings and four business buildings squatting on the intersection made by the crossing of two roads—a saloon called Denver Joe's Place, a hotel, a store, and a stable.

Neil dismounted and gave his mother a hand. "I'll put your horse away as soon as you get a room." Taking the saddlebags, he strode into the hotel.

The lobby was an indication of the hotel's poverty; an ancient desk under a bracket lamp, five chairs still on four legs along the wall and another kicked into one corner with three, a geranium plant in a coffee can on a window sill, one sorry salmon-tinted blossom hugging a fly-specked windowpane.

Neil tapped the bell, dipped the pen into an ink well, and handed it to his mother. She scratched her name and laid the pen down. Neil tapped the bell again, harder, its tinny jangle echoing through the lobby.

A man limped out of the hall behind the desk, calling in a high voice: "I'm coming, I'm coming." He reached the desk, saw Magda McKay, and stopped.

"I'd like a room, Giles," she said.

The man wiped a hand across his eyes and sat down. "Magda Rhule." He said it reverently as if her name and her face aroused old and gentle memories.

"Magda McKay," she corrected him.

"Sure, sure. I'd forgotten you married Phil."

The hotel man turned his gaze to Neil, and held there a moment. Then he looked again at Magda. "I heard Phil died."

"That's right." She laid a ten-dollar gold piece on the desk. "Anybody else here who would know me?"

"Reckon not. Most of the old-timers are dead or moved out to Granite City." The clerk pulled at an ear, eyes moving again to Neil. "Of course, old Sam's still out there on Wagon Wheel. Says he'll live forever, and danged if I don't believe it."

"I don't want Sam to know I'm here, Giles." She tapped on the gold coin. "Could you forget you know me?"

"Sure, sure. You bet I can, Magda."

Neil had stepped back, a mild amusement in his blue eyes. Now they narrowed. "Folks keep their say with me, mister," he said flatly. "This deal was made with me."

"Sure, sure." Uncertainty tugged at the man, and then he let his curiosity drive him into asking the question: "You Phil's boy?"

"The name's Neil Larkin." He picked up the saddlebags. "Which room?"

"Ten." The clerk jabbed a thumb toward the hall door. "Best we have, Magda."

Stepping around the desk, Neil followed the hall to the rear of the building, found the room, and lit the lamp on the bureau. He laughed and swung a hand toward the battered furniture. "You can't stay here, Ma."

"I'll make out." She studied him. "What are you going to do?"

"Visit Grandpa." He moved to the door. "I won't be gone long."

"Try to make him like you, Neil. You're his only kin."

"You reckon that old devil likes anybody?" Neil shook his head. "I keep thinking of that letter he sent you when dad died. I'll make him eat it."

To Magda he seemed old for twenty. Cheeks bronzed, wrinkles lined his forehead. His eyes, aged by rough experience, held too much wisdom for his years. Magda was thinking that as she looked at him, realizing he had missed his youth. Old Sam's iron had been fused into Phil's youthful body. He was neither of them—and both.

When he left, Magda stood there until the sound of his boots on the floor died, and regretted that she had brought him to Blackbow basin.

Neil stepped into Denver Joe's before taking the west road to the Wagon Wheel. He let his filled glass stand on the bar while he rolled a smoke. He was six feet of bone and hard muscle, eyes the color of deep ice.

"Kind of a lonesome place out here, isn't he?" he said to Denver Joe.

"It is for a fact. Don't see many strangers. No reason for a stranger to come here unless he's passing through, or tackling old Sam McKay for a job."

"Is McKay taking anybody on?"

"Now I doubt that. Kind of fussy, old Sam is. Got to know a man's pedigree like he would a bull's. Or maybe if you've got a recommendation. Like from Pete French over in Harney County."

Neil touched a match flame to his cigarette. "What makes the old gent so fussy?"

"He's crippled. Got bunged up more than twenty years ago. Before my time in these parts, but you hear the yarn yet. Seems like there was a bunch of theater players over in Granite City, and Sam fell in love with one of the girls. He brought her out to Wagon Wheel so she'd see the spread. Then he was gonna marry her." Denver Joe slapped the bar with a pudgy hand and laughed. "Funniest thing you ever heard. The woman fell in love with Sam's son, and they ran off. Old Sam was so mad he almost had pups. He slapped a saddle on a half-wild horse. Sam wanted speed, but that horse bucked him off and kicked him.

"Sam was stove up from that day on. He can stand if he holds onto something, but he can't take a step. Sits there on his front porch all day with a spyglass. Folks say he sees everything that goes on, and he even counts the flies crawling across the pies in the hotel dining room."

Denver Joe cocked his head at the sound of horses outside. "Might be some of the Wagon Wheel bunch. They ride at night a lot. If it is, don't say nothing about what I told you. It's a sore point with Sam, and I wouldn't want it to get back to him."

Neil nodded as the saloon doors opened.

Three riders came in. One was skinny and black-bearded, the second sleepy-looking with tiny red-flecked eyes, and the third was the squat, square-faced man Neil had seen moving Wagon Wheel cattle on the east slope.

The squat man called out: "Hurry it up, Joe!"

"What'll you have, boys?" the barman asked with quick deference.

"Whiskey, which same you know damned well. Ever see a Wagon Wheel man drink anything else?" His eyes moved to Neil.

"Wagon Wheel men do funny things," Neil said. "Like moving cattle into the mountains at dusk."

For the space of half a dozen clock ticks, none of them moved. Denver Joe licked his lips, prepared to duck. The bearded man exploded into action, hand whipping down to his gun butt. He wheeled to face Neil as the other two leaped back from the bar.

Neil Larkin fired from the hip. There was the dance of flame, a roar, and the bearded man went down as if his legs had been cut out from under him by the swing of an invisible scythe.

"You men want to play this hand out?" Neil asked.

"Who the hell are you?" the squat man demanded.

"Name's Neil Larkin. Heard McKay might be needing a cowhand. Thought I'd ride out there."

"I ramrod McKay's outfit." The squat man backed toward the door with the other rider. "Show up around Wagon Wheel, and I'll take a shotgun to you."

They went out and hit saddles before Denver Joe stuck his head over the bar.

"Friend, in case you don't know it, this jasper you shot is called Bannock, and he's just about as hard as they come. Some say he was a road agent. That dumpy jasper is Ike Kelly. The sleepy one goes by Smoky Peck, but don't let that slow, sleepy look fool you. He's bad."

Neil motioned to the dead man. "What was he doing with the other two?"

"I don't know. They've been in here several times together . . . only Bannock never went to Wagon Wheel with the other two. I watched. He always rode east."

"Thanks," Neil said, and strode toward the batwings.

South of a small butte he had seen from the brim earlier in the evening, Neil made camp, and as the first dawn light touched the sky, built a small fire from the limbs of a dead juniper, and cooked breakfast. Then, climbing to the top of the butte, he hunkered down in the sage and waited.

Full daylight flowed across the basin, the sun's early sharpness falling upon the western rim, shadowed purple on the eastern. Neil saw that Blackbow basin was all that his father said it was. Phil McKay had wanted to come back, but he had known he couldn't face his father. So, dying, he had told young Neil the story of how Sam McKay had changed a wilderness into an empire—the ruthlessness, the crimes he had committed, the selfish driving ahead to a goal he had set for himself.

Black timber ringed the basin. Neil could see the cut where the creek knifed its way into the valley from the south, the swinging meander that it made across the flat, the exit it had gouged out of the north wall so it could rush on to the John Day River.

Wagon Wheel centered the basin—the low log house, the stout corrals, the barns, the row of poplars running across the front. Upstream, alfalfa fields made a succulent green patch along the creek. A fence ran north and south a quarter mile east of the house, making that end a huge pasture. Here were the only cattle visible to Neil. The herd he had seen the night before had probably come from here. The cows and young stuff, he guessed, were likely in the high country.

Neil held his position through the morning. He saw smoke pillar up from the chimney, saw three men leave the bunkhouse and go in for breakfast. It wasn't more than another half hour before a man in a wheelchair rolled out to the front porch. The three who had come from the bunkhouse loitered for a moment beside him, then ambled toward the corrals, saddled, and, mounting, took a leisurely course eastward.

The man in the wheelchair remained on the porch through the morning, continually studying some part of the basin through a long telescope. More than once he fixed his glass on the butte top, and Neil wondered whether he had been seen. The man wheeled inside at noon, and came back in an hour to continue his study of the basin.

It was midafternoon when Neil slipped back to the far side of the butte and mounted. Swinging wide, he hit the road a mile east of Wagon Wheel and turned toward the ranch. It was an old spread, but well run. Womanless, because Sam's wife, Neil's grandmother, had died more than thirty years ago, it had the general appearance of neatness and masculine efficiency.

Neil knew he was watched from the moment he first came into view, but he looked straight ahead, giving the buildings an occasional glance as if they held little interest for him. He pulled to a stop in front of the house, still not looking at the man on the porch, racked his horse, and turned up the path.

His lean, leather-brown face inscrutable, Neil Larkin might have been another saddle tramp for all the interest that he showed. He was within a dozen paces of the porch when the man said testily: "Stand where you are. Who the hell are you?"

Neil stopped, his back to the sun. He stood spread-legged in the yard, his eyes now fixed on the man in the wheelchair.

In his day Sam McKay had been a bull of a man, big of frame and thick of muscle, wide-faced and blunt-jawed. Now he was half a man. Still beefy through the neck and shoulders, his legs by contrast were toothpicks. His eyes were his strength, entirely black, with all the startling menace of the twin bores of a double-barreled shotgun.

"Can't you talk?"

"Yeah, I can talk," Neil replied. "I was just thinking."

"Thinking what?" Sam demanded.

"That you're a hell of a busted-down critter to set yourself up as the baron of Blackbow basin and right-hand man to the Almighty."

McKay's breathing sawed into a sudden quiet, his shirt front moving with that breathing. Then words rolled out of him. "I may not be the Almighty's right-hand man, but I do run this basin. And now I'm running you off my land. Get out before I forget you're just a kid who isn't dry behind the ears yet."

"I'm not ready to leave," Neil said. He came to the porch. "I figured you'd be glad to see me, Sam."

McKay lifted a long-barreled Colt from between his right leg and the arm of the wheelchair. "Get out."

Neil made no move. He grinned at the old man, and what might have happened was entirely different from what did happen, for in that moment a young woman came out of the house. She lingered outside the doorway, dark eyes sweeping Neil, and then came to stand beside McKay.

"What is it, Sam?" she asked.

"I was just teaching manners to a young pup who never learned any," he said. "Now, go on, drift."

Neil drew tobacco and paper from his vest pocket. "The scenery around is interesting, Sam. Guess I'll stay."

Sam's face reddened until it was the color of freshly cut beefsteak. His gun was lined squarely on Neil's chest, but Neil wasn't looking at him. His head was bowed over the cigarette.

"Don't do it, Sam," the young woman said.

The old man lowered the gun. "Who are you?"

"The name's Neil Larkin." His eyes swept the

woman from her black hair to her feet. She was full-lipped and softly molded with a full measure of pride. She was definitely distracting to Neil and he knew she would be the same to any man. He touched a match flame to his cigarette and asked: "Who are you?"

"Bonnie Bradley."

"Bradley?" The name struck a familiar note in Neil's mind, but he couldn't tie it up to anything at the moment. He brought his eyes to McKay again, and it was with something of a shock that he discovered he didn't hate him the way he thought he would. He said with more sympathy than he had ever expected to have for Sam McKay: "I came here thinking I'd work you over, but I've changed my mind. Wouldn't be right to be rough on my own granddad, would it?"

"Granddad?" McKay shouted. "What are you working up to . . . saying I'm your granddad?"

"That's who you are. Maybe you forgot you had a son."

"Neil." McKay wiped sweat from his face. The black eyes raked the boy's slender figure. "Magda and Phil's boy. You look like Phil, but he never had the guts you've got."

"There's different kinds of guts," Neil said evenly. "Maybe you never understood Pa."

"I understood him, all right," McKay said bitterly. "I understand you, too. Came back to get the place, didn't you? Figured I was ready to cash in, didn't you? Well, you've guessed wrong." He jerked a hand at Bonnie Bradley. "If I ever die, this outfit goes to her."

"I'm not your flesh and blood," she said.

"Flesh and blood, hell," McKay spat. "Phil didn't act like no flesh and blood of mine, and in the pinch I don't reckon this kid will, either. Go on. Get out."

"I don't want your outfit," Neil said angrily. "I told you why I came back here. Now that I've seen what you look like, I'm ready to go."

"Don't let him go, Sam." Bonnie shook his shoulder. "I know what you used to be and I know how you are now. Let him see how you've changed."

Neil tossed his cigarette into the yard. "A mean horse never tames."

"Magda here?" McKay asked with the first hint of softness that he'd shown.

"She's in town. She didn't want you to know she's here, but I guess it doesn't make any difference."

"What'd she come back for?"

"She wanted me to butter you up so you'd will me your place." Neil shrugged. "I've got different ideas about that. I've made our living since Pa died. I can keep on making it."

McKay's face set stubbornly. "And I can keep on getting along without either one of you."

They faced each other now, eyes locking. It

was steel against steel, strength against strength, power against power. But there was an insight in Neil that had come to him from his father. He smiled now as if he saw something here that Sam McKay would never see.

"It's sure tough being all done up and not know it," Neil said. "Ike Kelly knows it, though. So does Smoky Peck. I dunno how many more. It's because you think you're so damned smart that they can rob you blind."

"Rob me!"

"They've been stealing your beef, probably some of the critters you've been holding in the east end of the basin, and selling them to a hardcase named Bannock. He peddles them to the Granite City butchers. A gold camp like that uses lots of beef, Sam . . . beef you never got paid for."

McKay scratched a bulging jowl. "You're just guessing. There ain't a move I miss in this basin."

"No guesses, Sam. Most of your hands are up in the hills with the she-stuff and the rest. That leaves Kelly and Peck to do what they like . . . while you sit here and think you know it all."

"I've told him," Bonnie said. "He didn't believe me."

McKay wasn't listening. He was staring thoughtfully at the east rim of the basin. Now he said: "There's a Canyon yonder I can't see from here. They could drift them up there for a piece till they was out of sight." He turned back to Neil. "And I reckon you figure you're man enough to stop them. Well, are you?"

"How many head have you got out there?"

"Five hundred. Maybe more. Good stuff I'm gonna market this fall. Granite City and the other gold camps will take 'em."

"If I rode out there and took a count, would you believe me?"

"Why should I?"

He gestured to Bonnie. "Would you believe her?"

"Reckon I would." McKay's eyes hardened. "Bonnie's got nothing to gain because she's gonna get the place. You'd like to change that, wouldn't you?"

Anger spurted in Neil. "I told you I don't want any part of your damned outfit. We'll ride out there and take a look. If we don't find five hundred head, we'll jump Peck and Kelly when they come in."

"There's three of them. A third one named Del Huber. Thicker'n tobacco juice with Ike." McKay glanced down at his gun. "Too many for you to handle."

"I'll handle them. How about it, Miss Bradley? Want to ride with me?"

She nodded. "I'd like to."

Neil lifted his eyes to the westering sun. "Then we'd better get at it."

Sam McKay sat motionless until Bonnie got her Stetson and left with Neil. Then he wheeled his chair into the house and picked up a hand-tinted portrait of a young woman with golden hair. He stared at it a long time.

They rode in silence, the sinking sun throwing long shadows before them. Old Sam, Neil was thinking, was as tough as he'd pictured him. He was uncompromising, yet willing to make use of a man he hated. Neil wondered what Bonnie had meant when she said she knew what Sam used to be and what he was now. Pride ruled him still. He had been as tough and selfish as a man could be. Now he made a show of that toughness because he was proud. How much of a thing like that sank so deep into a man that it became as much a part of him as the color of his eyes—something that death alone could change?

Hardly conscious of Bonnie's presence, Neil let his mind go back over the years. He thought of his father who had been sick as long as he could remember him, of the years when his mother had made a living of sorts by singing in mining camp saloons from one end of the Rockies to the other. The strange part of it was that Magda and Phil McKay had made the most of those years. He had been there to see it.

"It's been going on all summer," Bonnie said suddenly.

Neil looked at her, his mind jerked back to this moment, and wondered why Bonnie Bradley worked for Sam McKay. Her Stetson hung down her back from a chin strap; sunlight flashed against her dark hair. She was different, he thought, from any woman he had ever known, although he wasn't exactly sure what made the difference.

"Why wouldn't he believe you?" he asked.

"He'd like to think that anybody would be afraid to rob him."

Neil asked the question then that was in his mind: "What did you mean when you said for him to let me know how he'd changed?"

"He'd like to have you live here. It would take an earthquake to get him to admit it, but I know how he feels. He's a sick, lonesome old man who's found out he had his sights on the wrong things all his life. Hate has burned him out. He'd like to have some love."

Neil was puzzled. "How do you figure that?"

"From what my folks have told me, he never used to do anything for anyone else. The only thing that mattered to him was pushing everybody else out of the valley by any means he had. Then after your father and mother left, and he had his accident, he changed. He always covered it up by being crusty. I didn't understand that at first, but I did after I came to work for him. He doesn't want folks to know he's changed. It's pathetic the way he appreciates the things I do for him."

"He wasn't right glad to see me," Neil said.

"It's just his way," she said. "I don't want his ranch. My folks have enough. It's yours by rights. You're his only flesh and blood. He'd like to know his life's work won't go to someone outside the family." She gave Neil a straight look. "Why did you come back?"

"I wanted to make him suffer. Like he made Pa suffer." Neil grinned shame-facedly. "After I saw him, though, I kind of reckoned he'd had his share."

"Sam's suffered enough." She paused, and then said thoughtfully: "He could understand you and forgive you for coming here to kill him. He'd never forgive you for coming here to sugar him up so he'd will you the ranch."

"I'm not hanging around to prove why I came," Neil said. "I'll be riding on when I do this job."

They had reached the first of the cattle grazing along the creek. It was open flat country with scattered junipers, and Neil, riding in a wide circle, made a quick count.

"Reckon I didn't catch them all," he said to Bonnie, "but I didn't miss many. Might be a few up that draw." He motioned to a dry wash that cut through the eastern end of the basin. "I don't see any other place where they could be out of sight."

"What did you make it?"

"A little better than three hundred."

"That would be about right. The bunch they drove off last night was the fourth they've taken. They steal fifty at a time, which is all the butcher in Granite City can use."

"How did you know about it?"

"I listened under the bunkhouse window. They knew Sam wouldn't be around, and I guess they never thought of me."

They rode in silence for a time, Neil's gaze sweeping the valley. Suddenly he found himself thinking how Wagon Wheel could be run if it were his. Then he remembered Sam would never let Magda on the place, and some of his old hatred for Sam McKay was born again.

"I remember," Neil said suddenly, an old memory flooding back, "Pa mentioning a man named Oren Bradley. Said he was the only man in the valley Sam couldn't lick."

"He never did," Bonnie said with pride. "My folks still own the same place they settled on, but they wouldn't have if Sam hadn't given them a hand four years ago when we had the bad winter. That's what I meant when I said he'd changed. Look out, Neil!"

He saw the man just as she cried out, crouching behind a high sagebrush clump to the left. He dropped low along his horse's neck as he drew his gun, an instinctive move that saved his life. He saw the gun flash, heard the roar, and felt the whip of the bullet. Then he spurred his horse, driving straight at the man's hiding place, firing his .45.

A second bullet screamed high above Neil. Then his lead found its mark. The dry-gulcher lurched out of his hiding place, attempting to escape the thundering hoofs. He fired, wildly this time, a scared, frantic man sensing his destiny. Almost on him, Neil turned his horse and fired one last bullet.

"Del Huber!" Bonnie said when Neil wheeled his horse back to her. "Ike Kelly must have put him out here."

"That means Kelly's worried," Neil said. "Chances are, he and Peck are somewhere ahead of us."

A vagrant thought came to Neil Larkin then. If he stayed out of it, the odds were good that Kelly and Peck would get spooked and kill Sam McKay. Then the place would be his if the courts recognized him as Sam McKay's one legal heir. But it was only a passing thought, the notion of owning the Wagon Wheel carrying more bitterness than urgency.

It was deep dusk when they rode into the ranch yard, lamplight in Sam McKay's front room throwing long yellow fingers of light across the yard. They reached it and pulled up, Neil hitting the ground and running toward the house. It was an old game to Neil Larkin, and knowing men of Ike Kelly's caliber, he guessed the way the ramrod would play it. Del Huber had failed. Kelly would take no chances.

Neil stopped on the porch between the open door and the window. "Blow out that lamp, Sam."

Neil couldn't see the old man, but he heard the derisive snort. Bonnie came in behind him. Reaching out, he gripped her arm and pulled her to him so that she would not be in the light.

"You scared of something?" Sam jeered.

"You can stop a slug the same as me. No great trick for Kelly to make it look like we shot each other. They'd only have to get Bonnie then."

There was silence for a time. Neil couldn't see into the front room and he couldn't take a chance on going inside. Kelly or Peck or both might be there. Neil couldn't even be sure about old Sam.

Then Sam wheeled his chair to the door. He said in a low tone: "What was that shooting about?"

"A dry-gulcher made a try and missed. That's why I figured Kelly and Peck would be ready to call a showdown."

"Sam," Bonnie said, "it was Del Huber."

"Del," he repeated.

Neil added: "We made a count. You're short two hundred head."

Again the silence strung out. Neil stood

motionless, pressed against the outside wall, gun in hand. He saw one side of the old man's craggy face, enough to note the squeezing together of his lips, the narrowing of his eyes, but not enough to know what was going on behind those eyes.

McKay growled then: "Ike told me about you killing Bannock. Says you meant to kill him, and with my ramrod out of the picture, you figured I'd give the job to you."

"Why, you ungrateful old . . . ," Neil began angrily.

"Wait!" Bonnie whispered to him. "Maybe Kelly's inside."

Neil couldn't tell. Sam McKay might be saying what he meant—or he might be saying it because he had no choice.

"Come inside," McKay said. "Kelly's back in the kitchen. We'll get him in here and see what he's got to say. I told him what you said about me being short, and he allowed he'd gun whip you off the place. I want to see him try it."

"Sam," Bonnie whispered again, "is Kelly in there ready to gun Neil down?"

For a moment the old man hesitated, and Neil knew he couldn't wait. It was curtains for Sam McKay if he warned his grandson, and that was exactly what Sam started to do.

"He's . . ."

There was only one way Neil could play it. He plunged into the room, glimpsed the sleepy-looking Peck leaning against the kitchen door, and fired at him.

Peck fired quickly and missed. Neil nailed him with a second shot, his slug smashing the man's nose into bloody pulp and angling into his brain. He went down. Ike Kelly wasn't in sight.

Neil had gambled on the two men being together. He understood the value of violent and unexpected action. He'd counted on that action giving him the time he needed to get both of them. Now, in that one horrible moment, he knew he'd lost.

He wheeled back toward McKay. As he turned he caught Kelly's squat figure pressed against the far wall, caught the expression of triumph on his wide face. There was a gun in his hand, the barrel lined on Neil's chest. Neil felt a swift rush of panic—it lasted no more than a second—but it spun out into an eternity.

He thought he'd never been slower than he was now as he tilted his gun and pulled back the hammer. Kelly fired. Smoke ballooned upward, the room shook with gunfire, but Neil wasn't hit—for Sam MacKay's wheelchair rocketed across the room and smashed into Ike Kelly.

Kelly had taken his time to shoot and he'd used up one second too many. Sam had slid out of his chair and, standing beside it, had rolled it at Kelly. He tried to reach the wall for support and, failing, fell headlong. Bonnie rushed to him.

Neil's bullet caught Kelly high in the chest. He went down.

Neil watched the ramrod get to his hands and knees, eyes on Neil. The man held himself with tenacious strength, blood bubbling on his lips.

"You're tougher'n I figured," he said. "I should have . . . should have got the old man first. . . ."

Kelly's head lowered and he went flat, his face hitting the floor. Neil went over to him, retrieved the wheelchair, and helped Bonnie lift the old man into it.

"Had to say them things," Sam explained. "Had to. They said they'd kill me if I didn't. Didn't have no chance to warn you."

When the dead men were laid in the wagon bed, a canvas spread over them, Neil came back to the porch. Old Sam was sitting there, still muttering, "They aimed to kill me. . . ."

Neil said: "I'll be going now. I'm glad I came, Sam. You aren't half the hellion I figured you were."

Sam snarled. "What're you talking about? You can't hightail off and leave me."

"Reckon I can," Neil said. "Not too long ago, you'd have welcomed this news."

"All right, all right. I was wrong. Dead wrong. I figured you was after this place. I figured you wrong, and maybe I had my own son pegged wrong years ago. Your ma, too." He swallowed.

"Haven't had much to do for years other than sit here and think things over."

"You could have kept in touch," Neil said, "after Pa died."

Sam ran a hand over his face. "I know. I was just too damned proud."

Proud? Well, they all were, the McKays. Sometimes pride got in a man's way. Looking down at him now, Neil knew the hatred had left him, all of it.

"You can't go off and leave me," Sam McKay said again. "You're got a right to the McKay name, and I want you to wear it. This here place is half yours. Maybe it ought to be all yours, but Bonnie is deserving of half."

Neil saw her smile at him from the porch.

"I've got Ma to think about," Neil said. "She has a right to a home place, too."

"Why, damn it," Sam McKay bellowed, "she's got one if she wants it. Bring her out here!"

"She thinks you hate her," Neil said.

"Hell, that ain't true!"

Neil cast a doubtful look at him.

Bonnie said: "Neil, let me show you something."

He followed her into the house unwillingly, for he told himself that nothing could change his mind, ever. Then Bonnie picked up the picture of a young woman, dog-eared, tattered from much handling.

“He’s changed,” Bonnie said softly.

Neil stared at the portrait of his mother. She had been a beautiful woman then just as she was now. And now he knew she would come out to the ranch when he told her about Sam McKay.

Fugitive from the Boothill Brigade

It was almost lost in the sea of sage, this town so aptly named Sage, which was only a single short block of false-fronted buildings and a few shacks scattered without plan on the prairie. To the north the Blue Mountains made a straight-edged horizon of pine; in other directions buttes and rimrock stretched on and on to where the land lifted upward to meet the sky. Everywhere sage-gray cloaked the valley, except for the sharp green of an occasional greasewood or a black island of juniper.

Bunchgrass grew tall among the sage, and the grazing cattle stood out like boulders on the flat. This was a cattle town and these were cattlemen who stood in little knots along the street talking in low, tense voices. It was cattle country, so decreed by God but threatened now by the Pistol Valley Land Company. Foolish men, greedy men, with gold their master, were making wild promises to other men who followed the plow. Time had not taught them that those who spit upon the land in contempt of nature will see their spittle dried into dust while the will of nature remained unchanged.

Jeff Donner, loitering before the hotel, looked

upon the street and saw with prophetic eyes what lay ahead and felt his own inability to stop it. Drawing tobacco and paper from his pocket, he slowly rolled a smoke, making a ritual of it, while his mind searched for an escape and found none. They were the innocents, these cattlemen, snared by the land company that was taking advantage of a mistake made years ago by an ignorant or careless government. Pistol Valley, fraudulently bought a generation before for swamp land, would now be fraudulently sold as dry farm land, and there was no one who had authority to step in and avert the tragedy.

Vane Larson drifted by and stopped. "About time to go."

Jeff looked at his watch. "Ten minutes yet." He fired a match and held the flame to his cigarette.

"Stagecoach coming," Vane said. "Expecting somebody?"

"No. Just waiting."

Jeff stood under the wooden awning, lank body slack against the weathered wall. He was the only cowman on the street without a gun, a fact that gave him a strange, almost undressed look. Trouble had been his saddle mate since he had been big enough to mount a horse, and the years had disciplined him sternly. Now, watching the stagecoach wheel in from the north, there was nothing on his lean-jawed face to show the hopes or fears in him.

Larson, Jeff's neighbor to the north, was twenty-eight, but he was Jeff's age only in years. There was always a pressing violence about him. It showed in his bold blue eyes that were fixed in a direct stare at the stage as it rolled to a stop; it was indicated by the flame-red hair that lay against his forehead under his hat brim. His fingers were wrapped around the butt of his gun as he said in a tone whetted sharp by bitterness: "Reckon Tracy will send a gunslick. They say it's the way he works."

"Rufe Webb was in Canyon City a couple days ago."

"You know Webb?"

"I've seen him."

Larson drew his gun. "If it's him, I'll gut shoot him. Let 'em call it murder."

"Put that away," Jeff said quietly.

Swearing softly, Larson holstered his gun. Jeff Donner, who had less than a hundred cows under his JD iron and had not carried a gun since he had come to Pistol Valley, held a position of leadership far beyond his wealth or his years. It was that leadership that might save these men. He had seen the same preliminary events before, had seen them rush forward until they formed a swift, pressing stream bringing violence and murder. Patience now offered hope. Violence would bring a total loss.

The stagecoach had stopped, dust scudding

around it in a dirty fog. There was a single passenger, a young woman who stepped down and coughed and moved out of the dust toward the hotel door. She turned to wait for her luggage, her gaze touching Jeff. She was medium in height, perhaps twenty, with a woman's full-bodied maturity. In that one short moment Jeff saw that her blue eyes were shaded by some inner trouble. She faced the stagecoach, and then for a reason that Jeff did not understand, she brought her gaze back to him as if seeing something in him that provoked her interest.

Jeff swung away quickly. "Two o'clock, Vane."

Larson fell into step with him, looking at him curiously. "What's the matter?"

"Time for the meeting."

"Hell, yes, but pretty girls don't grow on sagebrush. Who was she?"

"How would I know?" Jeff asked, pushing open a swinging door as he entered the Longhorn.

The men who had been on the street a moment before were now bellied along the bar. Rick Sanders, at the far end, said: "We're all here, boys."

Sanders was the biggest cattleman within fifty miles of Sage and the rest of them backed any course he took. He had pioneered the valley twenty years before when he'd brought a herd and crew north from California. He possessed what he set out to get: money and position and respect, but the gaining of them had drained strength from him. Now he was paunchy and tired.

They moved away from the bar, picked up chairs at the poker tables, and formed an irregular circle. They had never formally organized a cattleman's association, but they came to meetings like this whenever Rick Sanders sent out the word. Now, as always, Sanders kept his feet, leaning on the back of the chair behind him, a cold cigar gripped in the corner of his mouth.

Nobody said anything for a minute. They all knew why they were there, they had been talking about it on the street, and none of them had found the answer. Then Sanders took the cigar from his mouth, ran the back of a hand across his tobacco-fretted lips, and said: "Boys, we're in trouble."

It was entirely unexpected. They had thought, all of them but Jeff Donner, that smart old Rick Sanders would know what to do. They stirred uneasily, seeing that he was as uncertain and puzzled as they were. Then Vane Larson took off his hat and slapped it down on a poker table. He ran a hand through his hair until it stood out in a ragged red fringe. His voice was biting and angry when he said: "What's the matter with us? We act and talk like we're licked. Hell, we've got more guns in the valley now than we've ever had."

It was what Jeff expected him to say. He saw their eyes turn to Larson, saw them nod in half-hearted agreement. They didn't want to fight, and without a leader they could not hope to fight the men Benson Tracy would hire.

"We've got guns," Rick Sanders agreed, "but from what I hear Tracy will have some, too."

"Sure," Larson cried, "but they're hired guns. It's different with us. We're fighting for our homes."

They nodded, knowing it was true. Sanders, touching a long jagged scar that ran across his cheek, said: "I got this from a Paiute bullet in Seventy-Eight. I tamed this valley, and what for? Just to see it torn up by plow-pushers who'll starve to death."

"And who gets rich?" Larson said. "A slick-tongued gent named Benson Tracy who never did a damned thing for anybody in this valley."

Sanders acted as if he hadn't heard. "We can drive our cows out of the valley. We can leave our houses for the grangers to move into. Some of us have enough cash to go somewhere else and start over again."

"Well, I don't!" Larson said. "Sixty cows and a couple horses and a shack on land I ain't got a patent for. I'll kill the first man that moves onto my place claiming he bought it from Benson Tracy."

He reasoned he would be right in that killing, and Rick Sanders and all the others felt the same way. All but Jeff Donner. He knew how it would go. Kill one man, and you'd have to kill another. Murder would become a disease; human life of less value than a bull calf. Always, when a man goes down before your gun, there was the aftermath of regret, soul-searching, and perhaps madness that the self-condemnation could bring.

Jeff was suddenly aware that Larson, Sanders, and the rest were looking at him. They had never seen him wear a gun, yet they would accept his leadership if he was willing to lead them. It was not a thing he sought; it was something they were pressing upon him. He knew, as his eyes swung around the circle, that he wanted this position of leadership they were offering, but he wanted it on his terms because he knew where Vane Larson would take them.

"I guess Vane could kill his man," Jeff said slowly. "Trouble is that man might have a wife and kids. Might have a sister or mother. Vane, are you willing to support those folks after you kill the man who's been making their living?"

"Why, hell . . . ," Larson began, and stopped.

"There you are," Jeff said. "We're caught like a cow in a bog. The grangers aren't to blame. They're looking for a living same as we were when we came here. Benson Tracy is the agent, but he'll sell and go on, and it's the grangers we'll fight."

Larson said: "Then we take out Tracy."

"As I told you, Vane, I hear Rufe Webb is in

Canyon City. You won't see Tracy without Webb or some other gunslinger like him backing his play and doing his fighting for him. I've seen Webb. He'll kill any of you if he thinks you'd pull a gun on him."

"Then he'll kill me," Vane Larson said. "They got the valley by fraud, but they own it just the same. We're squatters, whether we like it or not."

"But, damn it," Rick Sanders broke in, "I got here afore anybody. Mine was the first house between Denio and the Blue Mountains. This wasn't swamp land. Never was."

"We know that. Tracy knows it. Still that's the way it is. It's patented land and the land company owns it. We haven't had any law here but what we've made, but if we fight the company or the nesters who buy the land, we'll face federal law."

Even Larson was silenced then. Boot heels scratched along the floor. Their breathing was an irregular sighing.

Then Sanders said: "You're saying we're licked, Jeff?"

"We're not licked until we pull out and start over like you said. If we owned the land, it would be another story. Only thing I can see is for us to raise every nickel we can and make Tracy an offer."

"I'm cash-poor, same as Vane," Burl Haney from Angel Creek pointed out. Others agreed.

"We've all got some cattle to sell," Jeff said. "Sanders, here, has cash in the bank. If we stick together, we have a chance. We can draw up a contract with the land company and buy the valley over a period of years."

Silence again. Then Larson burst out: "With some dry years or low prices, we'd still be licked. I say fight!"

Jeff rose. He wasn't even sure Tracy would consider an offer from them. Or if he did, his price might be out of reason. Still, it was the only thing Jeff could think of and it was worth a try, but any sort of dicker with Tracy went against their grain and he could not blame them.

His gaze swept the circle again. He saw doubt and uncertainty, an inner clawing for some faint hope, but pride was there, too, the stubborn pride of men who thought it was better to die than compromise.

"You're talking too much, Vane, and too loud. Did you ever kill a man?" When Larson shook his head, Jeff turned to the others. "Any of the rest of you?" When they shook their heads, he went on: "There's a time to fight, but we're not there. Not till we've tried everything else."

"Maybe you're talking too much and too loud yourself!" Larson said angrily. "How many men have you killed?"

Jeff looked at the redhead, his weather-darkened face tight as old memories stirred him.

"More than I want to remember, Vane." Stepping around his chair, he moved to the batwing doors.

Before Jeff reached them, Rick Sanders called out: "Jeff, if Tracy gets into town today, see what kind of deal he'll make."

Jeff paused on the boardwalk and rolled a smoke in his slow, ritualistic way. The shadows were long now and a wind had come up, quartering in across the desert and sending dust along the street in a gray rush. Jeff cupped a match in his hands and lighted his cigarette. Then he turned toward the hotel, a sense of defeat crawling through him. He had gained a respite. No more than that.

This had been handled the way Benson Tracy handled things. He'd sent word that he'd be in Sage today, that if anyone wanted to talk to him this was his chance. He would pay for the improvements that had been made in return for a release of any claim to the land. Otherwise, all ranchers would be evicted without remuneration.

Jeff headed into the hotel lobby. Rufe Webb was there, a scrawny man with large hands and a pair of flat staring eyes. His black-butted guns, holstered low, clearly marked him. Behind him was Benson Tracy, stocky with thick shoulders and a blunt chin and straight brown hair that started far back on his head.

Webb rose from his chair behind a potted geranium. "That's him," he said, and moved toward Jeff, his walk casual but wary. Tracy stood.

"Howdy, Rufe," Jeff said. "Long ways from the San Juan."

"Yeah." His eyes went to Jeff's belt. "You forgot something."

"Haven't carried a gun since I've been here."

"I'll be damned." Webb's thin lips spilled into a grin. "The Durango Killer without a gun. That's something I never thought I'd see. You using a knife now?"

Jeff felt a sickness grow in him and spread as his hands tightened into white-knuckled fists. He had tried to put it behind him. He had built a wall across his mind and the deadly years in Colorado had been pushed behind it. He was another man, his name the only reminder of the hired gunman he had once been, his name and a memory that was shoving the wall back across his mind.

Webb turned to Tracy, his back to Jeff in bold contempt. "You don't need me for this job. I've seen it happen before. When a gunman loses his nerve, he's no more dangerous than a pup."

Tracy moved forward now, smiling easily, a confident driving man with the stamp of financial success upon him. He understood men, he understood the odds that favored him, and he played his game with calculated brilliance.

"Don't pay any attention to Webb, Donner.

He's like a mean dog. Just likes to fight. Now, I understand you are one of the small ranchers of the valley, and that you've made some improvements."

"That's right." Jeff looked at Tracy, trying to forget Webb stood there, but the man's presence was like a currycomb rasping along Jeff's nerves. "I'm one of a dozen. Some, like Rick Sanders, have lived here for twenty years."

"I know," Tracy said. "They have used company grass and paid no rent, but at the time the company did not plan to sell the land, so I have no intention of asking for past rent. That will be forgiven when you sign the lease."

It was bold and smart, and Jeff made no effort to argue over it. "We just had a meeting. We're willing to buy the land on a long-term contract. You'd sell to us instead of the Kansas farmers you've advertised to, wouldn't you?"

"Why, certainly," Tracy said. "If you have the money."

"What's your price?"

"Twenty dollars an acre. Cash."

Defeat was in Jeff. He had expected it, and now the certainty of it gripped him. "You're asking too much, Tracy. This is good grassland, but it will never be farm land. Those Kansas farmers have been lied to."

"I don't care to be called a liar, Donner," Tracy said. "If your bunch raises the money, I'll settle with you. Otherwise, tell them to see me today and sign their releases."

You didn't argue with Benson Tracy. You fought with his weapons or you gave up and crawled off and hated yourself because you were no longer a man. It didn't make any difference how deserving you were, how much of a mistake the government had made years before, the facts stood alone, and Benson Tracy had them on his side.

"How much are you paying for those releases?"

Tracy laughed softly. "One hundred dollars. You agree to drive out your cattle before the week's done. I want the grass to grow this summer so the valley will look good by fall when settlers arrive."

"One hundred dollars might be all my place is worth," Jeff said. "But what about Sanders?"

"Same price to all," Tracy replied.

"You're a thief."

Tracy chose to shrug and let it go, but Webb reached for a gun. Tracy gripped the man's wrist. "No."

Jeff swung toward the door, trying to forget the ghosts of men long dead that had been prodded into marching through his mind again. He heard Tracy's sure laugh, Webb's rasping guffaw. Then he reached the door, knowing that what he had to say to Rick Sanders and Vane Larson and the rest would result in more ghosts marching through his mind—if he was still alive.

"Jeff."

It was the clerk at the desk who called. Jeff swung back, irritated. "What is it?"

"Your wife's upstairs in your room," the clerk said. "She said she wanted to see you as soon as you came in."

"Wife?" Surprise jolted the word out of him.

"I sent her up to your room."

Somebody was running a sandy on him. He turned to Webb who gave back his flat stare. Tracy was fiddling with a cigar, paying no attention to what was going on.

Jeff went up the stairs and opened the door to his room. Inside he found the blue-eyed woman who had come in on the stagecoach.

"Shut the door, Mister Donner."

He obeyed, and then stood staring at her. He sensed again she was in some kind of trouble. She had taken off her bonnet. Her hair was auburn, shiny-bright with the afternoon sun slanting across it. Her blue dress made a tight fit at her bosom and waist. She was, Jeff saw, completely feminine and attractive, the kind of woman a man would be proud to call his wife. Stirred by her presence as he had been unaccountably stirred when she got off the stage, Jeff wondered why she had thus put herself into the hands of a man she had seen but once.

She bowed her head under his steady gaze. "I'd like to explain, Mister Donner. I hear you are the only man in Pistol Valley who doesn't wear a gun. That's why I picked you for my . . . husband."

She turned from him and stared out the window at the wind-whipped street. She had not unpacked her valises, but everything in the room was made different by her presence. "If you're terribly angry, I'll go . . . but he's here now, so I wouldn't know where to go."

"Who?"

"Benson Tracy." She explained, "I've worked for him for three years, Mister Donner. I overheard him and Webb talk about you. I want to see him beaten. When I saw you in front of the hotel, I knew you could do it."

"How did you know who I was?"

"You didn't have a gun."

"Who are you?"

She faced him. "Does it make any difference?"

"I should know my wife by name."

"Call me Mary. Mary Donner."

He frowned. He liked the sound of it, but the whole thing wasn't right. He wondered if the hand of Benson Tracy was somewhere back of this scheme. He said: "Tell me about it."

"There's nothing to tell except that I'm running away."

"From the law?"

"No. Tracy. Or maybe myself. I thought you'd understand because you're a fugitive, too."

"I never ran away from anything in my life."

"Now you're not being honest, Mister Donner. Why don't you carry a gun?" When he made no answer, she added: "You see? It's a little different with me. I've never killed anyone. Not directly, but I've been part of Tracy's organization. I couldn't stand it any longer."

He still did not reply. He hadn't run away from Colorado. He'd left because he was known as a killer. He had only wanted to go some place where he wasn't known.

"I'm not a fugitive," he said to her now.

She sat down on the bed, put her hands behind her, and leaned back. "You can deny it to me, Mister Donner, but not to yourself. You ran away from a reputation. Rufe Webb knew you when you were a gunman. When he heard you weren't wearing a gun, he told Tracy he'd break you the minute he saw you."

Rufe Webb had done exactly that, Jeff thought, and a strange feeling squeezed his insides.

"I suppose it was silly to pose as your wife, Mister Donner," she went on, "but it was the only thing I could think of that would put me out of Tracy's reach. I've been his secretary, but my duties were more than that. There were always important men at legislature meetings who must be influenced. At first I didn't know. Then I began to understand why cash was passed out. This deal is typical. Tracy doesn't care whether the men he sells to make a go or not. His only concern is how much he can make out of it."

"So you quit?"

She nodded. "In the Dalles, but he didn't know I was coming here. In fact, I didn't know myself until all of a sudden it seemed the thing to do. I can't go back and wipe out the crooked deals I've helped him pull off, but maybe I can stop him on this deal. It sounds silly, Mister Donner, but I want to cleanse my soul."

She sounded sincere, but he wasn't sure he could trust her. Benson Tracy would be the kind who would use a woman to do his dirty work. In the silence that followed, though, he knew he wanted to believe her.

"There's no way to lick Tracy," he said.

"Yes, there is. I can't promise it will work, but I think it will." She rose and walked back to the window. "I can't tell you how, not yet. We'll let it work out for a few hours. By morning I'll know." She must have seen something in his expression for she said suddenly: "You don't trust me, do you?"

He didn't lie to her. "I have no way of knowing you're on the level. I don't even know your name."

She turned away, hands clenched at her sides. "You've tried to correct something out of your past because you were ashamed. I'd like to have the same right to try."

He thought about that. If she was telling the truth—well, she had trusted him enough to come here. "All right," he said.

Her smile showed her relief. "I have nowhere to go. I couldn't help thinking I could find a place here if I helped you defeat Tracy. You were lucky. You found your place."

"What do you propose to do?"

"I want you to take me to supper," she said, "when Tracy and Webb are in the dining room."

Benson Tracy and Rufe Webb were still in the lobby when Jeff came down the stairs.

"Tell your friends what I said about signing up?" Tracy asked when he saw Jeff.

"I'll tell them you want twenty dollars an acre," he replied.

Shadows were shoved across the street and the wind had died, but dust smell was still in the air. Jeff walked swiftly, boot heels clacking on the boards. The drabness of the town struck at him, the isolation, the distance, the miles of sage piling up all around. Mary had said she hoped she could find a place here. That was crazy. She belonged where there were people and life, where there was less poverty and more of the goodness of living.

He went into the Longhorn. There was a poker game going, but most of the ranchers sat lifelessly, a few with beer or whiskey in front of them, all smoking and none talking. Attention gripped them when Jeff came in. Hope flared until he said: "Tracy wants twenty dollars an acre . . . which he may get from nesters."

"Thieving coyote," Rick Sanders said.

"Maybe he can be persuaded," Jeff said. "I've got a notion. You boys staying in town tonight?"

They nodded with Burl Haney saying: "No sense going home till we know where we stand."

Vane Larson placed his hand on his gun butt. "If we're gonna get shot up, might as well get it over with."

Jeff turned to him. "Damn it, Vane, I told you I'll work on Tracy. Start shooting, and we have no chance."

Larson looked at him defiantly. "You trying to save Tracy's hide?"

Jeff grasped his shirt and hauled him to his feet. "I won't take that even off a friend."

"What the hell is this notion of yours?" Larson demanded.

Truth was, Jeff didn't know. If these men knew that, or if they found out about Mary and grew suspicious of her, not only would the cattlemen lose, but he'd be finished in Pistol Valley.

"I've got to play it out alone," Jeff said. "We'll know in the morning where we stand."

They didn't like it. He knew that much by their stillness. Stakes were high. They had a right to know.

"I think you'd better tell us what you're shooting at," Rick Sanders said.

Turning, Jeff leaned back against the mahogany bar. "To be honest, I don't how it will go. I know Rufe Webb. Know what he can do. I've never met Tracy before, but I've been up against men like him. I know what he wants. What I'm asking is for you men to let me handle it."

In the silence Rick Sanders chewed his cigar. Vane Larson stared sullenly at the floor. But no one raised an objection because they could offer no alternative. Finally Sanders nodded, and glanced at the others.

"All right, Jeff. I can wait till morning."

The decision made, the group broke up. Jeff took Sanders aside.

"Keep your eye on Vane. He thinks he's a quick hand with the gun. I like the ornery son too well to let him get killed."

Rick Sanders nodded.

Jeff went back into the street. Men can be held back so far, and no farther. He had done all he could. It would break in the morning if it didn't break before. Pulling his hat brim low against the sun, he turned toward the hotel. He thought with some bitterness how much he had changed. If this had been in Colorado, he'd have had a gun on his hip. It would have been over by now, one way or the other.

He'd changed, all right. Mary thought he'd run away. Called him a fugitive. Well, he was. In that instant he was more honest with himself than he had ever been before. The ghosts of the men he had killed were again marching through his mind. Back of them, indistinct in the distance because he had never seen them, were the children he had made orphans, the women he had made widows.

His soul needed cleansing, too. He had tried to get away from his past by forgetting it, by running away and coming here where his reputation wasn't known. But it hadn't worked. Everything he had done to start new was destroyed the instant Rufe Webb had walked across the lobby and said: "You forgot something."

Jeff turned into the lobby, hoping Tracy and Webb would be gone, but they were still there. Webb's grin was a contemptuous taunt. Tracy's expression was carefree, as if he knew he held the top hand and this business of playing the cards was simply routine, a boring affair.

"Did you tell them?" Tracy asked.

"No."

"Why?"

"Because that was the way you wanted it played. You'd like to work up a little trouble just to let Webb earn his wages. I don't aim to let it happen."

"You've got this wrong," Tracy said. "I don't want trouble. If I did, I'd have sent a dozen men like Webb in here. Instead of that, I came myself so your friends would have a chance to get a little something for their work."

"Get this straight," Jeff said hotly. "If you make that offer to the cattlemen in the Longhorn, you'll have trouble . . . and it might not work out the way you figure."

Jeff went up the stairs. He was bluffing, and Rufe Webb would know it if Tracy didn't. Actually he was gambling everything on Mary, and right now it looked like long odds.

He reached the door and put a hand on the knob to turn it. Then he knew he shouldn't go in that way, and lifted a hand to knock. That, too, was wrong because someone was coming up the stairs and he didn't want anyone to see him knock on his own door. He dropped his hand to the knob and turned it slowly, the hinge squeaking when he pushed it in. He went in just as Tracy's head showed above the stair landing.

Mary was sitting in front of the bureau mirror combing her hair. "Hello."

As he eased the door shut, Jeff said loud enough for Tracy to hear: "Hello, darling."

She gave him a straight look, surprised. Jeff left the door open an inch. He motioned for her to keep still and waited until Tracy came along the hall and stepped into the room across the hall.

Then Jeff shut the door and locked it.

"Tracy's in the room across the hall," Jeff told her. "Reckon he fixed it that way."

Mary nodded. "Webb aims to kill you. That's the way they work. Webb kills one man after forcing him into a fight. That breaks the resistance of the others."

"But you said he knew I didn't carry a gun."

She nodded again. "Tracy's careful. He always sends someone into a community to see what the pattern is. In Sage he found out a man named Rick Sanders is the biggest cowman in the valley, but he's old. You're the one they listen to. Webb plans to push you until you take up a gun."

"Why didn't Tracy bring a bunch of gun-fighters?"

"One is cheaper," she replied. "If he's forced to, he'll bring in more hired guns. Besides there is a certain amount of bravado with him coming in with one gunman, and he likes that. It's always worked, Mister Donner. Of course, he has the law on his side, which is more important in the minds of those who are against him than in his own thinking."

Jeff sat on the bed. She was half turned to him; he saw the profile of her fine-featured face, the shape of her rounded form. He considered a new worry.

"How are you going to make this stick with

Tracy?" he asked. "Doesn't he know you aren't married?"

"A long time ago I told him I was married, that my husband was out of the country, and I had to work."

"He'll think it's suspicious if I don't stay here tonight."

She faced him. "There is good and bad in all of us, Mister Donner, but I am sure there is more good than bad in you."

He thanked her for that as she went back to brushing her hair. He still did not know what he would do. "I told the men to sit it out till morning. They didn't like the idea very well."

Her brush stopped half-way down her long hair. "Are any of them quick-tempered?"

"One."

"Webb will work on him if he can't goad you into a fight. Tell that man to stay out of trouble."

"I told him," Jeff said, "but there's no guarantee he'll hold his temper."

She laid her brush down. "There have been several instances of bribery at legislative meetings. It would be unpleasant for me if I told all I know, but exposure is the only thing Tracy's afraid of." She went on: "My own fear is the reason I took this risk of registering as your wife. I'm afraid of him. Fear kept me with him for months after I got to the point where I knew I couldn't go on."

Jeff rose and went to the window. That was it. She wanted his protection, and she was thinking he'd take up his gun. Well, she was wrong.

"No need to play this out till morning," he said, turning to her. "Will you sign an affidavit about the bribery you can document?"

"If I have to," she said. She stood and came to him. "Do it my way. Please."

After a moment he nodded.

She smiled. "And now it's time for supper, isn't it?"

That was when the gun sounded downstairs, one shot from a .45. Mary grasped his arm.

"Don't go down there. Your quick-tempered friend is dead."

Jeff cast a wild look at her. He jerked free from her grip, unlocked the door, and flung it open. He lunged into hallway and bounded down the stairs.

Mary was right. Jeff knew that even before he reached the lobby. Rufe Webb stood at the foot of the stairs, gun in hand, facing Rick Sanders and the other cattlemen.

"What about it, gents?" Webb asked.

"You had to do it," Sanders muttered. "Didn't you?"

Jeff stepped past Webb. Sanders and Haney and the others stood along the front wall, staring at the gunman as though held there by fear of him.

Jeff knelt beside Larson, thinking he was dead, for the bullet had caught him in the chest and blood made a widening stain on his shirt. Then he saw a slight movement.

"Vane."

Larson lifted a hand and clutched Jeff's arm. "You said he'd kill anyone who bucked him. I didn't believe you."

"He's bad medicine, Vane. He's a professional killer."

Larson stared at Jeff's face as if he was trying to see it and could not. "I meant it when I said I'd rather die than run away. . . ." His grip tightened. "See you one of these days, Jeff. . . ." His hand fell away.

Jeff slowly stood. He looked down at Larson's body. He had seen more dead men than he wanted to count, but few who had died for anything more worthwhile than their pay. Vane Larson was not like them.

"Well?" Rufe Webb's voice was scornful.

Jeff did not look at him. Another thought had come into his mind, thoughts of the woman who was ready to risk her life to cleanse her soul. Mary wanted more from life. It was different with him. The best he had been able to do was to run. He'd resented her when she called him a fugitive—but she had been right. Now, staring down at Larson's set, almost smiling face, Jeff realized that he had sensed all along the past would come to him.

"Vane jumped him," Burl Haney said. "Webb

called us squatters, hanging on for the hundred dollars Tracy hands out. Vane got sore and went for his gun."

The words were distant bullets of sound beating against Jeff Donner's ears. Stooping, he unbuckled Vane Larson's gun belt, pulled it away from him, and fastened it around his waist. He lifted the .45, pulled back the hammer, and then eased it down. Five rounds were in the cylinder.

He dropped the gun into the holster, and then lifted it. It came easily. A good gun, but Jeff Donner was out of practice. Still, there was no fear, no worry about the outcome in Jeff's mind. Live or die now, he was a free man.

He slid the gun back into the holster and turned to face Rufe Webb. Late sunlight cut sharply across his face; dust was tiny roving particles in the shaft of light, the smell of it was in the air, a strong reminder of the wind that had gone by, of the empty miles that ran on and on into the buttes and rimrock until it swelled against the sky.

"All right, Rufe," he said.

Hands flashed down and lifted guns. Red tongues of gunfire flashed into the late sunlight and was gone and the smell of burned powder filled the air. The room shook with the roar of those guns, the thin walls threw back the sound in prolonged echoes. Before the last of them had died out, Rufe Webb clutched his shirt, somehow surprised that this had happened to him. Then his hands fell away and he fell forward, hat knocked from his head and rolling across the floor toward the body of Vane Larson.

Jeff holstered the gun. Turning away, he climbed the stairs to Benson Tracy's room. He opened the door without knocking.

"Webb's dead."

Tracy stood at the window, trying to catch the last of the sunlight on the papers in his hands. He laid them on the bed and looked squarely at Jeff.

"That's too bad for Rufe."

Jeff studied him. "It doesn't make any difference to you because you can hire another gunman."

"Why, yes, that's about it."

Benson Tracy knew, and his lips showed it in a faintly mocking smile, that no matter how much Jeff hated him, he would not shoot him down. Nor would it solve anything if he did, for there were other men in the Pistol Valley Land Company who would take over its management and run it as he had.

"Go down and have a talk with Rick Sanders," Jeff said.

Tracy eyed him.

"You will agree on a fair price," Jeff went on, "and a damned sight less than twenty dollars an acre. We all will agree on a down payment, how many years to pay it off, and a fair interest rate."

"You're a little mixed up," Tracy said, as if talking to a boy who needed to be straightened out. "Killing Rufe doesn't change anything."

"I didn't kill him to get at you."

Tracy rubbed his chin, puzzled. "I've been in this business a long time, Donner. The law is on my side."

Jeff stepped back through the doorway. "Mary."

She came from his room across the hall, moving quickly, and stood beside him. Tracy was stunned by this blow he had not expected. Easy confidence washed out of him, and he sagged in that moment.

"She will sign an affidavit documenting bribery and a few other tricks you've pulled."

"She's in it, too?" Tracy said in disbelief. "She can't swear to anything without incriminating herself."

"That's the difference between the two of you," Jeff said.

"What?" Tracy asked, baffled.

"She doesn't think of herself first," Jeff replied.

Sweat beaded on Tracy's broad forehead as he stared at her. "I guess you are that kind of damned fool, aren't you?"

She met his gaze. "Make a deal here in Pistol Valley, or I'll testify against you in court."

"Sanders is waiting for you in the lobby," Jeff said.

Tracy nodded once.

They left the room and descended the stairs. From the lobby Rick Sanders looked up at them, his weathered face showing fatigue and discouragement. The bodies had been moved and the other cowmen had gone.

"Tracy's ready to dicker," Jeff said.

Hope brightened the man's lined face. "I'm listening."

Jeff turned to Mary. They looked at one another without speaking, each knowing the other had faced the past and had been freed from it.

"I'll listen in," he said, gesturing to Sanders and Tracy. "Then we'll get that supper we were talking about."

"The next stagecoach . . . ," she began.

"Mary, I had a notion," Jeff said, "that maybe you'd stay. Once you said something about finding a place here. You'll have it if you want to wait for it."

She smiled at him for that was what she had wanted to hear. She didn't believe, nor did he, that love was a tangible substance that could be packaged and bought. It grew with time and understanding, maturing with a man's and woman's need of each other.

She said: "I'll wait."

The Man Ten Feet Tall

The day Bill Linn married Vicky Shaw he became ten feet tall and he knew he could lick any man on the high Oregon desert. Not that he had a secret ambition to lick all humanity in general, for he was by nature a peaceful sort. There was just one fellow he wanted to lick, a gent named Curt Chandler.

Bill had left Ochoco City under conditions he wanted to forget. It worked mostly in his dreams. Chandler was a mean devil with big hands and a cannon-sized .45 who sat on the foot of Bill's bed every night and had the meanest laugh, the kind that caught hold of his spinal cord and jerked.

Bill would sit up in bed just as the devil swung his gun barrel down, a cold sweat breaking out all over him. Finally it got so bad he could hear the laugh in the daytime when the wind whistled through junipers.

When Bill married Vicky, he got rid of the devil and his laugh until Johnny Jones showed up riding the grub line. Johnny had been in Ochoco City the day Chandler had pistol-whipped Bill into the street dust in front of Hamil's Bar.

Johnny was the last man Bill wanted to see. Anybody from Ochoco City would have been the last man Bill wanted to see. The instant he saw

Johnny, the devil climbed up on the corral and started laughing. Bill had never seen the devil in the daytime, but he saw him now.

Johnny let out a squall when he recognized Bill, climbed out of the saddle, and mighty near shook his hand off at the shoulder.

"You ain't marked up much," he said in surprise. "Just got a little scar on your cheek and your nose ain't quite straight where Chandler cracked you with his gun barrel."

Bill's devil laughed so hard that he almost fell off the corral.

Vicky heard this from the porch. Bill never told her how he got the scar and why his nose was side-waddling the way it was. That night he told her. He had to. There wasn't a man living who could keep anything from Vicky when she made up her mind to get it out of him.

It did Bill a pile of good just to talk about it. Once he got started, he couldn't stop. He told her about the devil with the horns and tail, and how his laugh got hold of Bill's spinal cord and jerked. He told her about being ten feet tall after he got married and knowing he could lick any man on the desert.

Vicky looked at him, loving him, and telling him so with her eyes. "That devil's back right now, isn't he, Bill?"

He wondered how she knew. "Showed up the minute Johnny rode in."

There was a moment's silence.

"Bill, let's ride into Ochoco City tomorrow. I've got some shopping to do."

Bill didn't want to go to Ochoco City. He didn't want to see the town again. He didn't want to see Curt Chandler again. He didn't want to see the place in front of Hamil's Bar where he'd crawled through the dust.

"Bill, you hear me?"

He looked away. "You go ahead. I'll stay here with Johnny."

"You'd let me ride fifty miles across the desert by myself?" Vicky asked incredulously.

Bill squirmed some. "Johnny can go with you."

"No. Johnny can stay here and look after things."

He was caught. Nailed to the barn door. Even a man twenty feet tall wouldn't get loose after Vicky had roped and tied him.

"All right," Bill said.

Vicky kissed him and then pulled her head away so he could see the love in her eyes. "Bill, when we get there, don't forget you're ten feet tall and can lick any man on the desert. That's the only way you'll ever get rid of the devil."

Bill knew he'd be haunted until he licked Curt Chandler. He could do it. He knew he could. He'd just never had what it took to go back and do the job. Not until right then.

• • •

They rode into Ochoco City the next day an hour or so before dusk, took a room in the hotel, and Bill put the horses away. When he got back to the hotel, Vicky was gone, but there was a note.

First things first, Bill.
Remember you're ten feet tall.

Bill took a hitch in his belt and left the hotel in long steps, the kind of steps a man ten feet tall would take. He didn't see old friends who spoke to him. He shook off a man who wanted to know where he'd been. He went to Curt Chandler's cabin at the end of the street and walked in.

Chandler didn't seem surprised to see him. He was standing beside a curtain that divided the room, his face paler than Bill remembered it. Then Bill made a discovery. Chandler wasn't a devil. He was just another man who'd caught him in front of Hamil's Bar without a gun and slugged him with his Colt.

Suddenly Bill knew something he hadn't known before. The devil that had been haunting him was a creature that had been born in his own head, a combination of fears and battered pride and imagination.

"I came to lick you, Curt," Bill said. "I aim to do it with my fists. Come on out here."

Chandler said nothing. He stared at Bill, his

mouth a sullen, down-curling line. It puzzled Bill for an instant because Chandler had always been a sneering, contemptuous man whose laugh had been as wicked as the devil's. But Bill was not of a mind to waste time wondering what was wrong with Chandler.

"If you ain't coming, Curt, I'll give it to you here," Bill said.

Chandler went slowly, reluctantly, head turned toward the curtain until he was in the street. Then Bill hit him. It was a good, tough fight that attracted every man and boy in town, but it was nothing like the time Chandler had pistol-whipped Bill. Men who had seen the other ruckus said Bill was a different man, that he fought this time as if he had something to fight for. Might have been ten feet tall, they said, so tall that Chandler couldn't reach his chin.

They worked down the street until they got to Hamil's Bar. Bill knocked Chandler down. Then he knocked him down again. That was enough for Chandler. He wouldn't get up, so Bill grabbed him by the collar, hauled him to his feet, and flattened him again.

"Crawl," Bill said. "Crawl down the street to your house."

Chandler crawled and the townsmen laughed just as they had laughed at Bill Linn. Chandler didn't tarry in Ochoco City. He saddled up and left town with a devil that looked like Bill sitting on the saddle horn and laughing in his face.

That night Bill kissed Vicky and held her close and told her she could buy anything she could find in Ochoco City.

"You were wonderful," Vicky whispered, and kissed him again.

She would never tell him that she had been behind the curtain in Chandler's house, a gun in her hand, and that she'd told Chandler to make a fair fight of it or she'd shoot him. She would never know whether Bill won the fight because he fought like a wild man, or if Chandler lost it because he'd been afraid, but it didn't make any difference. Vicky was sure of one thing. Bill would never be afraid again. A man ten feet tall couldn't be.

About the Author

Wayne D. Overholser won three Spur Awards from the Western Writers of America and has a long list of fine Western titles to his credit. He was born in Pomeroy, Washington, and attended the University of Montana, University of Oregon, and the University of Southern California before becoming a public schoolteacher and principal in various Oregon communities. He began writing for Western pulp magazines in 1936 and within a couple of years was a regular contributor to Street & Smith's *Western Story Magazine* and Fiction House's *Lariat Story Magazine*. *Buckaroo's Code* (1947) was his first Western novel. In the 1950s and 1960s, having retired from academic work to concentrate on writing, he would publish as many as four books a year under his own name or a pseudonym, most prominently as Joseph Wayne. *The Violent Land* (1954), *The Lone Deputy* (1957), *The Bitter Night* (1961), and *Riders of the Sundown* (1997) are among the finest of the Overholser titles. *Bunch Grass* (1955) and *Land of Promises* (1962) are among the best Joseph Wayne titles, and *Law Man* (1953) is a most rewarding novel under the Lee Leighton pseudonym. Overholser's Western novels, whatever the byline, are based on a solid knowledge of the history and customs of the 19th-Century West, particularly when set in his two favorite Western states, Oregon and Colorado. Many of his novels are first-person narratives, a technique that tends to bring an added dimension of vividness to the frontier experiences of his narrators and frequently, as in *Cast a Long Shadow* (1957), filmed as *Cast a Long Shadow* (United Artists, 1959), the female characters one encounters are among the most memorable. He wrote his numerous novels with a consistent skill and an uncommon sensitivity to the depths of human character. Almost invariably, his stories weave a spell of their own with their scenes and images of social and economic forces often in conflict, and the diverse ways of life and personalities that made the American Western frontier so unique a time and place in human history.

Books are produced in the United States using U.S.-based materials

Books are printed using a revolutionary new process called THINKtech™ that lowers energy usage by 70% and increases overall quality

Books are durable and flexible because of Smyth-sewing

Paper is sourced using environmentally responsible foresting methods and the paper is acid-free

Center Point Large Print
600 Brooks Road / PO Box 1
Thorndike, ME 04986-0001 USA

(207) 568-3717

US & Canada:
1 800 929-9108
www.centerpointlargeprint.com